Cupid, Inc.

♥ ♥ ♥ ♥ ♥ ♥ ♥ ♥ ♥

Cupid, Inc.

MICHELE BARDSLEY

♠ ♠ ♠ ♠ ♠ ♠ ♠ ♠ ♠

A SIGNET ECLIPSE BOOK

SIGNET ECLIPSE
Published by New American Library, a division of
Penguin Group (USA) Inc., 375 Hudson Street,
New York, New York 10014, USA
Penguin Group (Canada), 90 Eglinton Avenue East, Suite 700, Toronto,
Ontario M4P 2Y3, Canada (a division of Pearson Penguin Canada Inc.)
Penguin Books Ltd., 80 Strand, London WC2R 0RL, England
Penguin Ireland, 25 St. Stephen's Green, Dublin 2,
Ireland (a division of Penguin Books Ltd.)
Penguin Group (Australia), 250 Camberwell Road, Camberwell, Victoria 3124,
Australia (a division of Pearson Australia Group Pty. Ltd.)
Penguin Books India Pvt. Ltd., 11 Community Centre, Panchsheel Park,
New Delhi - 110 017, India
Penguin Group (NZ), cnr Airborne and Rosedale Roads, Albany,
Auckland 1310, New Zealand (a division of Pearson New Zealand Ltd.)
Penguin Books (South Africa) (Pty.) Ltd., 24 Sturdee Avenue,
Rosebank, Johannesburg 2196, South Africa

Penguin Books Ltd., Registered Offices:
80 Strand, London WC2R 0RL, England

First published by Signet Eclipse, an imprint of New American Library,
a division of Penguin Group (USA) Inc.

First Printing, February 2006
10 9 8 7 6 5 4 3 2

Copyright © Michele Bardsley, 2006
All rights reserved

SIGNET ECLIPSE and logo are trademarks of Penguin Group (USA) Inc.

LIBRARY OF CONGRESS CATALOGING-IN-PUBLICATION DATA:
Bardsley, Michele.
Cupid, Inc. / by Michele Bardsley.
p. cm.
ISBN 0-451-21757-8
1. Love stories, American. 2. Las Vegas (Nev.)—Fiction. I. Title.

PS3602.A7753C87 2006
813'.6—dc22   200518134

Printed in the United States of America

PUBLISHER'S NOTE
This is a work of fiction. Names, characters, places, and incidents either are the product of the author's
imagination or are used fictitiously, and any resemblance to actual persons, living or dead, business
establishments, events, or locales is entirely coincidental.
    The publisher does not have any control over and does not assume any responsibility for author or
third-party Web sites or their content.

Acknowledgments

To my agent, Stephanie Kip Rostan. There is not enough Godiva chocolate in the world to thank you for your faith, diligence, and humor.

To my editor, Kara Cesare. You bought my book. And that is, of course, proof that you are an insightful and brilliant woman. Thank you so very much.

To my fabulous friends Jeff and Janice Strand, whose friendship strengthened me when I wanted to crumble. I can never repay that debt.

To Linda Eberharter, who is the reason CUPID, INC. exists. I'm eternally grateful for your encouragement and kindness.

To Rose Hilliard, the assistant extraordinaire. Thanks for your cheerful boot-in-the-patoots. I really do need a keeper.

And last, but never least, to my husband, Dean, and our children, who never, ever let me give up on the dream. I love you.

Prologue

"I don't believe it!" Aphrodite glittered into solid form and threw out her arms, nearly thwacking her companion, Grace. The goddess spun in a circle, her hands flying within inches of the young girl's porcelain-pale face, and appraised the lushly appointed lobby of Cupid, Inc.

"Good morning, Aphrodite. Grace." Psyche leaned against the receptionist's desk, her gaze drawn to the slender form dressed in the typical gauzy blue gown. Which Grace was it this time? All three looked and acted the same, and if she hadn't seen them together, she'd think there was only one. Aphrodite usually had a single Grace in tow unless she felt the need for an entourage.

"A lobby . . . with . . . with chairs and chrome lighting and magazines," Aphrodite said, infuriated. "Is that a clipboard and a pen? Paperwork? To create love between mortals?" She turned and gestured wildly. Grace retreated a few steps to avoid the flailing hands and the sharp ends of manicured fingernails. "What's next? Dating shows on that terrible invention, television?"

"If you watched TV, you'd know there are at least a dozen reality dating shows."

Aphrodite sucked in a fortifying breath and placed a hand at her throat. "What is happening to the world? In the old days, all you needed were a couple hundred young people, a roaring bonfire, Dionysus's vintage wine, and—boom!—orgies galore and love matches without cameras recording every move."

"Hey Di Di." A dangerously thin woman slunk to the open-mouthed goddess, a twiglike arm raised in greeting. Her hair and eyes were purple, and she sported a diamond-pierced nose. She wore a silver halter top, a skirt made of purple feathers, and silver thigh-high boots. "Last time you saw me, I looked like this." She crooked her limbs and struck a pose. The sheaf of papers in her left hand fluttered.

"Daphne?" Aphrodite's expression changed from amazement to shock. Her gaze landed on Psyche. "You hired a tree!"

"A nymph," corrected Psyche, even though she knew her mother-in-law intended to insult Daphne. She resisted the urge to point out that one of Aphrodite's rumored origins was the union of Dione, a nymph, and Zeus. "She gave up the tree gig to work for us."

Daphne assessed the goddess's mottled face. "Told you she'd be thrilled." She hip-bumped Grace. "What's shaking, doll?"

Grace blushed, her gaze seeking the floor. The Graces rarely spoke, choosing tender actions over brash words.

"Does Apollo know?" asked Aphrodite.

"Blech. Don't say the A-word." Daphne shuddered.

Nymphs cared little for the edicts of gods, as Apollo had

learned several millennia ago. His persistent love-crazed chase had made Daphne choose near eternity as a laurel tree rather than suffer another badly read poem or slobbery kiss.

"You haven't lost your spark, have you, Di Di?"

"For Hades' sake! Quit calling me that insipid nickname."

Daphne shrugged, a smile twitching on her lips, and sashayed to the desk, where she dropped into the chair. Psyche silently applauded her friend's taunting of the great love goddess, but she was careful to keep a neutral expression.

"Here are the applications, boss. Let the love games begin." Daphne handed Psyche the thick packet of forms.

"This is outrageous. You've opened a . . . a . . . *business*." Aphrodite pointed a slim bejeweled finger at Psyche. "This was your idea, wasn't it?"

"No, Mom. It was *our* idea." Eros appeared in the doorway that led into the conference room, looking yummy in his black jeans and black polo shirt. He wore black high-tops, which made him extra cute. "Spreading love in this day and age has been more challenging than in any other time. We needed to try something new."

"What's wrong with the old-fashioned way? Strike these nincompoops with your arrows!"

"My arms get sore," he lied with a grin. "How was Greece?"

"The Olympics were wonderful, though I do miss the male nudity. There's nothing like gorgeous naked men running and jumping and whirling to make a girl's heart go pitty-pat." She strode forward, all beauty and elegance and ire, stunning in a red Donna Karan pantsuit and a pair of diamond-studded Jimmy Choo heels. Diamonds glittered on her earlobes, and a ten-carat marquise-cut diamond nestled in her ample cleavage. She air-kissed her son's cheeks, then turned to Psyche. "Forgive me for not saying a proper hello."

Psyche inclined her head at the stiff apology. She was used to Aphrodite's begrudging politeness—and her fabulous fashion sense. Psyche fought the urge to assess her own clothing, since she had, like Eros, chosen casual clothes for their meeting. Her mother-in-law always managed to make her feel frumpy and un-worthy. She caught Eros's gaze, the ever-present glint of desire and affection in his green eyes as he mouthed, *I love you.* She smiled. Her husband, however, always managed to make her feel beautiful and valued.

"When Hermes told me you'd decided to open a sex-fantasy business in Las Vegas, I didn't believe him."

"You talked to Dad?" Eros sounded as surprised as Psyche felt. Aphrodite had briefly turned her attentions to Hermes thousands of years ago, and that torrid affair produced Eros. The goddess of love was purported to be a passionate bed partner, but nothing and no one kept her attention for long. Hermes had been dumped before Eros's birth, and even though it had taken a few centuries, the god had gotten over his heartbreak.

"He was at the Olympics. Most of the gods were there." She sent her son a pointed look. "It's tradition."

Eros smiled, choosing not to walk into his mother's verbal trap, and ushered her into the room. "Come to the meeting, Mother. We need your advice."

Psyche watched Grace take a seat in the lobby and pick up a magazine from a nearby table. "Would you like something to drink, hon?" she asked.

The girl looked up, surprised. "I require nothing, daughter of Aphrodite."

"Don't bother admonishing her about names, subservience, or the evil qualities of mothers-in-law," said Daphne. "You know how the Graces are. Better move your ass, though. Her highness hates to wait."

Psyche chuckled at the nymph's impertinence and strolled into the conference room, closing the door behind her. Because she knew it would annoy Aphrodite, she planted a lingering kiss on her husband's lips before sitting down.

"I'm the goddess of love," said Aphrodite. Hurt vibrated in her words, but her irritated gaze belied the emotion. "All love matches fall under my jurisdiction."

"Not according to Zeus," said Psyche, opening the folder and flipping through the applications.

"Don't throw that unfair decree in my face! I was making mortals fall in love before you were born."

"Way, way, *way* before I was born."

Aphrodite sucked in an outraged breath, and Psyche focused on the paperwork, trying not to laugh. The goddess was obscenely vain, and any aspersions on her youth or beauty usually got the insulting party a lightning bolt to the skull.

"Mother, we want you to be involved," soothed Eros. "That's why I asked you to join us." He turned to his wife, his gaze chiding and his half smile a plea. He made Psyche feel childish and petty, and at the same time, she knew he found her verbal sparring with his mother amusing.

"We welcome you, Aphrodite." She plucked the most interesting applications out of the pile and handed them to Eros. "We have several applicants who present exciting challenges."

Eros thumbed through the papers and paused. "Sara Beaumont." His brows rose. "Virgin."

Aphrodite snapped her fingers and the papers disappeared from Eros's hands and appeared in hers. She peered at the first page. " 'The Office Fantasy. Where would you like to have sex?' " She rolled her eyes. "There is no subtlety in this process you've created."

"Where *does* she want to have sex?" asked Eros.

"The desk, if you must know."

Psyche saw the hitch of Eros's mouth and knew he was remembering their interlude just this morning in his office. Her skin tingled as she thought about the way he'd taken her. With a whispered command, he'd made her clothing disappear, and before she could protest she found herself on the edge of the desk, naked before him. He'd spread apart her legs with those big, warm hands, seeking the wet heat between her thighs, his mouth descending toward her aching breast—

"Sweetheart?"

Psyche blinked. "Hmmm?"

"Mom wanted to know whom you planned to partner with Sara."

"Uh . . ." She glanced at the forms in front of her, unable to stop embarrassment from scorching her face. When she pushed several applications to her husband, she caught his gaze and knew by the ardor in his eyes that he'd known *exactly* what had distracted her thoughts.

"If one of you dares to utter a single sweet nothing or uses one of those atrocious pet names, I will vomit."

"Mother! You're the goddess of love. Doesn't it make you proud to see what your powers can render?"

"If you'll recall, I did not match you with Psyche. Who knew one little prick of the arrow would turn you into a bumbling love slave for all time?"

"Arrow or not, Psyche and I are bound." Eros's tone held a note of warning.

For all Aphrodite's faults—and the list was long—she loved her children, especially Eros. Psyche knew that the goddess had gone to great lengths and suffered many burdens to ensure she kept the love of her son. She probably considered one act the greatest sacrifice of motherhood: The day she bowed to Zeus's command and allowed Psyche to partake of ambrosia, and thereby accepted her son's eternal life mate.

"Sara Beaumont," said Psyche, breaking the tense moment between mother and son. "She was very specific with the physical characteristics she wanted in her partner. Out of three gentlemen I found suitable, only one matches her description, although not perfectly."

"I could change that," mused Aphrodite. "I could make her see what she wanted to see."

"We don't operate that way, Mom." Eros linked his hand with Psyche's and brushed a kiss on her knuckles. "Love matches can be made only if the people interact on a real level—imperfections and all."

"Oh, please." Aphrodite rolled her eyes. "If mortals didn't need our help, we'd be out of a job. A little change-a-roo here and there never hurt anyone."

"Αλήθεια, μητέρα," said Eros. *Truth, Mother.*

"Η αλήθεια είναι υπερτιμημένη."

"The truth is not overrated." Eros held his mother's gaze. "Η αγάπη είναι αλήθεια."

Aphrodite smiled and her expression softened. "Yes, you are right." She looked at the application. "Let's help Sara, shall we?"

Psyche stared at her mother-in-law and frowned. Aphrodite's sudden compliance was suspicious, and she knew the goddess well enough to believe the beauty was up to her old tricks. If only Aphrodite really believed Eros's declaration: *Love is truth.*

The Accountant and the Virgin

chapter one

"Hello, my name is Psyche."

Sara Beaumont took the woman's proffered hand. *Oh, heavens!* She was gorgeous—almost perfect in her beauty: blond hair, high cheekbones, silver eyes, tall, thin, graceful. Psyche was the epitome of her Greek namesake, and everything Sara would never be. She glanced at the door behind her; she could leave right now and forget she'd ever signed up for such a ridiculous, desperate—

"Please have a seat."

Her heart beat in her chest like a bird's wings beating against its cage in an attempt to escape. She glanced at the puffy white chair, took a fortifying breath, and sat down.

"Everything checks out fine. You've signed our contract, completed the survey, and chosen your fantasy. Our doctors say you're in the peak of health and that you're on birth control—though we still require use of condoms—and that you're . . ." Psyche looked up, surprise etched in her gorgeous silver eyes. "A virgin? We don't get many virgins at Cupid, Inc."

"Is there some sort of rule against virginity?"

"No."

"It seems, Miss . . . Psyche, that I must empty my savings account to get rid of mine," said Sara, unable to melt the frostiness of her tone.

"You're lucky, Sara. You get to choose how and where you lose your virginity. Though you won't meet your partner until the assignation."

"These are professionals?"

"No. They're clients. That's what we do—we match clients to fantasies. The man you meet will have also chosen the Office Fantasy."

Sara blinked. She'd read the contracts three times. How had she failed to miss that disclosure? "What about . . . what if—"

"Afraid you'll get someone old, fat, and ugly?" Psyche winked. "That's why you filled out the survey. We match you with someone who best fits your description of a partner."

She breathed a sigh of relief. That meant that if she couldn't have Zeth Peterson, her boss and her crush, she'd get the next best thing: his double. *Well, almost.* If only she had the nerve to initiate a relationship with Zeth, she wouldn't be here, losing her virginity with a stranger and hoping a sexual fantasy come true would turn her into some kind of vixen. A vixen Zeth would notice and fall in love with and marry.

Yeah. Right. "So what's next?"

"The fantasy. Here's our *Guide to Ultimate Sex.*" Psyche handed her a book about as thick as the Las Vegas Yellow Pages. "You can skip some of the chapters. Just read the information you're interested in. These are your complimentary condoms, flavored and regular"—Sara took the two boxes and tucked them into her

handbag—"and your fantasy date." She grasped the envelope between trembling fingers.

"It's in one week, on Monday. If you don't show up, you forfeit
your deposit. If you need to reschedule, call our office at least forty-
eight hours in advance."

"It feels so surreal . . . so sterile." Sara put the envelope into her
purse. "I'm nervous."

"Nervous is good. Those butterflies in your belly now are nothing compared to what you'll feel when you meet Mr. Make Me
Feel Good." Psyche laughed—the throaty, sexy laugh of a beautiful woman who didn't have to pay someone to sleep with her. "Do
you have any questions?"

Sara shook her head. "Thank you. I'll, uh, see you around."

"At the follow-up appointment. We want to make sure you
were satisfied."

A Week Later . . .

Mondays suck. Nic Anderson wanted to blow up the phone. It
had been ringing off the hook nonstop; some days he hated being
the boss of the accounting firm he'd started with a ledger and a
prayer five years ago. Now he had a six-room office, three full-
time employees, a growing clientele, and a lifelong migraine. He
picked up the receiver and buzzed his receptionist.

"Mandy, I don't want to take another call for the rest of the
day. And reschedule my appointments. I'm getting out of here before I take an ax to my computer."

"Gotcha, boss. But your noon appointment is here. Do you
want me to reschedule?"

Nic scrolled through his Palm Pilot. Cupid, Inc. One of his

biggest clients. They were sending over one of their employees to clarify some recent expenses. "No, Mandy. I'll take that one. After you're finished rescheduling appointments, disconnect the phone and get out of here. Tell everyone else to get out of here, too. I want the offices emptied in fifteen minutes."

"All right, Mr. A.! It's been a while since you gave us a Cheeseburger Day."

He laughed. Cheeseburger Day referred to the first time he'd told his staff to go get a cheeseburger and not come back until the next day. He liked being able to still say, "Screw it; let's party." He needed to do it more often. But he was getting more and more like his old man: working until the wee hours, giving up social engagements, forgetting special occasions.

"Mr. A.? Are you ready for me to send her in?"

No. "Yeah. Send her in."

Nic felt the woman's tension the minute she attempted to sashay across the room. She closed—and locked—the door, then wobbled toward him. Dressed in a trench coat, impossibly high heels—pink, no less—and clutching a gym bag, she looked scared, expectant, and cute as hell.

"My name is Nic Anderson."

"Sara Beaumont." She smiled. "I suppose names aren't necessary. It's not like we're ever going to see each other again."

"Uh . . . right." He gestured to one of the chairs in front of his desk, and she sat with a sigh of relief. The gym bag clunked to the floor. What the hell did she have in it? Bricks and steel rods?

"It shouldn't take long to go through the books."

"The books? Oh . . . *the books*." She blushed. "I was hoping it would take a long time. I overheard the receptionist telling everyone to take the day off, which was nice . . . it made me think you had, um, plans."

"I was thinking about having a beer and a sandwich after we're finished."

She blinked. "I . . . uh, hadn't thought about lunch." She licked full lips that glistened with pink lipstick. "I'm open to . . . whatever. I read the book—some of that stuff, well, I can't imagine doing. But we could talk about your ideas before we begin."

It was as if Sara Beaumont were talking about something other than answering a few questions about Cupid, Inc.'s expenses. "My idea is to clarify these line items. And there's some information I need you take back to—"

"Wow. You get right into it, huh?"

"Yeah." Nic resisted the urge to roll his eyes. He wanted to get out of this office and over to O'Riley's Bar for a draft beer and some serious flirting with the waitresses.

Sara leaned forward, her gaze filled with uncertainty and excitement. "So, boss, would you like me to take a little . . . shorthand? Or maybe we should call it *longhand*." She chuckled.

"Shorthand or longhand. Whatever you want." Why was she batting her lashes like that? What a ditz. *This is gonna take forever.* Good-bye, cold suds and beautiful blondes.

She drew in a deep breath and nodded. "Of course. I haven't had much practice—um, honestly, I haven't had any practice. After I read the book, I tried it with a zucchini, but it tasted weird."

Zucchini? *Oh, jeez.* "Er . . . okay. Don't worry. I'll go slow."

Those luscious lips thinned into a frown. "Does that mean I should go slow with the . . . with the *shorthand*, or that you'll go slow to keep from, uh, you know . . ."

As pretty as the girl was, she didn't have a lot upstairs. He was startled at his disappointment. Short, voluptuous brunettes weren't his style, even those with sexy mouths and eyes darker than midnight. "Tell you what: We'll both go slow, okay? Take it one step at a time."

She looked relieved. "That would be nice. Um . . . do you want me to start?"

So much for getting out of the office early. Unless she grew a brain within the next few minutes, they'd be here all afternoon. "Yes, Sara. I'm ready."

chapter two

Nic watched the crazy woman round the desk until she stood in front of him. Then she loosened the trench coat's belt and pushed the material off her shoulders. His heart stuttered to a halt. Other than the heels, she wasn't wearing anything. Not a damned thing. She was all lush curves and full breasts and smooth skin. Her shy smile belied the woman's body beckoning for his touch. Then she dropped to her knees and reached for his pants.

"Whoa." He scooted out of her reach. "What's going on?"

"You said you wanted me to take shorthand."

"Oh." He had warned Psyche about including him in any sex-fantasy schemes. He wanted the account badly enough to go through with their tests and surveys and updates. But to send one of their clients . . . *Wait a minute. Wait just a damned minute.* Psyche was an astute businesswoman; she wouldn't jeopardize a professional relationship.

He felt hands unzip his khakis and reach through the hole in his boxer shorts; the sweet, hesitant pressure of a woman's fingers around his cock fogged his brain. Then a warm mouth covered him, a tongue swirling around his length.

"Uh . . . w-wait." He contradicted his words by adjusting his position in the chair so she could take more of his penis into her mouth. She was inexperienced, but eager. And those cherry lips made him hot and hard. He clutched the chair's arms and nearly ripped holes in the fabric. "Sara. Wait." He grasped her head and tugged her away. She looked up at him, her eyes luminous with tears.

"I'm not doing it right, am I? God, I knew this was a mistake." She grabbed the coat from the floor and stood, shoving her arms into the trench coat. "I suck at this. . . . No, I don't. That's the problem."

Nic grabbed her hand and stilled her movements. "Have you ever swallowed cum, Sara?"

Her mouth rounded into an O and her cheeks flushed red. "N-no."

"Do you want to?"

"I . . . uh . . . maybe. Probably. Yes."

"Good." Nic rose and tugged at the coat; she allowed him to remove it. "Let me go to the restroom, then we'll start over."

The minute he entered his private bathroom, he grabbed his cell phone from his jacket pocket and dialed the number of Cupid, Inc. "Psyche. Now." The receptionist didn't ask for a name; his tone probably told her enough about his intent.

"Psyche," purred a sexy voice. "How may I fulfill your fantasy?"

"The question is, whose fantasy am I fulfilling?"

"Nic! I'm so glad you called. There's a young woman—"

"She just gave me a blow job, Psyche. I think I know why she's here."

"*What?*" He heard her suck in a breath. "My secretary switched addresses and sent a client to your office instead of to her assignation. I'm so sorry."

"Don't be. What's the fantasy and how much will it cost me?"

"You want to participate?"

"No offense, Psyche, but I'm not in the mood for a long conversation. Fantasy and rate. What are they?"

"The Office Fantasy. No charge. Ms. Beaumont had an interest in being taken on a desk and . . . well, I suppose you'll figure out the rest. This is highly unusual, Nic. I'm not sure it's advisable to—"

"Advise me later, Psyche." Nic turned off his cell phone, snapped it shut, then shrugged off his jacket. He looked at himself in the mirror. "What the hell are you doing, Anderson?"

His reflection offered no answers, but the hard-on in his pants had a response he couldn't ignore. Everything was great. Good. Fine. This was a legal encounter with a beautiful, willing woman. Who was he to give up no-strings-attached sex?

Leaving his jacket and cell phone on the counter, he exited the bathroom. The sight that greeted him made his feet immobile and his heart seize.

Splayed on the desk, Sara had opted for complete nudity except for those ridiculous pink high heels, which gouged the wood as she parted her legs and offered him a view of her shaved pussy. Then her hands cupped her breasts, pinching the turgid nipples, before coasting across her abdomen. Fingers slid down, down, down. A throaty moan escaped her.

The shyness, the uncertainty she'd displayed earlier had disappeared. She was a Siren, a sex goddess, and he was her willing slave. She opened the slick pink folds to reveal her clitoris to him. Her dark gaze found his. "I've always wanted to do it on a desk."

Her low voice shot sensual chills through him. He controlled the urge to run, but still managed to jog. He stood before her, gaping and damned unsure. He didn't know what the hell to touch first: pert breasts, round hips, or sleek legs.

Dear God. She was a delicious female buffet.

She robbed him of choice. Wrapping her arms around his neck, she pulled him down for a kiss that nearly sucked out his tonsils. He returned the favor, unable to get enough of the cinnamon taste of her lips.

"Naked," she murmured. "Too many clothes."

They both tried to unbutton his shirt, but fumbling fingers and stubborn buttons made it difficult. Nic solved the issue by wrenching open the shirt, buttons popping, and tossing it to the floor.

Her hands slid across his chest, her palms rubbing his flat nipples until tiny peaks appeared. She leaned down and suckled each one, her tongue swirling, her lips kissing. Her hands slid down his waist to his trousers, but he was way ahead of her. His pants dropped to the ground, followed by his boxers.

When she got to her knees and put that eager mouth on his length, he almost passed out. She licked him from tip to base, her hands cupping and stroking as she suckled, kissed, and at one point slurped.

"Sara. Do you want me to cum in your mouth?"

"Uh-huh."

"Do you want to cum in *my* mouth?"

"Uh-huh."

"Good." He tugged her by the shoulders until she rose, and led her to the couch at the other end of the room. He praised the furniture gods for his foresight in buying the black leather monstrosity, a purchase he'd bitched about in the past, but would never, ever regret again. He lay on it. He didn't have to give her directions. She got right on top, backward, and presented herself to him.

Nic wasted no time delving his tongue into her slit, giving the flesh long strokes of his tongue. She tasted as fresh and sweet as a peach. Her mouth on his penis was hot and wet and felt really fucking good. The more he licked, the more frantically she sucked. *Oh, hell.* Orgasm already threatened, but he wanted her satisfaction first.

He grabbed her buttocks and pressed her closer, suckling and stroking her clitoris, almost coming when she pumped her hips slightly, moving in rhythm with his tongue. Her moans and gasps vibrated down his manhood, her mouth matching the pace of her hips.

He knew when her orgasm claimed her because she sucked him, *hard*, and pressed herself against his face so that he nearly—and gladly—suffocated. Her cum coated his chin as he drank from her. She tasted like warm melted sugar. *Oh, yeah. Oh, damn. Oh, God.*

Pleasure crashed through him and held him hostage. His entire body tensed as he emptied his seed into her mouth, and she drank from him like he was the ice-cream flavor of the month. She licked and tasted and, yeah, slurped, until he thought he might have a heart attack and die from the bliss of it all.

After several long seconds of deep breaths and heavy shudders, she escaped the couch and stood, looking down at him. "That was fun."

"Better than a roller coaster."

She laughed, and the sound of it turned his already mushy insides extra gooey. He liked her laugh, her smile, the sensuous twinkle in her eye as she assessed his nakedness.

Turning, she presented him with her gorgeous ass and tottered on those ridiculous heels to the gym bag abandoned on the floor.

She squatted near the bag and unzipped it. His penis twitched with an eagerness he hadn't known in a long while. His naughty, perverted, brilliant mind came up with all kinds of ideas about her in that position. His gaze traced the curve of her spine, the rounded flesh of her buttocks, and just underneath, he knew, was the smooth skin of her womanhood.

He was so busy conjuring pornographic scenarios about Sara that he failed to realize she'd found what she was looking for and had turned to look at him. The heat of embarrassment spread up his neck to warm his face. "What?"

"I've always wanted to do this." She swept her arm across the desk. The ledgers, paperwork, and knickknacks displaced by their earlier actions fell to the floor. Thank God his laptop was set up in the area behind his desk—not that he cared if she threw the damned thing out the window at this point. He wanted her again at any cost.

She climbed on it, giving him an excellent side view of her body. Her breasts were beautiful—full and heavy and just the right size for his hands. Her coral nipples were hard, either from the chill in the room, or, he hoped, those succulent peaks represented the rousing symbols of extreme horniness.

He set the world speed record for leaping off a couch and crossing a room. He grabbed her hips and pulled her to the desk's edge, allowing his length to tease open her entrance. He breathed hard, grabbing gulps of air to steady his pulse. "I have never wanted anyone like I want you."

She smiled, her gaze soft with desire. "Ditto."

He took it slow, wanting to make it good for her, wanting to torture her just a little longer, and knew his efforts were appreciated when she moaned.

He slid inside a teeny bit farther. Damn, she was tight. "What the . . ." His gaze locked with hers. "Are you a virgin?"

chapter three

"You knew that," Sara said, her voice breathy.

Nic hesitated. A virgin. Indulging in an impromptu office fantasy with an attractive, experienced woman was one thing, but taking her virginity was something else entirely. Why would a woman with her considerable charms buy a Cupid, Inc., fantasy to make love for the first time?

"Don't stop," she begged.

Her restless hands floated to his shoulders, down his chest, until her fingers wrapped around the part of his penis not yet embedded inside her. He made the mistake of looking down. *Oh. My. God.* His manhood pierced that glossy smoothness, and her wicked fingers stroked the exposed hardness.

"I think— Whoa. Don't stop. Wait. No. *Damn.*" He dragged in some oxygen. "Sara, are you sure you want to do this? I want you—I *really* want you—but I don't want you to regret losing your virginity this way. With me."

"You're very gallant. I appreciate it." She gazed into his eyes, her lips pulled into a tiny frown. "Now shut up and fuck me."

That settles the issue. His mind whirled with sensations. The creamy paleness of her smooth skin . . . the lustful spark in her eyes . . . the soft mouth nibbling his jaw. And she smelled like hot cinnamon. His brain fogged, leaving only one discernible word: "Condom."

Slowly, reluctantly, he withdrew, shuddering as his penis left the warm tightness, and watched her sit up. She scooped up the items she'd taken from the bag. In one hand dangled a bullet-shaped vibrator with a small black control box, and in the other she fanned out three condoms. "Maximum Pleasure, Ultimate Pleasure, or chocolate."

"Save the chocolate. What the hell's the difference between Maximum and Ultimate?"

"Would you like me to read the information on the backs so you can decide?"

"God, no." He plucked one from her fingertips, and she dropped the others.

As he rolled on the condom, he watched her turn on the minivibrator and circle her left nipple with it.

"Hmmm . . . the book recommended trying this. You'd be amazed how many places you can put this device. The vibrations are nice." She cupped her right breast and rounded the hard peak with the bullet. "You know what would be good?"

Nic blinked, realized his mouth was watering with the need to taste those perfect breasts, and managed to stutter, "W-what?"

"If you'd play with me."

He leaned forward and took a nipple into his mouth as she teased the other one. He suckled it like it was the last butter-scotch in the candy dish. How was it possible for her to taste this sweet? He turned to lavish attention on the other nipple, and she lowered the vibrator between her legs. With her free hand she cupped and kneaded the breast he'd abandoned.

He curled an arm around her back, scooted her until she wrapped her legs around his waist, and slowly, oh-so-slowly, pierced her virgin flesh. "You're so wet, Sara. So tight."

"It hurts."

"I'll make it good," he promised, feeling like the jock lying to the cheerleader. He slid in deeper, regretting the way she flinched, the way she stilled. The vibrator dangled from its cord in her hand. "Tighten your legs around me. Put that vibrator on your clit. Remember how good we make each other feel."

She replaced the vibrator she'd let fall away, and, by her little gasp of joy, he knew the tiny machine was doing its job. He sheathed himself all the way, allowing her to adjust to the feel of him inside her. He kept his pace slow, though it damned near killed him. She rubbed the bullet on her clitoris, moaning, and several times she slid it over the exposed part of his penis. *Oh, damn. That feels good. Too good.* He resisted the temptation to fuck her fast and hard, because he wanted to; he wanted to slam into her and take her to the stars.

Soon she got wet and wiggly, encouraging his thrusts. Her legs tightened, pulling him closer, and one of her arms flopped around his neck in an attempt to hold on, but then her inner muscles clenched him and she came, her scream of completion driving him over the edge. Her orgasm milked his, and the intensity of his pleasure nearly blinded him.

It took nearly a full minute to regain his breath, and another thirty seconds to open his eyes and unclench his teeth. Both of them were sweaty, breathless, and limp, but her gaze was dreamy and her lips drifted upward into a cat-that-ate-the-canary smile. "That was fantastic."

Machismo nibbled away his doubts about taking her virginity, and he grinned, planting a quick kiss on her lips. "Ditto."

In her palace on Mount Olympus, Aphrodite peered into the silvery liquid of her Love Glass, and whispered, "Sara Beaumont."

Lonely Sara's dreams of love and marriage flickered and formed, showing Aphrodite all she needed to know. She smiled. Her son and daughter-in-law still had so much to learn. "Sex fantasies for sale. Puh-leeze!"

She had created love between mortals since . . . well, for a long time. Did it matter that one was married, another engaged, yet another widowed? No. Love spoke to the heart and did not care about the constrictions of the mortal world.

"Zeth Peterson is who you want? Yet you settle for the second best. Tsk, tsk." With a wave of her hand, the Love Glass changed and Zeth Peterson winked into view. He sat in his corner office, his floor-to-ceiling windows offering a distant view of the Las Vegas Strip. He looked over a report, a frown playing around his lips, and sipped coffee. She sensed the coldness in him, and the lack of true purpose in his life.

"Not exactly warm and friendly, are you, Zeth? And you know nothing about women or how to please them." Aphrodite pursed perfect, lush lips and tapped a finger against her chin. "Ah, we shall have to fix you." Her gaze turned to the frozen image of Sara's deepest desire: She and Zeth stood at an ornate altar under an arbor of roses and pledged their vows. "Eros thinks Nic is for you, Sara, but don't worry, m'dear. You can count on me to give you what you really want."

Sometimes Aphrodite liked the hands-on approach. When she was feeling particularly good-natured, she'd talk to her targets over an espresso at a coffee shop, or sometimes she'd lure a female into an upscale shoe store so they could gossip about men while trying on Jimmy Choo stilettos. Because her trip to Greece had mellowed her mood, and because Zeth Peterson was not a mortal she felt deserved her direct contact, she decided to make him fall in love with Sara the old-fashioned way.

She zapped him.

Watching through the Love Glass, Aphrodite pointed, aimed, and *zap!* A gold-and-pink ray traveled from her forefinger to Zeth's heart. Though invisible to humans, to immortals it looked like a laser, and it had the same pinpoint accuracy. The instant it touched the man he fell hungrily, selfishly, deliriously in love with Sara Beaumont.

chapter four

On Tuesday, the morning after she'd lost her virginity, Sara entered her office cubicle, dumped her purse and convenience-store coffee on the desk, sat down, and turned on her computer. She'd been unable to stop smiling, unable to stop doing a happy jig when she walked short distances, and unable to stop thinking about sex with Nic. He reminded her of a shaggy lion, with his blondish-brown hair and his hazel eyes. He'd taken her like one of those fearsome beasts, too, when they'd had a third session on the couch, and a fourth on the floor. Dear God, she never thought physical relations would be that damned fantastic. The only thing better than having sex with Nic was having lots of sex with Nic. Yeah, she was sore, her thighs hurt, and her muscles ached, but every twinge was worth it.

He said he would call her. Said he wanted to take her to dinner. She found that funny. Didn't guys usually foot the bill for a date in the hopes they'd get laid? He had it backward. But she didn't care. She wanted him to call, wanted to see him. Oh, well. If her luck with men held, he wouldn't call and she wouldn't see him again. Ever. At least he'd given her some wonderful memories to relive.

Splaying herself on the desk and Nic, there, pulling her toward him.

His wet mouth on her breast.

His hand on her hip.

His cock slipping inside her.

Her heart tripped . . . her nipples hardened . . . an ache spread between her legs. *Whoa, girl.* The fantasy date was over. Reality had returned, but she felt good. Powerful. Beautiful. Like she could take on the world. Like she could tell Zeth Peterson to go fuck himself because she was soooo over him. Yesterday's news, baby. Not that he'd ever known about her crush on him. She had never even been a blip on the man's radar. No, she was too broad in the hips, and had not a single strand of blond in her mousy locks. But Nic had wanted her, as she was, and he had proven it on five—or was that six?—different occasions in the same afternoon.

Still grinning like a silly idiot, she lifted the lid from the Styrofoam cup to pour in the tiny creamers she'd snatched from the break room.

"Sara?"

Zeth Peterson's deep voice startled her, and she dropped the little plastic container into her coffee.

"You scared me," she said, digging out the container and placing it, dripping and sticky, onto her desk. She looked at him over her shoulder. "Is there something you need, Mr. Peterson?"

Her heart pounded and she felt light-headed. Maybe she wasn't over Zeth, after all. She'd had a crush on him for more than a year—since the day he'd hired her. He had a staff of fifty, and she was just another minion, but she'd pined away for the man who rarely noticed her. She'd woven a very nice fairy tale for the two of them: marriage, children, parties, friends, and vacations in Europe.

"There's something different about you." He tilted his head and looked at her as if she were the girl on the cover of *Playboy*.

Her pulse stuttered, but she shook off the reaction and frowned. What game was this? Despite her desperate attraction to the man, she hadn't been blind to the way he stalked around the office making conquests of the prettier women. She had wanted to be one of those conquests, but no amount of lipstick or horizontal stripes would fix her features and her body.

"I heard you were out yesterday," said Zeth. "Is everything okay? You're not sick, are you?"

"No, I had to take a personal day. Was there something I left unattended yesterday, Mr. Peterson?"

"Of course not. I care about my staff's welfare."

Since when? Sara pushed aside the uncharitable thought. She'd been out with the flu just the month before, and being gone for an entire week hadn't brought about this kind of solicitous behavior from the man. Despite his good looks and his reputation as an outstanding lover, Zeth rarely displayed emotion in the office. Sometimes he snapped out orders like a drill sergeant, but most of the time he was distant and polite—an animated statue with a great ass and eyes the color of a Tahitian sea.

"I'm supposed to attend a dreary charity event Friday night. I thought I might be able to tolerate it if you came with me."

"Me?" She licked the sudden dryness from her lips. "What's the charity?"

"Hmmm. I don't remember. Orphans or something. It's a thousand dollars a plate; it's a good cause—probably." He laughed as if he'd made a joke. "Despite all the hobnobbing required and the tiresome speeches, the food is decent and they serve alcohol. What do you say?"

Zeth Peterson was asking her out to a really swanky affair where he'd be seen with her as *his date.* She'd never known him to publicly date his office "girls." She blinked. Twice. Then she assessed him to see if the man before her was really Zeth and not an android look-alike. Tall, broad shoulders, wavy brown hair, handsome face—the poor man's Mel Gibson, but a looker all the same.

"Friday night. In public. With me?"

He grinned, his pearly whites gleaming. "The limo will pick you up at seven o'clock."

That night after work, the first thing Sara did when she entered her apartment was check her answering machine.

Nada.

Disappointment sat heavy and thick in her chest. Nic hadn't called. She toed off her low heels, stripped off the friggin' hot panty hose, and walked into the kitchen to pour a glass of wine. Another night of television, going over unfinished reports, and dreaming about men she couldn't have.

Except now she sorta had Zeth. But she wanted Nic. Maybe she wanted them both. She closed her eyes and tried to imagine what making love to Zeth would be like. Every time she envisioned a hand cupping her breast, a mouth kissing her lips, it was Nic, not Zeth, giving her the pleasure she craved.

She carried her full wineglass to the little antique table by the door. On it sat the stupid phone and its stupid answering machine. She glared at the little red light and cursed it for not blinking. Maybe it was broken. She pushed the button. "No new messages," trilled the electronic voice.

"Yeah, yeah. Don't rub it in."

She raised her glass to take a long drink of wine. The phone rang and its shrill bell startled the hell out of her. Her hand shifted and merlot splashed onto her white silk blouse.

"Goddamn it. *Now* you ring."

But still, despite wine dribbling down her shirt and soaking her skin, her heart lightened. *Nic, please be Nic. . . .*

"Hello?"

"Sara? It's Zeth."

"Oh." Her excitement plunged. "Hi, Mr. Peterson."

"Call me Zeth. We're not at work, are we?" His chuckle was low, intimate. "I was wondering if you'd like me to take you shopping."

"Do you need office supplies?"

"Oh, Sara, you are such a darling. I'm not interested in talking about work. I wondered if you'd like to go buy something suitable for the charity dinner. My sister shops at this marvelous store . . . what's it called? Dina's . . . Dinkie's . . . ."

"Diva's?" Sara sucked in a breath. Diva's was a very exclusive, appointment-only, you'd-better-have-gobs-of-money-to-set-foot-in-the-door woman's clothier. It was the kind of place women whispered about in the same tone reserved for Sunday Mass and for ordering a dozen Krispy Kremes. It was reverent, holy, and unattainable.

"You want to take me to Diva's? I'm sorry, Mr. Peter—Zeth. I can't afford it."

"I can. I'll buy you whatever you want. Dress, stockings, shoes, jewelry. We can go on Wednesday. We'll take off the afternoon and have lunch out, too."

Her boss wanted her to ditch work to go shopping and out to eat. *Holy shit.* Sara wished she were the kind of woman who could take Zeth up on his offer. If only she were a heartless slut, she could date him and run amok with his credit card.

"I'm sorry, Zeth. I'm not comfortable spending money that's not mine or getting to take half a day off because I have a date with the boss."

"I admire your integrity, but you're making me feel helpless. A man wants to provide for his woman."

His woman? Unease snaked up her spine. What was he doing? Did he want to get up her hopes, make her believe he wanted her, then pull a *Carrie*-prom-night scenario on her? Maybe getting pig's blood dumped on her head was better than getting her heart stomped on by Zeth.

"I promise not to embarrass you by showing up in jeans and a sweatshirt."

He laughed, but the sound rang hollow. "I have no doubts that I will have the most beautiful woman in the room on my arm this Friday night."

"I thought you were taking me?"

"Sara, Sara, Sara. You don't give yourself enough credit. We'll talk more about Diva's later. I'll see you tomorrow. Sleep tight, sweetheart."

"You, too . . . er, cupcake." She dropped the receiver into the cradle. What was that all about? Going out to a charity event was one thing; moving on to credit-card abuse and tender endearments was another. Everything she'd wanted with Zeth was unfolding—too fast and too furious, but still progressing in a very dreamy, delightful way.

So why did her mind insist on ruining the moment by torturing her with images of Nic?

chapter five

On Tuesday evening, just shy of five o'clock, Nic picked up the phone to call Sara and leave a naughty message on her answering machine. He wanted to see her again. Naked, yes, but more than that, he wanted to spend time with her, even if that meant a table and two plates of pasta between them.

As the receiver dangled from his hand, he realized the worst thing *ever* had just happened. Before now, the worst thing ever had been relegated to fifth grade, when Todd Malloy had punched Nic in the face and he went down like a big ol' sissy, blubbering all the way. That painful humiliation remained a blight on his manliness, but this . . . *this* was far more heinous.

He'd lost Sara's phone number.

Five hours of the hottest sex Nic had ever had in his entire life with the most delectable female on the planet and he couldn't find her fuckin' phone number. What had she written it on? A Post-it? A napkin? His sock? The details were fuzzy because as he watched her pull on the trench coat and pack up the toys, he'd been fantasizing about her naked and sweaty and moaning. He liked her naked. A lot. So he got distracted when she was writing down the phone number for him.

"Damn it." He crawled under his desk and combed the carpet for a little piece of paper. Instead he found the chocolate-flavored condom.

"Uh . . . boss?"

Nic raised his head and smacked it against the underside of the oak desk. "Godfreakingdamnit."

"Did you lose your pen or your mind?"

"My mind. What is it, Mandy?" He pocketed the condom and scooted out, standing up and rubbing the sore spot on his skull. His secretary, God bless her, handed him a packet of Tylenol.

"Psyche with Cupid, Inc., wondered if you'd drop by tomorrow morning around nine A.M."

"I'll call her."

"She seemed insistent you come by the office."

Nic ripped open the square plastic packet, downed the pills, and swallowed them with a swig from the half-full water bottle on his desk. "Don't I have some clients coming in?"

"No . . . well, you did, but both of 'em canceled their appointments, and, weirdly enough, just minutes apart. You don't have anything else scheduled until after lunch."

"Okay. Fine. Whatever."

His secretary left. Nic dropped into his chair and stared at the desk, remembering how he'd taken Sara's virginity right there. She had the greatest laugh, the cutest smile, and a wicked sense of humor. She was beautiful and curvy . . . *Oh, yeah.* She had the most curvaceous ass he'd ever laid eyes on. His penis hardened, and he sighed at the ache throbbing in his groin.

Damned if he wasn't half in love with her already.

*   *   *

When Nic entered the Cupid, Inc., offices, he wanted one thing: Sara's freakin' phone number. Last night he'd searched the Las Vegas Yellow Pages and the Internet, and he'd called every Beaumont in the city, to no avail. He even tried to get in touch with Psyche only to hang up on her voicemail. It was as if his dream girl had disappeared. He didn't know where she worked, though they had talked about her job, briefly, before she stopped the conversation by bending over the desk and wiggling her ass. He'd shut up and taken the invitation.

Yowzer. He swallowed the knot in his throat and silently begged his libido to stay in check. He didn't want to face Psyche with a hard-on tenting his pants. He shoved his hands into his pockets and grimaced. When he had dressed this morning, he'd tucked the chocolate condom into his pocket. *Sheesh.* Did he miss Sara that much? Even if he were to miraculously bump into her today, it didn't mean he could stick her in the nearest dark corner and make love to her until she screamed with pleasure.

His dick responded with rabid interest to that little fantasy, and Nic turned his thoughts to ice cubes. *Snow. Glaciers. Antarctica.*

"Mr. Anderson? Psyche's ready for you."

He crossed his legs and glanced at the secretary, Daphne. She was tall and leggy, Cameron Diaz gorgeous, and sported purple hair like few other women dared. Her nose was pierced with a tiny diamond, and he suspected contacts made sure her eye color matched her hair. She looked like a nymph—the kind he'd been forced to read about in Greek literature during high school English.

His stomach lurched. In all his worrying about Sara, it hadn't occurred to him to wonder why Psyche wanted to see him. *Shit.* Did she want to fire him? Did she want to make sure he didn't sue her for the mistaken Office Fantasy? Did Sara call and demand a refund? To his relief, his penis reacted to the idea that Sara hadn't enjoyed its thrust-joy by wilting like a summer rose.

"Mr. Anderson?"

"Yeah?"

Daphne's purple eyebrows rose to her hairline. She tilted her head and jerked it toward the office door. "Go in."

Heat flushed his cheeks. He grinned sheepishly as he rose from the chair and tried to keep his walk casual as he entered Psyche's office.

"Nic!" Psyche rounded her desk and embraced him, then held him at arm's length. "Oh, my. You do look well. Perhaps you should take advantage of our discounts and schedule another fantasy."

"With Sara?"

"Oh, no. We're not a dating service. We try not to pair couples more than once." She led him to the opposite side of the room. A small antique table held a tea service for two; on either side of the table sat fat pink wing-back chairs with lace doilies on the arms. Nic tried not to shudder as he settled into the frilly seat.

"What happened Monday was our fault, Nic. I've been uneasy about the entire situation, particularly since Sara doesn't know you weren't her original assignation. I fear what might happen. . . . She has every right to sue us."

"I don't think she'd do that."

"No?" A thin blond brow rose. "Perhaps not. But all the same, I'll have to tell her." She poured fragrant tea into the cup nearest to him and, without asking, added cream and two cubes of sugar. "Go ahead, Nic."

He picked up the china cup, shuddering at its delicate and entirely too girlie shape, and sipped. Surprised, he turned to her. "My mother used to make this tea for me. What was it called? Jasmine chamomile. With just about the right amount of cream and sugar, too."

"What a lovely coincidence." Psyche sipped from her cup and smiled at him over the rim. "Usually there's a long and involved process with our clients, and you've skipped over the formalities. One thing we do is a follow-up interview. Why don't we do that now?"

"Psyche, it was a happy accident that Sara Beaumont walked into my office. I have no intention of sharing with you what happened between us." He took another drink of tea before putting the cup onto its matching plate. "Are you planning on finding another accounting firm?"

"No. We like you very much. But I will need you to sign some papers put together by our lawyer, basically agreeing that you don't hold us accountable, you participated of your own free will, and so forth."

"I don't have a problem with that." Nic cleared his throat and tried to calm his nerves by inhaling a deep breath. "So . . . um, you said you don't pair couples up more than once?"

Psyche laughed. "We provide the pairing up for fantasies, sexual or otherwise. Marital status isn't an issue, mind you."

Marital status? For a moment his mind blanked. Sara married? Then he remembered he'd been her first man—and, if he had his way, her *only* man. No way was she married.

"What if your clients want to date?"

"If our clients wish to carry on a relationship outside the confines of the fantasy, we have no problems with that. Our contract includes a clause that once the fantasy has reached its conclusion, Cupid, Inc., has satisfied its promise."

A whoosh of relief made his limbs tremble. "That's great. That's really, really great. So all I need is Sara's phone number and I can move on to the dating part."

Psyche frowned, her gaze suddenly sympathetic. "Oh, dear. I'm sorry, Nic. I can't give you that information. Only Sara can."

"She did, but I . . ." He sucked in a breath. "I lost her number."

"The best I can do is to tell Sara you'd like to see her again. In the meanwhile, maybe she'll surprise you and call."

"I doubt it. She probably thinks I don't want to talk to her again. The guy always has to make the next move. It's my move." He knew his desperation showed in his gaze. "I can't tell you how much I want to make the next move."

"I'm truly sorry. I'll convey your enthusiasm to Sara." Psyche rose, as regal as a queen, and crossed the room to her desk. "Let me make it up to you, Nic. There's a coffee shop around the corner that has the most divine lattes you'll ever drink. I'll give you a gift certificate."

Nic rose, too, and resisted the urge to tell Psyche where she could put her gift certificate. He knew she was protecting her client, but surely she could see his intentions were good. And it wasn't like he was Joe Schmo off the street. He was Cupid, Inc.'s accountant. *Aw, crap.* Waiting for Sara to get in touch with him would be like waiting for it to snow in the Bahamas.

"Oh! I forgot about this." Psyche frowned as she pulled out a square black invitation from the same drawer from which she'd withdrawn the gift certificate. "The Las Vegas Children's Charity Fund. It's this Friday, and I have an extra ticket. Are you going?"

Nic took the invitation, looked at it, and whistled. "It's too fancy for me, Psyche. My accounting firm is doing well, but a thousand dollars a plate is too much moola." He saw the look of censure in her eyes, as if his not giving to charity were a strike against his humanity. "My employees and I pick a charity each month to donate our time to. We've held picnics and softball games, been Special Olympics coaches, read books to underprivileged kids. Right now it's the best I can do."

Psyche's smile nearly blinded him. "Dearest Nic! Eros was right. You are the one."

The one what?

"Would you like this ticket? It might be a good place to network and find more clients. You never know who you might meet."

Unless his psychic pleas to call him reached Sara, he had nothing planned for Friday. He wasn't in the mood to be social today, and he seriously doubted that the sentiment would go away in time to enjoy the weekend. He wasn't so flush with success and money he could afford to blow off an event where he could network.

He nodded. "Thanks, Psyche."

"Wonderful!"

He took the invitation and turned, but Psyche rounded the desk and grasped his arm. "Don't forget your gift certificate for Dionysus Café. It's the best coffee you'll ever drink, I promise."

"Dionysus? Isn't he the Greek god of wine?"

"And of merriment. These days he's in love with coffee."

chapter six

Zeth Peterson didn't understand his obsession with plain and pudgy Sara Beaumont. Up until yesterday the woman rarely, if ever, crossed his mind. She was good at her job and presented no problems as an employee. She wasn't exactly beautiful, though her eyes were a nice chocolate brown and her lips full and kissable. Her body was too curvy, too lush. Usually his women were bone thin and tall. And blond.

Sara was none of the things he liked in a woman.

But he had to have her.

All of her.

Forever.

That was why he'd spent the last hour picking out her wedding gown from the Paris fashion magazine open on his desk. He knew he couldn't pop the question right away. Maybe in a week or two. He was handsome, well educated, charming, and rich. Women loved him. Always had. Until now, until Sara, he had cared nothing for women other than what they could give him. They were, in fact, very expensive toys, and he didn't mind paying the high prices if he got what he wanted.

He looked at the gold clock on his desk, the one attached to the expensive pen set his father had given him when he'd taken over this small section of the company. Nine thirty A.M. He had a sudden, inexplicable desire for coffee. A peppermint latte. From Dionysus Café. What the hell was Dionysus Café? Another thought entered his mind: *Send Sara.*

He buzzed his secretary. "Mattie, please tell Sara Beaumont I need to see her."

He was surprised at his nervousness. He put away the magazine, squared up the paperwork on his desk, made sure his tie was straight, and slicked back his perfectly cut hair with his hands. As the door opened and Sara came in, his pulse raced and his heart *tha-thump*ed.

"Hello, Sara."

"Hi, Mr. Peterson." She stayed near the door, looking cute and uncertain, so much so that he wanted to take her in his arms and reassure her that everything was okay. She looked at him, then down at her sensible low-heeled shoes. He frowned. Those sort of shoes would never do for his bride-to-be. He made a mental note to take her shopping as soon as possible.

"Did you want something, Mr. Peterson?"

"Must I send you a personal memo to call me Zeth?" He winked, disappointed when she didn't react with the usual twitter and blush he'd come to expect from the women he flirted with. "I find myself craving a peppermint latte. Would you mind running to Dionysus Café for me? You're welcome to get anything you like as well."

Her mouth rounded into an O. "I have a report to finish, Mr. Pe—Zeth. It's due today."

"I'll reassign it to someone else."

"Please don't do that, sir. The employees might get ideas. . . . I don't want to cause any interoffice resentment."

"If anyone says a bad word to you, Sara, I will fire them." He crossed the room and pressed a twenty-dollar bill into her hand. "Dionysus Café. You can look up directions on MapQuest. Like I said, I want a peppermint latte, and please get something for yourself."

He leaned forward, because he couldn't resist, and brushed a soft kiss on her cheek. "You smell good. Like cinnamon peaches."

"Th-thank you."

He let her go, immensely satisfied with the blush staining her cheeks. Then she turned and escaped through the door, leaving him with fantasies of his bride in white. Hmmm . . . maybe they'd wed in Paris.

Sara stood in line at the very crowded Dionysus Café and silently grumped about Zeth Peterson. Something about his sudden attention made her wary, nervous. The man hadn't looked at her for the entire year she'd worked for his company. Why the tender looks, the soft kisses, the invitations to fancy-schmancy events?

You should be thrilled. This is what you wanted, remember? How many times did you plan the wedding? Envision the children? Think about the parties and the vacations?

Foolish, that was what she was. Dreaming a little girl's dreams instead of creating the life she wanted with someone who wanted her. Someone like Nic. Her stomach felt like it had plunged to her toes. Disappointment wedged itself into her heart, right alongside the unacknowledged thought that she might be in love with Nic Anderson.

Stupid, Sara. You thought you were in love with Zeth, but now he's just creeping you out. Nic took your virginity. That's all. If he wanted a relationship, he would've called. He didn't. Live with it. And don't cry!

The tears welled anyway, and she blinked them back. If their liaison hadn't been a paid arrangement through Cupid, Inc., she could go to Nic's office and demand an explanation from his promise-breaking ass.

Ten minutes passed. Then fifteen. The line inched forward. Sara wondered just what the hell was in the coffee. Gold flakes? Soon only two people were ahead of her, and she tried to curb her impatience. Already the rumors about her attending the benefit with Zeth zoomed around the office. She could just imagine what her coworkers were saying now that she was on an extended personal errand for the boss.

She felt a hand wrap around her arm; then she was yanked out of her precious spot. She looked over her shoulder and tried to step back into her space. The guy who'd been behind her, a geek with a long ponytail, fake Ray•Bans, and a pierced eyebrow, smirked as he stepped forward and closed the distance between him and the guy placing an order for his coffee. *Damn it!*

Anger pumped through her and she turned, ready to kill the inconsiderate SOB with a plastic spoon if necessary. "Why the hell did you . . ." Her mouth dropped open and her breath hitched.

Nic.

"Sara! I almost didn't come here. I mean, these kinds of places go out of their way to ruin a good cup of coffee, but Psyche gave me the gift certificate and I thought Mandy might like one. Truth is, I had this strange urge to come here, so I did, and I'm really glad I stopped, because here you are! Right here!"

Nic beamed at her. She stepped out of his embrace. Crossed her arms. Jealousy jabbed her. "Who the hell is Mandy?"

"My secretary. I didn't think I'd see you again."

"You would've seen me just fine had you called."

Nic nodded. "Yeah. Except I lost the number. I stayed up until two A.M. last night trying to track you down through the phone book and the Internet."

"I'm unlisted."

"I figured that out." Obviously ignoring the coldness of her tone and of her stance, Nic dragged her into his arms and kissed her with such passion she dropped the pretense of her anger. She was glad to see him, glad that he was thrilled to see her.

He lifted his head, his eyes sparkling with desire. "C'mon." He led her through the crowded tables to the back of the small shop, into a hallway, and down a flight of stairs. They left through a door marked EXIT, and Nic dragged her to a Jeep Cherokee and helped her into the backseat. She scooted until her backside met the opposite door and she stretched out her legs. Nic opened the driver's door and started the car. Air-conditioning blasted through the warm, stale air. Then he jumped in the back, slammed shut the door, and crawled on top of her, laying another mind-numbing kiss on her that left her breathless and needy.

"What do you think you're doing, Nic?" Her heart raced at the look in his eyes. He looked . . . hungry. *For her?* "I'm supposed to be getting coffee for my boss. I don't have time to—"

He shut up her protests with another kiss. His tongue traced the seam of her lips, and she opened for him, as greedy for his taste as he was for hers. Her breasts tingled, her very core ached, and she pressed closer, moaning when he deepened the penetration of her mouth, twirling his tongue with hers. His hands slid to the waistband of her gray skirt and untucked her red blouse.

Sara broke the kiss and looked at his strong, tanned hands as they unbuttoned her top. She grabbed his wrists, stilling his movements, and looked at him.

His gaze was opaque with desire, the intent glittering there so ravenous, she felt her heart stall, then triple its pace. "W-what do you think you're doing?"

Nic leaned forward, his breath brushing her lips when he whispered, "I'm going to ravish you."

S ara almost swallowed her tongue. The ache in his voice, the roughness of his request, made her pulse stutter. He wanted her. Just as she was. No dieting or makeup or better clothes or spa treatments necessary. His raw need made her wet and wanting. But making out in the backseat of a car like two horny college students?

"In here?"

"It's private."

"It's not really that—"

He cupped the back of her neck, his fingers warm and strong, and leaned close.

"It's quiet."

Sounds filtered into the interior: the rumbling of the Jeep's engine, the traffic whizzing by on the street, and the far-off voices of people walking into the café. His lips moved along her jaw; then she felt his teeth nibble her earlobe.

"It's not that—"

"Yes, it is. Work with me."

She laughed and he captured the sound with his lips, his hand drifting to cup her breast. He palmed the nipple, rubbing it with small, sensuous circles. Then he held the hardening nub hostage between his fingers, rolling and pinching. Little zaps of pleasure pierced her.

"Oh . . . uh . . . Nic." Her mind fogged, and she couldn't formulate a thought. What did she want to say? *More, please.* She couldn't utter the words.

Her blouse fell open and revealed her lacy front-snap bra. With two fingers Nic unhooked it and revealed her breasts; the cool air in the car stroked the nipples to full hardness. His mouth closed over one taut peak, and she groaned at the sensations prickling through her.

"Nic!" Encouraged, he suckled it harder, then flicked the tip quickly with his tongue. She clutched his shoulders and arched, panting and writhing under him. He turned his torturous attentions to the other nipple and committed the same felonies.

When he lifted his head, she inhaled some air. He left her so breathless—his mere presence destroyed her ability to take in oxygen. She felt dizzy and light-headed and utterly wanton.

"Sara . . . oh, Sara." He pulled her underneath him; his hands dipped to the edge of her skirt and he pulled it up to her waist. He grabbed the top of her hose and panties and pulled down, while she lifted her ass off the seat and tried to wiggle out of them.

"Hurry," she said. "Hurry!"

Nic yanked on the stubborn hose, dragging them down to her feet, where her low heels held firm. With a growl of frustration he took off her shoes, then ripped off the hose and panties, flinging everything onto the floor. "Never wear hose again."

"Okay."

"You can skip underwear, too."

"On special occasions."

"Honey," he said, unzipping his trousers and letting them and his boxers fall to his knees, "every day with you is a special occasion."

Her gaze stroked his hard-on, and she watched in eager anticipation as he rolled on the chocolate condom. "Maybe I should get a taste of that," she purred. "Chocolate is my favorite food group."

She sat up and scooted close, wrapping her fingers around his hips and allowing her thumbs to trace circles on his tense thighs. Slowly she took the tip of his cock into her mouth. . . . *Ew!* The sticky sweetness of the condom violated her taste buds. She lifted her head and looked at Nic. "This rubber has desecrated the holy taste of chocolate."

His expression was half pain, half amusement.

"No worries. *You're* my favorite food group," he said, and he pushed her down and covered her, slipping his cock along her clit. Tormenting her with long, slow movements, he brought a delicious ache to her core, rubbing and teasing until bliss electrified her, frying her brain and making her flesh sizzle with need.

"Nic, please!"

"I promise to buy you chocolate," he whispered in her ear.

She felt his length slip inside her until he was fully sheathed, and he stopped, kissing the side of her neck as she adjusted to him.

"I'll get you bonbons and ganache and truffles."

He moved as he uttered the promise; the measured strokes drove her insane with lust. Little orgasms trembled, rolling like tiny waves and breaking with each penetration. She wrapped her legs around him and urged him with her hips and whispered admonitions to move faster and harder. She shuddered as he complied, his delicious cock pumping into her.

The slap of flesh on flesh was accompanied by the squeak of the seat springs and the scrape of his shoes against the door, which he used for leverage. The smell of sex mixed with the light scent of pine from the air freshener. But what Sara noticed most of all was the warm, hard feel of Nic on top of her, inside her, around her. She held on to his shoulders, her fingers sliding into the damp tendrils of hair clinging to his neck. She whispered into his ear.

"What did you say?" he asked, his voice hoarse.

"I said fuck me, Nic."

"That's what . . . Holy . . . Don't say . . . Damn, you're going to make me cum."

"Don't say what?" she whispered. "Fuck me?"

He groaned, dropping his head to her neck and slipping his arms under her shoulders. He pounded into her now, his cock slick with her juices, her moist heat welcoming every stroke. The soft cloth of his shirt rubbed her nipples raw until they tingled. As sensation after sensation pierced her, she moved with him, meeting his every thrust with one of her own.

He felt so good; *this* felt so good.

She felt the rising of ecstasy and moaned as the little earthquakes melded into a huge wave of lusty delight. "Nic . . . yes . . . *fuck* me."

"Oh, hell, woman!" He groaned and shoved his dick hard inside her. She felt the milking of his cock as he came, his shuddering release melding with her own. Sara's orgasm exploded, a million sparks of pleasure sweeping over her, burning through her, leaving her thick and weighted with total satisfaction.

After a long moment of heavy breathing, closed eyes, muttered phrases of thanks, and another toe-curling kiss from Nic, they sat up. Sweat pearled their skin despite the coolness of the air-conditioning, and once again Sara's muscles ached—in a good way. Sex with Nic bordered on an exercise program. Maybe she could give up her gym membership and just work off the calories with him.

Nic disposed of the condom by wrapping it in her underwear and tucking it under the driver's seat.

"Nic!"

"Gee. I'm sorry. Did you need those?"

She batted at him playfully, though she'd never gone without underwear in her life. "Well, at least I have my . . ." Her jaw dropped as she watched him ball up her hosiery, roll down the window, and chuck the wad into the parking lot. Walking into the office sans panties and hose? Instead of feeling uncomfortable with the idea, she felt deliciously naughty.

Nic grinned at her as he pulled up his boxers and pants and tucked in his shirt. His look of regret as she resnapped the bra was almost comical. His fingers brushed the collar of her still-open shirt. "Need help?"

He buttoned her blouse and pushed the ends of it into her skirt. The feel of his fingers circling her waist made her feel tingly. How could pressing fabric into a waistband be such a sensual act? Who was she kidding? Everything with Nic was a sensual act.

"I want to see you tonight," Nic said.

"Okay."

"I want to see you Thursday night."

"Okay."

"I want to see you Friday night."

"Oh—Oh, no!" She laid her head on his shoulder so she wouldn't have to look into his eyes. She didn't want to admit she had a date with her boss. It shouldn't be a big deal. It wasn't like she and Nic were exclusive . . . or were they? Maybe great sex addled her brain, but waking up to Nic every morning for the rest of her life sounded like nirvana. She sighed. "I've got a . . . a thing on Friday."

"I've got a thing on Friday, too. Maybe I can escape early. We could meet at my house or my office." His tone turned wicked—and Sara laughed.

"Is your desk clear?"

"It won't even have a paper clip on it. So what do you say?"

"Okay."

Dionysus, known as Dion to the mortals who worked for him, was a jolly man with apple cheeks, sparking green eyes, a wide girth, and fire-red hair. He watched the two lovers enter the main coffee shop from the back stairs and exit through the front door. He suspected they might have gone through the alley had it not been blocked off. They looked happy and tousled. Through the picture window of his café, he watched the young man walk the woman to her car parked on the street in front of the café and kiss her good-bye. Dion chortled and slapped his round tummy like a drum. His staff, and even some of his customers, knew he was prone to laughing without any obvious reason, so no one stopped and wondered about his outburst.

"Hermes!"

A tall, thin man with long silver hair appeared in a shower of silver sparks. A row of seven silver studs graced his left ear, while his right held only one. He wore a loose white shirt with silver biker pants, and an odd-looking pair of silver sneakers. "You bellowed, my liege?" His reedy voice dripped with sarcasm.

Dionysus pounded the god on his back with jubilant abandon. "Take a message to Psyche. Tell her, 'Mission accomplished.' "

"There is such a thing as a phone, you know. Or e-mail. Ever heard of instant messaging?"

"You're more fun to send. And I know that you like any excuse to see Psyche and Eros. Besides, technology"—Dionysus waved a chubby hand in dismissal—"is just a fad."

Hermes rolled his eyes, but his lips betrayed a smile. "Anything else?"

"Nope. Not unless you're willing to drink a lukewarm peppermint latte."

chapter eight

*I*thought I would be fired when I returned to work on Wednesday, but it was as if no one realized I was gone. Zeth didn't even ask about his latte. That night Nic and I met at an Italian restaurant. We ate spaghetti and drank wine, but we couldn't keep our hands off each other. By the time we reached the car, he was so hot and bothered, I gave him a blow job right there in the parking lot! I think I'm getting better at those.

On Thursday all I could think about was seeing Nic. He is a big distraction. So is Zeth, but in a more annoying way. I had to tell him, repeatedly, that I did not want to go shopping. After I got back from lunch yesterday I found a bouquet of red roses on my desk. I might as well wear a sign that says, DATING THE BOSS. Except such a declaration wouldn't be true. My crush on Zeth Peterson was such a childish infatuation. What I feel for Nic is different. It's real.

So anyway, after work I met Nic at his office and we had

sex on the desk again. Damn, I love that thing. It's huge. Both of us can get on it and there's still plenty of room.

Now it's Friday. I wish I could tell Zeth I didn't want to go tonight, but it would be unfair to leave him in the lurch. I just wish he'd back off. It's funny—a year ago I would have lapped up this kind of attention from him, but now he's creeping me out. All I have to do is get through this evening. I'll give Zeth the "let's be friends" speech, but if I break up with the boss, I should probably start looking for another job.

I wish I could see Nic tonight. We have a date tomorrow morning—at Dionysus Café. I think he's hoping to get a little nookie in his Jeep again. Ha. Ha. I couldn't bring myself to tell him about going to this event with my boss. I don't want him to think I'm seeing anyone else. I'm not, really. I shouldn't be so worried. Once the evening is over I'll tell Zeth so long, and that'll be that. There's only room in my heart for one man: Nic Anderson.

Sara closed the journal and stared at the glittery floor-length black dress draped across her bed. She had spent an hour at the hairdresser's getting her mousy brown locks cajoled into an upswept hairdo, which included a row of rhinestones up the side of it. Then, completely unskilled with the level of makeup required for high society, she'd paid an outrageous sum for a professional to create a very un-Sara glam look. Her head felt strangely heavy. She never realized how much mousse and hairspray and really expensive makeup could weigh. Wearing only a black silk bra and matching thong, she stretched out her freshly waxed legs and assessed her red-painted toenails. *I wish I were dressing—and undressing—for Nic.* She'd gone to a lot of trouble to look good because Zeth was still her boss and she didn't want to embarrass him. But the whole thing felt wrong.

She used the pen to beat a tattoo on the journal's worn purple cover. It was a sure sign of her stressed-out mental state that she'd pulled the ratty thing out of the nightstand drawer. Writing in it usually calmed her, but she still felt restless. Foreboding whispered through her, touching her belly with cold fingers.

The journal held pages and pages about Zeth Peterson. She'd written down her fantasies about him, her dreams about their lives together . . . just like a silly schoolgirl. Embarrassment and shame heated her cheeks. *Pathetic, Sara.*

Maybe she'd needed those fantasies because they saved her from taking a real risk on love. She wasn't someone who enjoyed the rituals of dating, or maybe it was just the jerk factor of the men she'd gone out with that had made her spend a fortune at Cupid, Inc. She knew now that she'd hidden her fears about relationships, choosing false longing over trying, *really* trying, to find a man worth having.

Like Nic.

"Problem solved." She rose from the bed and took the journal into the kitchen. She tore out all the pages about Zeth Peterson and dumped them into the metal sink. In a drawer she found a book of matches. She lit one and dropped it onto the papers and watched, in supreme satisfaction, as they burned to ashes.

When Nic spotted Sara at the charity dinner, his tongue nearly dropped out of his mouth and rolled across the floor. *Hubba-hubba!* Then he noticed the tall, blond, handsome man next to her, his possessive hand caressing the small of her back as they maneuvered through the tables.

I've got a . . . a thing on Friday.

The charity dinner was Sara's thing?

Or was her *thing* the guy?

He felt like someone had ripped out his guts and filled the gaping hole with acid. Despite the burning ache eating away at his insides, he felt cold—cold and frozen. What should he do? Confront her as she stood next to Mr. Suave? Or skulk away like a wounded animal and pray she didn't see him?

Okay, okay. So Nic and Sara hadn't agreed, formally, to be an exclusive couple. They'd had great sex, lots of laughs, and good conversations. He never thought she was seeing someone—if she had a boyfriend why did she pay for a fantasy to get her cherry popped?

Clenching the stem of his champagne flute, he tracked the couple's progress. Sara seemed distracted, and more than once she frowned at the man who could not keep his goddamned hands off of her. He rubbed her shoulder, trailed his fingers across her hip, rubbed her arm. Nic noticed that Sara tried to put distance between her and the dickhead, but he was too slick. He found a way to get into her space almost as soon as she found a way to part from him.

Nic put the glass on the nearest table and straightened his tuxedo. The one-plus-one equation equaled three . . . except someone was getting subtracted from it—and now.

"Isn't he dreamy?" The lyrical voice directed the question at Sara. She turned to look at the woman who'd just joined the circle of small-talking rich folks and gasped. She was the most beautiful woman Sara had ever seen. Tall and thin, yet somehow curvy and lush, she wore the simple white Versace gown with a grace no other woman ever had. Her ash-blond air was piled high with ringlets dropping just so down her neck. She wore a diamond affixed to the indentation at the base of her throat—no chain at all. She looked like a Roman princess. No, maybe more like Helen of Troy might've looked . . . and if so, the reason Paris kidnapped her was entirely justified.

The woman's perfect lips curved into a half smile. "Call me Helen."

Sara's eyes widened at the coincidence of the lady's name. She blinked, feeling dowdy, fat, and ugly. A cold knot of envy lodged in her throat. "Sara Beaumont." She flicked a glance at Zeth, who was bending the ear of some poor elderly gentlemen about stocks and bonds and God knew what other boring subjects.

"How did you manage to tame Zeth Peterson? He's been a bachelor for so long—no one believed he'd settle down."

"I . . . uh . . . we just work together."

"Oh, pish-tosh. I've seen the way he looks at you. Believe me, darling, I know when a man is in love. And you? You must be ecstatic to be engaged to such a catch."

"*Engaged?*"

Sara whirled, the dread lodged in her stomach all evening blooming into fireworks of shock and guilt. "Nic!"

"You . . . you're engaged to this guy?" His gaze was dark and dangerous. Anger vibrated from him, but she saw the hurt in his eyes before he masked it.

"He's my boss. He asked me to come, but we're not engaged. We're not even dating. *Really.*" Desperate, she cast her gaze around the room as if proof of her innocence would suddenly appear.

"Sara! Nic!" Psyche and Eros stepped into the circle of people, beatific smiles lighting their perfect faces. Psyche squeezed between Helen and Sara and jostled her closer to Nic. "It's such a pleasure to see you."

Sara saw Helen scowl fiercely at Psyche and Eros and swore she saw the woman jab Eros in the ribs with her elbow. *What the heck?*

"Hello, Psyche," said Sara, nodding to the handsome man next to the blonde. She knew he called himself Eros, like the Greek god of love, and she'd seen his picture in Psyche's office. She attempted a smile, but knew her effort failed when Psyche glanced at her husband and gave a tiny shrug. *Damn it!* Sara felt so nauseous about Nic's reaction to Helen's loudly voiced assumption, she couldn't stand the idea of polite conversation.

Screw societal mores! Sara turned to Nic, her arm on his sleeve, and stared into his eyes. His gaze was filled with both longing and despair. Why hadn't she told him she was attending this stupid charity dinner with her boss? Better yet, why hadn't she told Zeth to take a hike? An ache welled in her chest, clutching at her throat, bringing tears to her eyes. What could she do? Say?

"Nic, I—"

"Forget it. I don't need an explanation. It's not like we're . . . Damn it." His jaw clenched and he shook off her hand. "You don't owe me anything. We both got what we wanted, right?" He spun on his heel and stalked away.

Sara turned and saw that the circle of people chitchatting had dispersed, except for Zeth, whose gaze followed Nic's erratic path to the exit. His fingers slid up her neck; then he whispered, "I'll be right back, darling." Sara nodded, though she didn't much care where Zeth went.

Psyche and Eros stood next to her, their avid interest in what had transpired obvious in their expressions. With self-pity creeping through her, she looked at Psyche. "He . . . he just paid for s-sex like I did. I shouldn't expect him to . . . care." Tears welled, but she sniffed them back.

"I was going to tell you at our follow-up appointment that Nic . . . Oh, dear. Sara, I'm truly sorry. It was a mistake sending you to his office. He's our accountant. His address got mixed up with the address of your real assignation."

"You sent me to the wrong office?" Sara tried to process the information. *Wrong office, but the right man.* "Nic wanted me? Not because . . ."

Psyche smiled. "What are you waiting for, my dear? He's getting away."

Sara ran as fast as her heels would let her and caught him at the door. This time she grabbed onto his arm with both hands and held tight. "We've known each other less than a week and we met through a sex service and maybe I'm stupid for saying it, but it's true nonetheless. Nic, I'm falling for you."

His gaze softened, but his expression remained inscrutable. Sara's breath hitched as he leaned forward, his lips a whisper away, and said, "I don't think your fiancé would appreciate the sentiment. Good-bye, Sara."

chapter nine

Nic whirled away from Sara, her stunned expression making him feel like a world-class jerk. He hurried through the open double doors and into the large red-carpeted hallway. As he stomped toward the bank of elevators, he heard a man call out, "Excuse me!"

He turned around and felt gut-punched. The octopus who couldn't keep his hands off Sara stood in the shadow of a large potted palm tree and motioned Nic to join him. Nic did so reluctantly, fisting his hands at his sides so he wouldn't knock the guy's teeth in. "What do you want?"

"We need to talk about Sara."

Nic shrugged. He wasn't telling this asshole anything. His heart felt cleaved in two. *Why, Sara? Why sleep with me and marry him?*

"I don't know what's transpired between the two of you, but I'm willing to make it worth your while to stay away from her."

"You're trying to *bribe* me?"

"I think of it as insurance. You don't distract Sara with your charming presence and she will focus on what's important: me."

"You son of a bitch!" Nic advanced and the creep backed against the wall, an expression of alarm crossing his handsome face. "There is nothing—*nothing*—you can give me that will make me stop . . ." He hesitated. Stop what? Falling for Sara, too? He backed away as hurt crushed his chest and threatened to cut off his oxygen. What kind of manipulative, cold bitch lost her virginity with a complete stranger instead of the man she was marrying? He clenched his jaw against another wave of stagger-ing emotional pain.

He's my boss. He asked me to come, but we're not engaged. We're not even dating.

The words ricocheted in his mind over and over. He'd been so outraged at the thought that she had a secret fiancé, he hadn't heard what she was telling him. The Sara he knew, the one who laughed so freely, who gave herself to him without reserve, who made him feel so alive, was the real deal. He didn't care that he'd known her only a week. In the depths of his soul he knew she wasn't the kind of woman who trashed a man's dignity and stomped on his heart.

Octopus Guy straightened, though he stayed as close to the wall as possible. "Everyone has a price, my friend."

He glared at the cowering jerk in front of him. "Fuck off."

Sara watched Nic march into the hallway and go right, toward the elevators. She couldn't draw a steady breath, and her legs felt welded to the floor. What was wrong with him? Did he really be-lieve she was engaged?

Then the horrible realization hit her.

He thought she'd played him.

They hadn't known each other long enough to establish a

deep, abiding trust, the cornerstone of any relationship. Still, he'd leaped to the wrong conclusion without allowing her to explain, and he didn't seem to care that she had admitted her feelings for him. The fact that he believed she could do something so heinous to another person—marry one while she made love to another—sliced her to the core.

She heard raised voices and looked over her shoulder. Psyche, Eros, and Helen were having a heated discussion. Helen looked pissed off and gestured wildly at Psyche and Eros; the other two reacted with more calm, but she noticed Eros kept a restraining hand on his wife's arm. Words floated above the din of the crowd.

"You can't just zap people."

"She's marrying the man of her dreams."

"Nic is her match."

"Mortals must always have a choice."

After another round of furious arguing, Helen waved her arms in apparent surrender and yelled, "Oh, have it your way!" Strangely, she pointed her left forefinger at the wall behind Sara and made a poking motion. Then, disgust marring her beautiful face, she pivoted on her heel and disappeared into the milling people.

Sara frowned. What an odd conversation . . . and she was sure they were talking about her. Zap? Match? Mortals? What did it all mean? She glanced into the hall, harboring a small hope that Nic had reappeared. No such luck. She looked at Psyche and Eros again, only to find that they, too, had left. Zeth, her date, had finally done what she expected—abandoned her for a thinner, blonder, sexier woman. *Hell, he's probably forgotten he even came to this shindig with me.* She didn't need to see the evidence to assess the crime, and honestly, she was relieved. Wanting the dream was not the same as having the reality.

Feeling morose and terribly unwanted, Sara trudged into the hall and headed to the elevators. She walked about five feet and stopped. Amazement and relief rushed through her. Nic stood over Zeth, who was unconscious on the floor, his tawny head resting on the rim of a potted palm tree.

Nic turned toward her and put up his hands in a gesture of surrender. "I swear to heaven, Sara, that I didn't touch him. I was thinking about punching out his lights, but the next thing I knew his eyes rolled back into that thick skull of his and he collapsed."

Before she could bend down and check his pulse, Zeth's eyes fluttered open. He stared at her in confusion. "Sara?"

"Yes, Mr. Peterson?"

"What the hell am I doing on the floor?"

"Uh . . . too much champagne?"

He blinked a few times, as if he couldn't get his bearings, and then climbed unsteadily to his feet.

Nic touched her shoulder, and when she turned to him he cupped her chin, his gaze apologetic. "I'm a fool. I heard what you said—about not being engaged to this asshole—but I didn't process it. I just . . ."

"Got hurt and ran away like a wounded bear?"

"Yeah."

"What asshole?" asked Zeth in a dazed voice. "Wait a minute. Me? I'm the asshole? Engaged to Sara Beaumont? I barely know her, and . . . and she's not even my type!"

"That's true," said Sara, nodding. "Thin, blond, and shallow, that's his type."

Nic frowned. "But he was just blubbering about . . . He said . . ." He shook his head. "What the hell is going on?"

"I have no idea," said Zeth. "Sara, I appreciate your attending the charity dinner with me, but I believe this is where we will part ways."

"That's probably a good idea."

He scuttled past them, straightening his tuxedo as he hurried away from them, casting scowls over his shoulder.

"I'm sorry." Nic kissed her softly, and all her angst melted under the tender assault. "You mean more to me than how I just treated you, Sara. I should have given you a chance . . . I should have given us a chance."

Sara smiled and wrapped her arms around him. "Why not take a chance now?"

Staff Meeting
Conference Room B
Eight A.M. (This means you, Aphrodite)

Eros looked up when Psyche entered the conference room and waved a thick cream envelope at him. "It's a wedding invitation from Nic and Sara. They're getting married."

She danced a sexy jig to his desk and grinned with such silly, carefree abandon, he felt his chest constrict. *Psyche—my heart.* He would never forget the day he saw her, the day he fell in love with the mortal woman who gave him such joy . . . he never regretted his path on the rocky road of love.

"Can you believe it's been a year since they met?" She glanced at him. "I'm still annoyed with you. To mix up the addresses on purpose and not tell me! Daphne almost turned into a potted plant because she didn't want to hear me bitch about it anymore."

"There should still be some surprises between us, don't you think?" He smiled wickedly, and she dropped the pretense of annoyed spouse, leaning down to give him a kiss that seared him to his toes. "What should we send them?" he asked when his breathing returned to normal.

Psyche chuckled. "A bed, I think. Made from a very large desk."

The door to the room burst open and Aphrodite breezed in, a look of pure torment creasing her beautiful face. "Holy Zeus! Why do we have these meetings so early?"

Eros lightly pinched Psyche's arm to keep her from uttering whatever insult hovered on her lips. Her mouth snapped shut, but her eyes sparkled with humor. He'd have to ask her later what she intended to say. The reason they had early-morning meetings, according to his beloved, was to maintain the appearance of a real business. But he knew Psyche just liked to rile his mother in whatever way possible—and he had to admit, he enjoyed his mother's melodramatic responses.

"Good morning, Mom."

"Whatever. Grace!"

The slender young woman—one of three identical females who obeyed Aphrodite's every whim—entered the room, her eyes downcast.

"Yes, goddess?"

"Darling, get thee to the Dionysus Café and bring me a large mocha with extra whipped cream."

"Will you have sustenance, too, son and daughter of Aphrodite?"

"Oh, yes. Yes, get them something, too."

Eros sighed. He knew his mother adored the Graces, but she took them and their service to her for granted. "Thank you for volunteering Grace to do our bidding, too, Mother."

"It is with great joy that I serve Aphrodite and her children." Grace meant every humble word. Eros looked at Psyche and she inclined her head.

"Bring us the same, Grace. Please accept our thanks."

She smiled, leaving as quickly and as silently as she had entered.

"We were just talking about Sara and Nic. They're getting married in a month," said Psyche, dropping a quick kiss on Eros's lips before scooting into her own chair. "Remember them?"

"No." Aphrodite concentrated on the paperwork in front of her as if trying to memorize each paragraph word by word. After a long moment she sighed. "Oh, all right. Yes, I remember them. I'm thrilled they're getting married, blah, blah, blah." She looked at her manicured nails. "I don't make mistakes. Sometimes wires get crossed or mortals get stubborn. It would've worked out just fine between Sara and Zeth."

Eros rolled his eyes. She would never, ever admit that he and Psyche had made the better match. His mother's arrogance was one of her less-than-stellar qualities. But even with her vanity, Aphrodite also harbored a generous and kind spirit. "I am sure Zeth is quite happy with the wife you found for him. They moved to Paris, didn't they?"

Aphrodite stopped admiring her nails and looked at him, her eyes glinting with pride. "Yes, they did. And that marriage worked out well, didn't it? I . . . I guess it was just as well Sara and Nic stayed together, for Zeth to attain his own happiness."

Psyche had a coughing fit of epic proportions. Her eyes streamed with tears as she struggled to regain her breath or, more likely, prevent the peals of laughter threatening to erupt. Eros poured his wife a glass of water from the pitcher on the middle of the table and handed it to her. She sipped the refreshing liquid and smiled. "Thanks. Something got caught in my throat."

"I hope you're all right, my dear," said Aphrodite, suspicion tingeing her concern. "Perhaps we should get started on today's matches."

"I picked out someone special," said Psyche. "Janie Brown. Recently divorced. No children. She was married for five years to a lawyer—a real sleaze, too—who couldn't keep his dick in his pants. Irony of ironies, she owns one of the independent chapels downtown—the Wedding Veil."

"Celebrity Fantasy," murmured Aphrodite as she read over the application. "She wants a date with Kevan Rune? Ha. Her and every other female in the known world."

"We've set this one up in a special way," said Eros. "It's a promotion for Cupid, Inc., but it gives us an—"

Psyche cleared her throat. "Er . . . let's take a break."

"What?" Aphrodite tapped impatient fingers against the steel conference table. "If you insist on early-morning meetings, you should be prepared."

His mother sounded particularly sulky. Eros hoped Grace appeared with the coffee soon. Dionysus's mochas always put her in a better mood. He looked at his wife, his brows raised. "Anything you need to tell us, dear?"

"Be right back!" She popped out of sight before he could follow up on the sneaking suspicion that Psyche had forgotten a rather important errand.

Private Meeting
The Trailer of Kevan Rune
8:06 A.M.

"Me? The prize of a win-a-date contest?" The mellow voice held a note of ire. Kevan Rune's shaggy dark hair fluttered into his face and he shoved it back, revealing almond-shaped, melted-chocolate brown eyes. "Psyche, I can't take off to Las Vegas so I can wine and dine some starry-eyed housewife."

Psyche silently assessed the movie star. Seconds ago she had zapped herself just outside his trailer door on Trillion Studio's back lot. Kev let her in, appearing unsurprised to see her. The man spent more time in the trailer than he did in his multimillion-dollar home in Beverly Hills.

As she expected, she found him alone, in his usual morose mood, reading *Macbeth*, or as actors called it, "the Scottish play." He slouched in the leather chair, barefoot, his ripped jeans clinging to long, muscled legs. He wore a black T-shirt that molded his chest and stretched tight enough to show off his six-pack abs. The infamous patchy beard shadowed his angled cheeks.

"You don't have a girlfriend. Your sister is in Paris. And you just finished a film." Psyche plucked the tattered book out of his hand. "Janie is a nice woman."

"All my fans are nice."

Psyche's brows lifted. "How would you know? You don't read fan mail."

Kevan shifted uncomfortably. "It's not because I don't appreciate their . . ." He waved a hand, unable to articulate the right word; then he shrugged. "I'm just a meathead—"

"Oh, puh-leeze," interrupted Psyche. "If I have to hear or read that stupid quote one more time, I'll shave your head and make you wear pink high heels to your date with Janie. You hate the thought of people getting close to you. Zeus forbid someone gets to know the real you."

"I value my privacy."

"You owe Eros."

She watched Kevan's gaze slide to the book she held hostage, and he sighed, giving a slight nod. Grinning in triumph, Psyche returned the ratty tome to him and left. The minute the door slammed shut behind her, she disappeared in a shower of gold sparks.

Staff Meeting
Conference Room B
8:11 A.M.

"He's agreed to wine and dine her for one night. He will submit to our tests, questionnaires, and medical exams, but he insists: no sex." Psyche sent her husband a pleased but sheepish smile. He shook his head, a grin tugging on his lips.

"We can't promise they won't have carnal relations," said Aphrodite.

Eros's brows rose. *"Carnal relations?"*

"The horizontal bop? The mattress mambo? Plowing the fields of—"

"Point taken, Mom."

"We cater to a variety of fantasies, not just sexual ones," said Psyche. "Janie will win the contest and meet the man of her dreams."

"You think this is a match?" Aphrodite sounded doubtful, but Eros wasn't offended. Mom always expressed cynicism for his and

Psyche's pairing of humans. "A movie star and a wedding plan-ner." She chuckled, shaking her head at the apparent idiocy of the choice.

"It has a good probability as a match, but Mother, the mortals must choose their own life mates. If they don't fight for love, they don't deserve to have it."

"That means no zapping," clarified Psyche.

"Oh, for Hades' sake! Fine. Whatever." She waved her hand in dismissal. "Do as you like, and when it falls apart, I will mend the pieces."

"Yes, Mother." Eros winked at Psyche, grinning when she winked back.

The Stars in Her Eyes

Kevan Rune sat at a table for two near the restaurant's bay window, which faced the Las Vegas Strip, and regretted for the thousandth time his acquiescence to Psyche and Eros's insane scheme. If Eros hadn't saved his life five years ago on the set of *Fast*, the action thriller that made Kevan a star, he would've told the couple to take a hike. But, no matter what anyone else believed about him, Kevan was a man of his word.

He fingered the soft petals of the dozen white roses on the table and sighed. Had he really consented to a whole evening with a female who would simper and flatter and ask personal questions? He loved acting, and, in some ways, he liked being a star, but he hated the invasion of his privacy. No one had the right to delve into the areas of his life not related to the craft or to the business.

"Angela Marleaux with *StarNews*. Who are you meeting tonight?"

Oh, crap. His friends had nicknamed her "Angela Marlowdown," and for damned good reason. For all his desire to avoid bad press and journalists like Angela, it was impossible to have a career without media coverage. Unfortunately, for every well-written article, there were ten pieces of malicious, untrue dreck. Angela specialized in dreck. She had been the first reporter to make a deal with his ex-girlfriend Bonnie Braden for the nitty-gritty details of their rocky romance.

Kevan inhaled a fortifying breath as he turned to face the worst of the worst reporters who covered celebrities, and forced a smile. "Are you eating here, too?"

"You know I can't afford a ritzy place like this, Kevan. I'm a working girl." Her gaze was riveted on the rose bouquet. She grinned, showing shiny rows of teeth—white just like a shark's.

Why was Angela in Las Vegas? She was way outside her usual beat of Hollywood hot spots. Surely she didn't know about his deal with Cupid, Inc. If she had her way, she'd take another huge bite out of his reputation and plaster any indiscretion across the front page of the rag she worked for—like she did, week after week, with Bonnie's tell-all.

Angela kept grinning at him, obviously hanging around to see who showed up at his table. "Who was the woman you were seen shopping with at the Place Vendôme in Paris?"

Damn it! The press had hounded him so relentlessly that he'd gone to Paris to visit his sister Kimmie and chill out for a few days. He needed a break from the publicity that, after six months, still had not died down—thanks to Bonnie's constant stoking of the media fires.

"What is the blonde's name? Is she your new girlfriend?"

The woman was his *sister's* girlfriend, not his. They lived in Paris happy as clams, and he'd be damned if he'd set reporters loose to investigate his sister's sexual preferences. No one should care about bedroom politics in this day and age, but he knew better. Everything was a scandal—from the chipped polish on Paris Hilton's toenails to the drunken nuptials of an NCAA basketball player and his Mercedes-Benz.

"Oh, c'mon! You were photographed coming out of Van Cleef and Arpels, one of the most exclusive and expensive jewelry stores in Paris. Now here you are in Las Vegas. Do I hear wedding bells?"

Where was her logic? She believed he had gone to Paris to buy an engagement ring, but instead of marrying his so-called bride in one of the most romantic cities in the world, he took her to Vegas for a quickie wedding? *Riiiiight.*

Kevan's smile felt brittle and fragile, but he kept it in place and stayed silent. Angela knew this tactic, and rolled her eyes. "Gimme a break, Kev. If you won't tell me who you're dating or marrying, at least answer one question for me. How do you feel about Bonnie's six-figure book deal, where she promises to reveal the sins of the Hollywood sect, especially those of you and your friends?"

He felt like shit that someone he had cared about and trusted screwed him over for money. Hell, if all Bonnie had ever wanted from him was cash, he should've paid her outright instead of dating her. When he'd found out about Bonnie's book, he got righteously pissed off and called his lawyer, who was fighting the publication deal tooth and nail.

"You are so freaking tight-lipped. Can you tell me if you've signed on for *Flames of Rhapsody*? I hear Nicole Kidman is playing the blind ex-assassin."

"Why don't you go ask her?"

"I will. Are you playing the CIA operative bent on revenge?"

"Are you sure that's what the movie is about?"

Angela stilled, her eyes widening as she shoved her unruly red curls away from her face. "Are you saying *Flames of Rhapsody* has an alternative plot?"

Kevan shrugged, his smile nearly melting under the pressure of aiming it at Angela. She took the opportunity to snap his picture with a palm-size digital camera. "Gotcha! Pictures may be worth a thousand words, Kev, but yours are worth a thousand bucks."

"Excuse me."

Kevan turned toward a tall brunette wearing a shimmery silver dress and black lace wrap. She stood next to the table, her gaze twinkling with mischief as Angela almost tripped trying to shove a minirecorder in her face. "Are you Kevan Rune's date?"

"No. Are you Angela Marleaux, the famous reporter with *StarNews*?" The woman's soft voice had an accent he couldn't place. It wasn't the deep drawl of the South, but there was a definite twang.

When Angela didn't respond, Kevan glanced at the reporter. Her mouth was open, her eyes wide. He'd never seen Angela speechless before, and it was terrific to watch the tables turn. One thing celebrities knew about their media tormentors was that their driving motivation, other than money, was getting a taste of the fame. After a second the reporter shook off the daze of being recognized and once again presented the microphone. "And you are?"

"Nobody at all, Ms. Marleaux. I swear—and I can't be sure, mind you—that I saw Nicole Kidman sneak into one of the private dining rooms, and again, I don't really know, but I think she's with her ex-husband. They were talking. . . . You know, it's strange. Do flames or blindness or CIA agents mean anything to you?"

"*Flames of Rhapsody!* Tom and Nicole in a new film together? Oh, my God!" Angela hurried off in the direction the woman had pointed without so much as a good-bye.

"Hello." She smiled at him, and he noticed the genuine quality in the curve of her lips and the cute dimple near the left corner of her mouth. He felt a faint stirring of admiration. "My name is Janie Brown."

His date. Politeness forced Kevan to stand and reach for the wrap across her shoulders, but she stopped him with a wave of her hand. "I don't think we have much time, Mr. Rune. I just lied my ass off, and chances are good little Miss Nosey will return with questions blazing if we don't skedaddle."

"Skedaddle?"

"Leave the premises."

He grinned and handed her the roses with a flourish. "Let's go."

He'd made arrangements to leave through the kitchen. He had, with major reluctance, left his Kawasaki 750 Vulcan in the valet parking of the Bellagio's garage and opted for a limousine, an ode to ostentation he usually tried to avoid. To his surprise, Janie scooted across the gray leather seats without uttering a single "ooh" or "aah." He sat across from her, not wanting to crowd her, or worse, risk her sidling up to *him*. And yet . . . he had to admit she didn't seem like the type of female his sister called "strut-'n'-slut."

He watched her place the bouquet on the seat beside her. "Thanks for the roses. They're lovely."

"Roses are small thanks for your very timely rescue."

An awkward silence descended as they stared at each other, though from the congenial expression on Janie's face, he guessed it was awkward only for him. The limo pulled smoothly out of the parking lot and onto the Strip.

"How did you know what to say to her?"

"I hid by a potted palm tree and listened to her harass you."

Janie's gaze was warm, and her smile hinted at secret amusement. Her eyes were brown and reminded him, for some odd reason, of autumn, apple cider, and bonfires. She was pretty, not in the gym-and-Botox way he'd come to expect from so many of L.A.'s beauties, but in a way that suggested a natural comfort with herself. Her body was all lush curves and sumptuous possibilities. *Sumptuous?* What was wrong with him? He shook off the ridiculous thought and smiled at her. "I appreciate your coming to the rescue, though that's supposed to be my job."

"I'll return the white steed to you later." She grinned; then her gaze turned sympathetic. "It must be difficult for you."

"Dealing with reporters?" He shrugged. "It's part of the business."

"But offering yourself as prize for a silly contest is not."

Surprised by the gentle reprimand in her tone, he grinned ruefully. "It's a long story."

"The good ones always are." She stared out the window at the glitter and glam of the hotels lining the Strip, and Kevan used the opportunity to compose himself. He reached into the small black fridge to his left and pulled out a can of Pepsi. "Would you like a soda?"

"No, thanks."

"If you think the contest is silly, why did you enter it?" He popped the top and sipped the cold, sweet drink.

"My sister thinks I need excitement in my life, so she filled out a gazillion entry forms in my name." Janie glanced at him. "I'm supposed to indulge in hot sex, if, and I quote my sis, 'You even *breathe* in my direction.' "

Kevan almost choked on his Pepsi; liquid spewed from his mouth. He grabbed a napkin from the minibar next to the fridge and wiped his face, then patted dry the spots on his blazer. At Janie's look of astonishment, he smiled weakly. "You, uh, want to have hot sex with me?"

One corner of her mouth quirked and she winked at him. His heart skipped a beat at her sexy flirtation and her wordless, *You betcha*.

Hot sex with Janie Brown was not on his agenda.

Not that she didn't look great in the dress that clung to her delicious shape, and . . . well, he noticed, now that the wrap had slipped off her shoulders, that she had a great pair of— *Whoa. No, no, no.*

The rush of blood to his groin forced him to cross his legs and think about Canadian winters. He couldn't help but wonder what she was doing here if she thought the contest was silly—and it was—and she didn't even enter it of her own accord. Part of acting was confidence, and sometimes unchecked confidence turned to arrogance, but like most human beings, and actors in particular, he needed validation and appreciation. *Aw, hell.* He caved in to his ego and to his curiosity. "Why didn't you make your sister take the prize? Or give it to the second runner-up?"

"Maybe I should have auctioned you off on eBay. Would've made a bundle." Her brown eyes displayed the same mischievous twinkle he'd seen when she'd fibbed so gleefully to Angela. "I'll tell you a secret, Mr. Rune. I've had a crush on you since *Fast*."

"Um . . . thanks." The disappointment startled him. He had thought that maybe Janie wouldn't be like other female fans. He sighed, looking out the window, but without really seeing the flashy hotel casinos and tourist-crowded sidewalks.

It unnerved him how an autograph or a picture or just standing three feet away from him made people crazy. He did the red carpet at premieres because he knew the value of promoting the work. He wanted people to go see his movies. He just didn't want them crawling in the rosebushes underneath his bathroom window or chasing him down the street with their cameras. He dealt with screaming, crying, stars-in-their-eyes women by staying away from them.

"Do you wonder why people like you?"

Kevan blinked at her uncanny comment, which so closely echoed his own thoughts. "They believe what they see in films."

"Isn't that what you want as an actor?"

"Yes. But I want to be the character, not the movie star playing the character."

The corner of her mouth tilted, revealing the cute dimple. "I'm afraid you don't get to choose what people see or believe about you." Her gaze met his and she chuckled. "Thinking about Kevan Rune is simply thinking about how to create the perfect man. He's loyal and kind and enigmatic and gracious and handsome. He's unattainable, too, so I will never see the chinks in his armor. I will never be disappointed."

Kevan wasn't sure if he felt complimented or not. She liked the *idea* of him. Then again, how could she or anyone else like anything but the man he projected on-screen and whom the press wrote about?

"Maybe that's the real fear we all have, Kevan. We don't want to disappoint the people who admire us or who love us." Sadness shadowed her gaze, and she turned again to the window. The hunch of her shoulders suggested self-protectiveness. He wondered who had hurt her and why.

Maybe it was ego again. Maybe it was the way she'd rescued him from Angela. Or maybe it was that tiny seed of lust planted when she'd winked at him. Whatever the reason, he wanted Janie to know that he wasn't some asshole movie star reluctantly serving out a one-night sentence. Maybe that was the way he'd felt—and acted—minutes before, but now he realized the truth. He liked her. She was candid and funny and sexy in that lush way that made him think about the four-poster bed in his suite.

He leaned toward her. She was still staring out the window, her head slanted in a way that suggested befuddlement. He glanced out the window and saw that the limo had pulled into his hotel's driveway. Okay, so the Bellagio *was* impressive up close.

Kevan looked at Janie's face, the soft curve of her cheek, the sleek line of her neck, and the oh-my-God cleavage revealed by the V-necked dress. Forget Bellagio. Janie was impressive up close. He touched her knee, gaining her attention. She opened her mouth, but he held up his hand. "I've been—"

"A meathead?" she asked sweetly. "I'm quoting someone famous."

He laughed, delighted with her quick wit. Before he could respond, the door next to him flew open. At least fifty people tried to cram their heads inside. All were female. All were screaming. Some were crying.

One girl managed to pop through the mass of squirming women, grab his arm, and screech, "I love you, Kevan Rune!"

chapter two

J anie flicked the switch that locked the door next to her, then lunged to other side of the limo and did the same to the remaining two doors. She turned to Kevan and blew out a steadying breath. Those female minions of Fan Hell mauled him and screamed, trying to drag the poor man out of the car.

She grabbed Kevan's left arm with both hands and yanked with all her might. The strength of the teenyboppers pawing the actor, however, overwhelmed her efforts—and his. He kept trying to pull away, but even with his feet anchored on the floor and his shoulders leaning back, he was no match for the maniacally adoring women.

"Please, ladies. I'm not a piñata," said Kevan. His gaze looked as tormented as that of a dieter faced with a chocolate sale at Godiva. No wonder the man hated to deal with fans. They were nuts.

She let go of Kevan, looking around the limo for some inspired way to free him. Her gaze landed on the roses. The plastic covering crinkled in her hand as she gripped them, and she swung forward, yelling, "Duck!"

Kevan failed to heed this warning and got thwacked across the skull.

"Ouch!" White rose petals fluttered into his hair. His shocked gaze captured hers for an instant before his attention was diverted by a dozen pairs of hands grabbing his shoulders.

Oh, hellfire and damnation. Janie jumped onto the wiggling arms and snaky hands. The weight of her body broke their contact with Kevan's mangled blazer. Kevan remained behind her, reaching over her shoulders to push and pull away various appendages while Janie applied the roses to the girls with a force that dismantled the petals and bent the stems. She managed, with flying roses, curses, and sheer willpower, to get the idiots out of the way. Just before she grabbed the handle and slammed shut the door, she saw the harried limo driver and three Bellagio security guards attempting to subdue the little mob. She smacked down the lock and fell against the seat.

Kevan sprawled next to her, sweeping back his shaggy locks and inhaling deep breaths. He looked at his wrinkled black blazer, worn over a black designer T-shirt, and frowned at the missing buttons.

She elbowed him and he looked at her, embarrassment red slashes on his cheeks. She grinned. "You sure know how to show a girl a good time."

He laughed so hard he turned redder still. "You're something else, Janie Brown." Then he leaned down and kissed her.

Holy freaking moly. Kevan Rune is kissing me.

Her heart thrilled in her chest, doing a triple-beat mambo that threatened to leave her breathless. Grasping the lapels of his blazer, she drew him closer, sighing in delight when his arms slid around her waist, pressing her tight against him. The sweet movement of his lips against hers sparked a fire low in her belly. Wanton. God, she felt wanton. *Wanted.* Sexy and oh, so divine. She didn't care if this kiss wasn't real, wasn't truth. If Kevan had turned on his acting skills to give her this gift, then God bless him.

His tongue slid into her mouth, flicking against hers in an erotic display that turned low flame into high heat. She moaned, the sound echoing into him, and he pushed her down to the seat, releasing her mouth to nibble the line of her jaw, the column of her neck, the base of her throat.

"You smell good. Like cinnamon. And apples."

"I . . . uh . . . oh, God, can you do that again?" He kissed a slow trail to the place under her earlobe, suckling the spot gently, and she shivered. Tendrils of lust clung to her, tightening their grip with every touch of Kevan's mouth.

He buried his face into her neck, breathing in the scent of her hair before lifting his head. "What kind of perfume is that?"

Dazed, still riding the train to Lustville, she blinked up at him. "I don't wear perfume."

"It's gotta be your shampoo. It's driving me crazy." He dipped down for another taste of her neck; then she felt his tongue trace her collarbone.

"Natural, unscented. I buy it at the health-food store."

"Then it's *you.*" He sat up abruptly, leaving her flat on the seat, limbs askew. "*Shit.* What am I doing?" He looked at her, utterly appalled, and grabbed her by the elbows, jerking her upright so fast she nearly got whiplash. "I'm sorry, Janie. Damn it. I shouldn't have done that."

Janie wanted to laugh and to cry. She wasn't one of those teenyboppers dreaming impossible dreams about a movie star.

She wasn't wishful or foolish, either. Only someone living on Mars could escape the media-covered battle going on between Kevan and his ex-girlfriend. The silly bitch did everything possible to keep her name in front of the celebrity-greedy public—all in the name of making a buck. The last thing he'd want was the possibility of another scandal. *Kevan Rune Ravishes Fan in Limo.* Yeah, that was exactly what he didn't need. He was already fighting to maintain his dignity against Bonnie's crass revelations. What little privacy he'd had before she'd done the talk-show circuit had been shredded.

For all Kevan's glamour and good looks, she'd glimpsed a terrible loneliness in his eyes. Not even his considerable skills could hide that kind of unhappiness all the time—at least, not from someone who'd known the same kind of pain. And still her heartbeat refused to slow, and the burning desire to jump his bones rioted through her.

"It was a helluva kiss—one that didn't happen," she said, straightening her dress and forcing a grin to her lips. "Don't regret a second of it, you hear?"

"Didn't happen, eh?" He smiled, shaking his head as a chuckle escaped. "Like I said, Janie, you're something else."

"C'mon, Ralph from *Morocco*." Angela Marleaux peered at the young man's gold tag, then at his pale Anglo-Saxon face. "If you're from Morocco, I'm from Mars."

"Welcome to Earth," he said, flashing a polite smile.

The security guard wore a tuxedo and stood strong, tall, and stoic in front of an elevator. The very elevator she'd seen Kevan Rune and his mystery date enter just a few minutes ago. She hadn't gotten a good look at the woman's face, but she recognized the silver shimmer of the dress. Anger surged anew as she thought about the "aw, shucks" lady from the restaurant who'd sent her on a wild-goose chase. Honestly, when would she learn to spot a liar? With all her coverage of the Hollywood set, it should be second nature to spot a fake. *Ha.* If everyone acted fake all the time, what the hell *was* real?

"Look, Ralph. I'll slip you a hundred bucks." The last hundred bucks she had in her bank account. The *StarNews* didn't pay for lowly reporters like her to go on trips to Las Vegas. She was here on her own dime trying to snoop out a story that would get her noticed in the more respectable papers. She wanted to be the next Liz Smith, damn it. So far her single biggest accomplishment was being the lucky reporter to answer the phone when Bonnie Braden had called. She'd spent the last six months converting Bonnie's whines into juicy scandal. *Blech.*

Ralph remained stoic. In fact, she swore she saw amusement flicker in his blue eyes. *Crap on a cracker.* Who was she kidding? Ol' Ralph from Morocco wouldn't tell her where the restrooms were located for one measly Ben Franklin.

"Mind if I hang out?" she asked.

"You can do whatever you want, ma'am." He grinned, baring his teeth like a growling dog. "Except enter this elevator."

When the elevator to his private suite slammed to a knee-jolting stop, Kevan found his arms full of the luscious Janie Brown. Her purse flew out of her hand, and the black lace wrap slithered to the floor. *Oh, no.* Surely this wasn't—

The elevator joggled and squealed upward another couple of feet before halting roughly. He and Janie fell to the floor, a tangle of snagged clothing and bruised shins. He found himself on top of her, his face pressed into her ample cleavage as he fought for breath. He sucked in the scent of Janie—the scent that made no sense and shouldn't exist, because she didn't wear perfume or scented lotions, soaps, or shampoo. He'd already asked. "Gotta be the detergent," he muttered, his lips scraping the soft skin just above Janie's breasts. *Washes her clothes in cinnamon-apple Tide. Yeah. That's it.*

"Oh. My. God."

He lifted his head and looked at her. "Crazy, isn't it? The elevator stalled." He was such a liar—even though it was fib-by-forgetfulness.

"It's not that. It's w-what you just did." Her hands fluttered around her face like escaped birds. "The breathy-kissy thing."

Kevan noticed the sensual flush of her skin from cleavage to neck. *Whoa.* Passion thickened within him and arrowed straight into his hardening cock. He cleared his throat. "Yes. Well."

"Either get off me or do it again. If you do it again, *don't stop.*"

She wasn't moving suggestively, wasn't trying to sexily influence him into losing his mind. No. He was losing his mind all on his own. After what Bonnie did, he'd be an idiot to trust another woman he knew well, much less a stranger who inspired such mind-fogging lust. It was stupid and insane to slide his palm up, up, up the sparkly dress that denied him direct access to her body.

Stupid to allow his restless fingers to stroke the underside of her breast.

Insane to scoot up so that his hard-on nestled against the vee of her thighs.

Stupid to lower his head against her neck and nibble the flesh.

Insane to flick his tongue against the sensitive spot behind her ear.

Her moan sent pleasure-heat surging through him, filling him with a primal desire to claim this woman.

Fuck it. Stupid and insane would be his mantra for the next few hours . . . because he was taking Janie Brown to his bed, damn the consequences.

"Are there surveillance cameras in here?" asked Janie as Kevan rained tiny kisses on the swell of her cleavage, stopping only to dip his tongue in the space between her aching, way-too-sensitive breasts. Her nipples tightened. *Oh, baby.* She wasn't out of her dress yet—hell, he hadn't even touched a naked boob—and she felt ready to go over the edge. Then he did the breathy-kissy thing again and she nearly melted into a puddle of lust-delirious ooze.

"Kevan. The, uh, wow . . . yeah, that's good." Spine-shivering excitement clawed through her, and she dipped her hands into his open blazer, stroking the hard muscles hidden by his T-shirt. "Oooh. Right there. Could you—oh, yeah. That's the spot." His tongue inched under the black lace bra, teasing her poor neglected nipple by only swiping the areola.

Wait, wait, wait. Cameras. Getting filmed having wild monkey sex in an elevator might distract the press from Kevan's fight with Bonnie, but he didn't need another scandal—and neither did she. Her wedding chapel business was already on the skids because of her ex-husband's petty revenge schemes. She didn't need to complicate matters by giving the bastard more grist for the mill.

Kevan pulled down the dress just enough to reveal her nipples straining against the bra. He stroked one taut peak through the lace, agitating it with the pressure of his fingers and the abrasion of the material. Sensations ricocheted—an onslaught that left her trembling with fiery need.

"I think we should stop." The words issuing from her mouth were low and hoarse and unconvincing. "In a minute. Or five hundred."

Kevan didn't answer. His mouth surrounded the aching nub and began a sensual attack that left her mindless with pleasure. She untucked his T-shirt and dragged her hands across his six-pack stomach. Smooth skin and hard muscle quivered under fingertips. She snaked along the edge of his jeans, sliding her hands over his tight ass and squeezing. *Yowzer.*

He switched his attention to her other breast and, with unerring aim, his hard-on pushed against her clitoris in just the right way. Little orgasmic waves quaked. She couldn't believe how close she was to coming, and damn, if he kept rubbing his cock on her like that, she just might.

"You have the most beautiful breasts," he muttered before beginning another dizzying wave of nipple torture. His pelvis moved slowly, dragging his jeans clad cock across her dress-protected but throbbing clit. *Wham!* She grabbed his buttocks and ground into his cock, flying over the edge into an orgasm that left her breathless and blind.

When she floated down from the euphoria, she found Kevan staring at her. She was grateful to see the desire-drugged look in his eyes. He was as turned on as she—thank God.

"Did you just do what I think you did?"

She nodded; the back of her skull thwacked the floor. *Ouch. Shit.* "It's been a while."

His pleased expression was rife with manly pride.

She smiled at the typical male reaction and patted his behind as if to say, *Good boy.*

Whew, doggie. What a fine ass. Her body was ready for round two, but her thoughts remained sluggish. What had been so important just a second ago?

"Cameras!" she shouted.

Kevan was so startled by her scream that he toppled off her. He laughed as he scooted into a sitting position. Janie sat up, too, and leaned against the back wall of the elevator. Her thighs still trembled. In fact, most of her still trembled. "What's so funny?"

"There aren't any cameras in this elevator. My suite is exclusive—not even the whales get to use it."

Whales referred to the über-rich gamblers that every Vegas hotel catered to. They spent thousands—sometimes millions—of dollars, and in return they got exclusive perks no one else could hope to have. If the suite was off-limits to whales . . . She swallowed the knot in her throat.

She'd been so busy trying to act cool and collected around a man most women would never get to meet, she hadn't thought about the fact that he was a millionaire. Not only a millionaire, but Kevan was also one of the world's most popular actors, and one of the hottest bachelors in Hollywood.

The nervousness she'd avoided most of the evening slammed into her. *Kevan Rune just gave me an orgasm.* How could she have lost sight of the fact that she was with a megasuperstar? One who wouldn't have looked twice at her on the street or in a bar or . . . or anywhere. She'd thought she wasn't wishful or foolish. *Ha.* She was both!

"What's wrong, Janie? You look pale."

The concern in his voice sounded real. Was it? Could a man like Kevan who faked emotion for a living mean what he said or did? She nibbled her lip. "I-I just realized I was rolling around on the floor with Kevan Rune. I'm sorry. You made it very clear you weren't interested, and I—"

"No. Don't." His gaze darkened, but with what emotion she couldn't name. "I can't make you any promises. But . . . but for tonight, if you want, I'll just be Kevan and you can just be Janie. No regrets, you hear?"

Janie smiled at his use of the same words she'd said in the limo. God, she was so relieved that he still wanted her. Her ex-husband had accused her of being a cold fish in bed, one of many excuses he had used to justify his affairs. She'd learned through painful experience that almost nothing Dale said was true. Why had she believed it when he called her frigid? That lie was now revealed. A handsome man, a near stranger, had just brought her to an amazing climax without taking off her clothes.

She looked at the row of numbered lights above the door. They were three floors away from the P. *Wow.* Penthouse suite. Of course, she might not get to see it. Now that she and Kevan weren't attacking each other, she realized they were trapped. Where the hell was the rescue squad? "Good thing I'm not claustrophobic. How long does it usually take for someone to notice there's a problem?"

"Damn. I got distracted." He opened a small panel just below the elevator buttons and picked up a red phone. "Hey, Fred. It's Kevan. We're stuck. I didn't pull the stop switch. You what? Er . . . yeah, I can see why you might think that. Thanks."

He hung up the phone and cleared his throat. "Apparently Fred got us confused with . . . another couple—yeah, some *other* people—who, um, usually request that the elevator stop working for about half an hour."

The poor dear looked way too embarrassed. Dared she think Kevan was the one who enjoyed an "accidental" stalled elevator?

Clunk! The car wrenched for a split second, then began a smooth ascent. Kevan rose and helped her to stand. The mere touch of his palm made her tingle with excitement. He picked up her purse and wrap, handing them to her and allowing his touch to linger before slipping his fists into his jeans pockets. Then they stood side by side, waiting in companionable silence.

"No cameras, eh?" she asked.

"Nope."

"Security mistook us for a *different* horny couple."

"Seems so."

Janie quelled the laugh bubbling in her throat. "Forgot to tell them not to do it, didn't you?"

"Yeah." He sighed. "I swear, it wasn't a cheesy play to get into your panties. I haven't been to Vegas in a long time, and the last girl was . . ." He stared at the rows of elevator buttons, studying them as if they were a complex math problem. *Oh-ho.* So the last girl had been that insipid Bonnie Braden.

"You shouldn't worry about getting into my panties. You know why?"

Kevan looked at her, his head tilted, his gaze questioning. "Why?"

A soft ding announced their arrival, and the doors opened. Janie sashayed into the foyer, pausing to look over her shoulder. "I'm not wearing any."

N*o panties. No panties. No panties.* Kevan stumbled out of the elevator, barely noticing its doors swooshing closed behind him. Under that . . . that . . . that dress she'd been walking around bare-assed and . . . His heart stuttered as he considered what else under the dress was uncovered. He staggered forward like he'd had one too many martinis; then, strangely nervous, he halted and watched Janie's progress across the foyer.

If he hadn't known better, he'd think she was an actress playing to the camera. The sexy walk, the eyes glinting with naughty promise, the careless tossing of her wrap, purse, and heels onto the floor—she didn't bother to look back at him. She strode through the right doorway, into the living room, and left him standing there like a dumped prom date. His gaze strayed to the left doorway, the one that led to the bedrooms, then returned to the foyer.

What the hell did Janie expect him to do? Collapse to the floor in a lustful faint? Possible. The blood had already seeped from his brain into his penis. He was man enough to admit to some dizziness. Or maybe she wanted him to run after her, rip off his clothes, and tackle her onto the nearest piece of furniture.

His aching hard-on jerked inside his jeans, an enthusiastic "yes" from the organ now controlling him. *Did you see that luscious ass? Good God, move it, you idiotic bastard. Do you want her to start without us?*

A vision of Janie doing wicked things to her own body while he watched overtook him. Maybe she would strip for him . . . slink out of that dress . . . s-l-o-w-l-y peel down that bra to reveal those big, beautiful breasts. *Oh, hell, yeah.* Her hand would slide down, edge into her panties, one slim finger dipping inside the lace, touching the slick folds hidden within . . . except . . . except—*dear God*—she wasn't wearing panties. Lust shuddered through him, heating his body until he felt trapped in a skin-melting fire. His too-eager cock was harder than the marble floor of the foyer and protested the confines of his jeans with vigorous pulses.

"Kevan? Are you coming?"

Almost.

Desire was heavy and thick, a metallic longing that weighed him down and made him feel sluggish and weak and stupid. He walked, zombified, until he made it into the living room.

It was empty. *Er . . . empty?*

He stopped a couple of feet from the huge couch that bisected the cozy space from the bar area with its cushy stools, black marble countertop, and liquor-loaded shelves. In front of the bar were several groupings of chairs and tables—all sizes and shapes and colors—meant for partygoers to relax, mingle, and converse. His gaze floated over the empty chairs. No Janie lounged on that curved red chaise, the one with infinite possibilities as a sex chair.

He imagined her there—a come-hither look in her eye, her dress hitched up just enough to reveal the pale slope of her inner thigh.

He turned to the other side of the room. The large brown leather couch faced a white-marble fireplace. On either side of it were two wing-back chairs, one burgundy, the other striped with colors that matched other decorations in the room—dark red, rich gold, deep brown, hunter green. The fireplace was empty, cold; though several fragrant logs stacked on the left meant instant romance, if he wanted to go through the effort of making a fire. In June. In the Vegas desert. *Yeah, right.* He was hot enough, thanks.

To the left of the setting were three tall cherry-wood bookshelves crammed with popular fiction, biographies, classics, and many pretentious, expensive leather-bound hardbacks that had authors like *Shakespeare* and *Aristotle* written in scrolled gold. A singular chair, large and puffy, its covering green crushed velvet, waited forlornly for a reader to settle down for a quiet evening. No Janie, though, so he lost interest in the charming library.

To the right of the fireplace, close to the floor-to-ceiling windows with a view of the Strip, was a baby grand piano, its white keys gleaming in the low lighting of the room. The shiny black bench probably hadn't had a butt on it since Liberace—who had owned the piano and the bench for a brief time. At least, that was the story the bellboys always told him.

"I hope you're envisioning all kinds of sexually interesting positions."

Kevan turned and saw Janie behind him—still clothed, damn it—watching him with a wet look in her eyes. What had she seen in his expression while she watched him consider his surroundings? She looked as if she wanted to cry, but not in a my-cat-just-died kind of way—more like . . . I'm-sad-for-you. Why? *Oh, no!* Had she changed her mind about sex? Then her words filtered into his brain and he smiled, relief bubbling through him. Sexually interesting positions? Ah, if only she knew the deviant thoughts he entertained at this moment.

"I had a thought or two about bending you over the couch."

"Really?"

"Mm-hmm."

To his astonishment, and the approval of his dick, she bent down and lifted the edge of her dress until the silver material danced around her thighs, hiding the evidence of panties. Had she been serious about lack of underwear?

"I want to see your pussy."

She grinned, apparently undeterred by his raw language. *Well, damn.* That was how he felt. Raw.

"How will you manage that if you're fucking me from behind?"

His brain exploded. Or at least, it felt like a watermelon bludgeoned by Gallagher. Too many images of naked, aroused, beautiful Janie assaulted his mind. In desperation, his brain had made a deal with his cock. *Must. Have. Janie.*

White-hot longing burned through him, more intense than the sizzling hunger that had claimed him minutes ago. He'd made love to beautiful women. To famous women. To rich women. He'd never felt this . . . primeval. *Me Tarzan. You Janie.* He didn't want to make love to this woman; he wanted to claim her. He wanted to own her—body and soul—even if it was for just one night.

"Do you want this?" he whispered, hearing the ache of need in his own voice. "Do you? Because if I touch you again, I won't stop."

She backed out of arm's reach. *No! Oh, Janie . . . no.* He howled silently at the loss, at the terrible agony that clenched him. His gaze tracked her across the room. She wasn't going out the doorway, wasn't running toward the elevators. She still held the dress in her hands as she walked to the couch and leaned against it, facing him. The fabric bunched in her fists . . . inched . . . upward.

Anticipation rocketed through him. He rubbed his cock, shivering at the sensitivity. It strained against the confines of his clothing, maybe harboring the idea that it could perform the impossible act of piercing his silk boxers and jeans. He stared at Janie's thighs, at her fingers sliding up her legs. Was she trembling? Oh, yes. He detected the tremors in her arms. Was she nervous? Or turned on?

Higher . . . higher . . . the lace edge of her black stocking appeared.

His heart almost stopped. She was wearing stockings. Not panty hose. *Stockings.* He toed off his loafers, ripped off his socks. He unzipped his jeans, pulled them down, and flung them away.

He noticed the quick rise and fall of her chest and realized she was breathing hard. She *was* turned on. *Damn right!* Was her heart pounding as roughly and as loudly as his own? Licking his lips, he looked at the progress of her body pictorial.

Attached to the stocking he saw a thin black strap. . . . Up went the sparkly cloth . . . just enough to tantalize.

He shucked off his boxers. Tossed his blazer to the floor.

The black lace garter was revealed, a wisp of lace clinging to her hips.

Good-bye, T-shirt.

He let his gaze travel along the garter, afraid to look, to know if she'd lied about the panties. Then . . . he dared. His breath left in a whoosh. No panties. When she went bare, she went *bare*. She'd had a Brazilian bikini wax—the kind of painful removal of pubic hair that left a woman's nether regions smooth and naked. Except—he swallowed hard—for a thin strip of light brown hair that arrowed to her vulva.

"Did I . . . did I mention my mother was a biology teacher?" he asked, afraid to move. His cock throbbed, ached, and promised ejaculatory punishment if he teased it just one more time with image, touch, or word.

She arched an eyebrow, then shoved up her dress, her coy manipulation gone in a flash. "Biology, eh? What do you call this?" Turning so that her hips met the top of the couch, she bent over and presented her gorgeous ass.

He lost it. His thoughts vaporized; his body went from white heat to inferno. He strode to her, his hands grasping her buttocks, kneading the flesh, his shaking hands lifting her just enough to slide his cock between her thighs. Her toes still touched the floor, but barely. Hell, she wouldn't need leverage. He'd make sure she stayed put. Just the pressure of soft thighs on his manhood was enough to send preorgasmic frissons ricocheting from balls to bone. *Shit. I'm going to come before I even get inside her.*

Then he saw it.

A yellow circle of plastic clasped between two of Janie's fingers. She waved it at him like a tiny round flag. "Hel-lo," she managed to say despite the large pillows pressed against her face. "You wanna take this before my arm breaks?"

"Less talk, more naked." He grabbed the condom and shoved it onto his dick. He lifted her higher. God, she was wet. He smelled her, too, the cream of her sex, the impossible apple-cinnamon scent mixed within it. His cock pushed inside the tight, warm sheath and rejoiced. *Slow, man. Do it slow or you'll scare the hell out of her.* He sucked in a breath and squeezed his eyes shut.

A gliding press in, an agonizing withdrawal . . . another long, unhurried stroke . . . and another . . . Damn, he was going to die from this torture. . . .

"Um, Kevan?" He heard the hesitation in her voice. *I can't go any slower. Please don't ask . . . .*

"Yeah?"

"Would you mind . . . I don't mean to tell you how to do it or anything . . . but, would you *please* fuck me hard and fast?"

"Arg-ugh," he agreed.

He slammed into her once, clawing at her waistline as he penetrated deeply. Then, with the blessings of Janie, if her growly moans were considered amens, he pounded into her slick flesh—hard, fast, *and* deep. The *slap-slap* of his hips against her buttocks revved him into overdrive. His cock pulsed with imminent release, too stimulated to hang on for an extended performance. She smelled so good, that strange sugar-spice scent—like gingerbread, like autumn, like home.

"Janie!" The orgasm rushed through him, an endless wave of light and sound and pleasure, while his cock jerked with release.

"Thafwafreaffygoofaf."

Wha . . . ? Kevan blinked and looked down. He was still embedded in the delicious Janie, and he was damned reluctant to move. Her ass looked great propped in the air, pearled with sweat and flushed red from his enthusiastic pounding.

"What did you say?" he asked.

"Thafwafreaffygoofaf!"

Janie formed a lopsided triangle; her feet dangled about half a foot off the ground. Her dress had been shoved to her shoulders. *Whoa.* He'd nearly fucked her off the couch. He withdrew, looking with remorse at the happy organ tucked in the yellow condom. The damned thing was *so* happy, it had shrunk to half-mast.

Kevan wrapped his arms around Janie's stomach and righted her. She grabbed the couch and sucked in a shaky breath. Her hair was a wreck, her makeup smeared, and her dress wrinkled. She was befuddled and disheveled and cute as hell. His cock perked with renewed interest.

"You were saying?"

She looked dazed. "That was really good."

"Yeah," he said, grinning. Despite her sensual haze, he knew she probably hadn't come, and he wanted her to have another orgasm. And another. And one after that. And if he hadn't died from sexual ecstasy, he'd give her *another* one.

"Take off your dress, but don't move. I'll be right back." He hurried to the bathroom, disposed of the condom, cleaned himself off, and returned to the living room.

"Wow. That was fast." She stared at him with raised eyebrows. He saw the appreciation in her gaze as she looked him over. He refused to toast his skin in tanning beds or blister under the hot sun in nothing more than a Speedo, so his skin wasn't basted brown like some of his contemporaries. However, his body was toned and muscled. Whether he was tan or not, Janie obviously enjoyed his form. Her gaze went dark and her tongue flicked out to wet her bottom lip. He promised never again to give his personal trainer so much shit for those harsh workouts.

She smiled, revealing that cute dimple, and crooked a finger, wiggling it in the universal female language that translated to: *Come here, big boy.*

Desire shot through him. He advanced toward Janie like a lion stalking a gazelle. She looked . . . scrumptious. She wasn't bone thin, thank God. She was curvy—as in "Dangerous curves ahead." The garter belt encircled her waist, the straps attached to the silk stockings. . . . *Hot damn!* The getup really showcased that beautiful pussy. She wore nothing else except the sexy black lace bra. She had such gorgeous, big breasts—he had to admit, at least to himself, that he was a typical, slobbering male when it came to boobs. Her large, luscious nipples protruded beneath the thin material. He wanted to play with those breasts, taste the oversize areolae, suck the nipples. . . .

"Kevan? You look like I do when I go to Ethel M's Chocolate Factory."

"How's that?"

"Hungry."

"We skipped dinner," he said. "Maybe I should have a bite." He dropped to his knees and kissed the area just above her pubic hair. He showered slow kisses between her thighs, his tongue sliding on the smooth flesh, tasting the cinnamon of her skin.

She smelled good, she tasted good, she *felt* good. His cock zoomed from "perked" to steel rod. Later, he'd take the time to explore Janie's womanhood centimeter by centimeter—to torture her into mindless pleasure. For now . . .

He moved his hands up to her buttocks and squeezed, pushing her closer to his mouth. His tongue swirled up her outer labia— one side, the other side—and down again. Her juices coated his chin as he sucked the sweet inner lips. He feasted until his tongue reached the sensitive knot waiting like a diamond on a gold crown. Just a tease, a quick swipe . . . down again, delving into her vaginal entrance . . . thrusting his tongue inside the warmth . . . sipping her nectar.

She shuddered; he felt the rough dive of her fingers into his hair.

Slow licks up, up, up . . . then he took the hard little nub between his lips and swept his tongue across it.

Flick. Suck.

Her thighs trembled.

Flick. Suck.

She moaned.

Flick. Suck.

She came, a violent release that had her grabbing his skull and bucking against his face. His mouth flooded with her nirvana. He gladly drank from her, greedy for her taste, and all the while her cries of completion reverberated through him.

"I might need a chiropractor," said Janie, collapsing against Kevan. They sat on the red chaise longue. Rather, she sat on top of him, his cock embedded inside her, her vaginal contractions slowing as her orgasm faded into exhausted bliss.

"I might need a priest," answered Kevan, wrapping his arms around her. "Because I think I'm about to die happy."

She laughed against his chest, then swiped a bead of sweat with her tongue. She kissed her way up his breastbone, tasting the salt of his skin, until she got to his neck. *Nibble, nibble, nibble.* God, he smelled all manly and felt all musclely and looked all yummy-sweet.

"Why don't we take a shower, snuggle into bed, and get some rest?" asked Kevan as his hand coasted down her backside to cup her buttocks.

"Hmmm. That's *kinda* like my plan."

"Yeah?"

"Take a shower, snuggle into bed, have wild monkey sex, *then* get some rest."

"I vote for your plan."

She laughed and sat up, stretching her arms over her head.

"Whoa." He cupped her breasts, brushing his thumbs across her nipples. "Have I told you that I love your breasts?"

"Once or twice."

He leaned forward and licked her left nipple, then blew on it, causing it to tighten. That sexy move was an extension of his patented breathy-kissy thing. "Did I mention that your breasts are so beautiful they should be cast in bronze and put on special display at the Louvre?"

"That's the nicest compliment my mammary glands ever got."

He couldn't stop playing with her boobs, and that was fine by her, but he managed to pry his gaze from her chest to look into her eyes. "You are a fabulous woman, Janie Brown. All of you."

"Thanks." Her heart stuttered. The reality hadn't hit her yet—but it would in the morning. She'd have this one night with Kevan Rune, movie star, and he'd have one night with Janie Brown, forgettable woman.

But at this moment, he thought she was fabulous.

And that was enough.

chapter four

When Janie awoke in the heavenly four-poster bed, she found the strong arms of Kevan Rune wrapped around her waist. She was tucked into the crook of his body, held like Kevan's personal teddy bear. He felt warm and hard against her—a shield of manly reassurance. Early in her marriage to Dale she had felt this way, protected and comforted and loved. It had been a pleasure to wake up next to him, a joy to feel his body stretched next to hers. But, like this time with Kevan, that had been a lovely and short-lived dream.

She managed to scoot out of his embrace and get out of the tangle of sheets. The bed was huge! She had to crawl at least three feet to reach its edge.

"Where're you goin'?" croaked Kevan.

She looked at him over her shoulder. He hadn't cracked open his eyes, but he managed to gather one of the pillows into his arms as her fluffy replacement. Not a morning person, was he? She grinned. "I'm going to take a shower."

His eyes sprang open and interest shone in his gaze. "You mean you're gonna be under a spray of water soaping yourself . . . everywhere?"

"It's not pay-per-view," she said, chuckling. "Besides, you saw me wet and soapy last night."

"Hmmm."

"Go to back to sleep, Kev."

" 'Kay," he murmured, and his eyes fluttered shut. She hadn't walked ten steps before she heard his light snore. *Definitely not a morning person.*

After a quick shower, she toweled dry her hair and belted herself into one of the comfy hotel bathrobes. For the hell of it, she tucked her feet into the luxurious matching slippers. She entered the bedroom and stopped short. Kevan was not only awake, he'd also managed to get breakfast.

"I was only gone twenty minutes," she said, plunking onto the bed and crawling toward the feast he'd laid out on a big, round tray. His naked chest gleamed in the slant of sunlight penetrating the gauze curtains; her heart quickened. A thin sheet covered him to his waist, but she knew what was underneath and what it was capable of. Kevan Rune's talents were many. She bit back a smile. No need to give his ego a boost on that score. Still, she felt the tingling pleasure of arousal, the flush of heat in her core as she considered the man's skills.

"There are perks to being Kevan Rune, movie star," he said in a deep announcer's voice. "Have no fear. I use my powers only for good . . . and, occasionally, for ordering breakfast to arrive in record time."

"No argument here." She plopped a berry into her mouth and eyed the waffles. "Is that whipped cream?"

"Yep."

She picked up the bowl of fresh whipped cream and peered at it. "It's missing something."

Kevan's brows rose as he considered the snowy concoction. Janie shimmied out of the robe and, with Kevan's questioning gaze on her, brought the whipped cream to her breasts. The toast on the way to his mouth halted its progress as he watched her dip one nipple, then the other into the cold froth.

"What do you think?" she asked, considering her breasts with the same scholarly attention given to study of the Mona Lisa. She put the bowl on the tray and cupped her breasts, bringing them together and boosting them. "Too much?"

Janie looked at Kevan through her lashes and quirked one corner of her mouth. She watched the bread fly out of his hand, hitting a lamp shade before spiraling to the floor. He dove on her, knocking her flat to the bed, his hot mouth on her nipples, licking and sucking off the cream. The breakfast tray tilted, dumping its contents onto the burgundy silk comforter. Silverware clanked in protest.

"You turn me on," he muttered against her flesh, his tongue swirling around her areolae, his lips dragging across her breasts. His hand plunged between her legs, his palm coasting over her clitoris before two fingers tested her readiness.

Janie felt the length of his cock against her thigh and reached down to wrap her fingers around the solid flesh. Her thumb swiped the tip; the dew of his desire was evident.

Rubbing down the shaft, she brought her grip to the sensitive area just below the head and let her fingers dance across the bumps. His penis jerked; his moan vibrated on her skin. She grasped his cock again, stroking it as she maneuvered herself to a more suitable position. The firm, rounded flesh teased her opening. She slid her fingers over his hard-on until she reached his balls. She massaged the tightened sac, gripping lightly as he pushed slowly inside of her.

"I've had you all night, in almost every way, and it's not enough," he said, an ache in his voice.

"Take me again," she whispered. "Take me now."

He sheathed himself fully and paused. They both shuddered at the sensations, both gulped breaths. His head dropped to her neck and he blew out a sigh. "Shit."

"What?"

"It feels too fucking good." He lifted just enough to look at her. "Because I'm not wearing a condom. I know we both have Cupid, Inc.'s stamp of approval . . . ."

She heard the unvoiced *but*. "I'm on birth control," she said. "I have a clean bill of health. No diseases, ever. I can count on one hand how many lovers I've had—including you."

"I'm healthy, too," he said, "but I've had, um . . . more than five lovers."

He actually looked embarrassed about his sexual past. *Aw.* He was *so* cute. Janie swallowed her laughter. "How far away are the condoms?"

"I don't know."

"Soooooo . . . we'd have to do what might be a very long search to find one?"

He nodded, his expression a mixture of misery and frustration. She felt the same way: horny and needy. Willing to trust Kevan at his word? Yes. And she could only hope he trusted her as well. But . . . they were adults, *responsible* adults. Responsibility. Hot sex. Responsibility. Hot sex. *Oh, hellfire and damnation!*

"Slide out of me," she ordered, "and put that big cock between my lips."

She wrapped her legs around his waist and pressed upward. "How's that feel?"

"Arg-ugh."

Her own juices provided plenty of lubrication, and he lost no time thrusting his cock between her sensitized labia, bumping deliciously against her swollen clit. Sweat slickened their bodies as they moved in frenzied harmony with each other. Pleasure blossomed quickly, a fire flower that sparked and burst.

"Kevan," she screamed, slamming against his cock, her nails biting into his hips as she pushed her clit against his manhood. The orgasm overwhelmed her and blocked out everything but the bliss pulsing through her. She was mindless with it, writhing with it, and had barely begun the soft float back to earth when she felt Kevan stiffen.

His cock jerked against her clitoris, causing another riot of sensations. He rose on his elbows, his face buried against her shoulder, his groan trapped against her skin. Then she felt the warm liquid of his release spurt onto her stomach.

Kevan rolled to her side and sank into the mattress, causing dishes to rattle. He sniffed her neck. "Is there cinnamon soap or shampoo in the bathroom?" he asked. "Or maybe you scrubbed with some apples or found a cider switch on the shower controls?"

Janie looked at him and laughed. "You are so weird."

He plucked a napkin from the breakfast carnage behind him and placed it on her stomach, rubbing her flesh clean. "Looks like you'll have to take another shower."

"Guess so. Wanna join me?"

*   *   *

Janie stood in the library section of the living area, looking at all the books. It was an impressive amount of material—from literary masterpieces to the latest paperback best sellers. After a long and enjoyable shower with Kevan, she'd gotten dressed sans stockings and garter belt—those went into her purse. The silver dress was wrinkled and the black lace wrap felt itchy. She wished she could wear the soft hotel robe all the way home. The high heels on her bare feet felt too tight, and again made her wish for the plush slippers she'd left in the bathroom.

Kevan's agent had called, and he'd been in the bedroom for the last ten minutes. Should she leave him a note? A thank-you, good-bye, and mum's-the-word reassurance penned before she left? Or should she wait and tell him in person?

"I know what's not under that dress," said Kevan.

Janie whirled around and found him lounging against the doorway to the foyer. He looked good . . . oh, Lord above, *really* good . . . in a plain black T-shirt and raggedy blue jeans. His dark hair was wet, combed back from his face, highlighting his cheekbones, scraggly beard stubble, and those expressive, sad eyes.

"I had a great time," she said, walking to him. "It was beyond my wildest dreams."

"At least your sister will be happy you had hot sex with me." He smiled, but she saw the doubt and mistrust lurking in his gaze. She knew what he was wondering. Would she rat him out to the *StarNews*? Had their night of fun included a price he'd be forced to pay? Her heart ached for him, and tears pricked her eyes. He had every reason to believe she'd behave like Bonnie or those rabid fans who managed to pilfer his blazer's buttons.

"I have nothing to tell Bev. You see, we had a nice dinner and

I drank too much champagne. You left in your limo and I walked to Motel 6. I have a really good friend who manages that place—it's just off Trop and Las Vegas Boulevard, not far from where we almost had dinner. She'll swear sideways to Tuesday that I stayed the night there, too tipsy from champagne to drive home."

His gaze remained enigmatic, but he seemed to relax—a smidge.

"I signed confidentiality papers with Cupid, Inc.," she reminded him. "But if you like, you can have your agent or your publicist fax me more specific documents relating to our date and I'll sign them. Please do whatever you need to feel more comfortable about what happened between us." She rummaged through her purse and pulled out a business card.

He pocketed it without looking at it. Then his hand snaked out and cupped her cheek. "You'd do that?"

"I'm selfish. The memories I have of you I want for myself, and I refuse to share them with others." She leaned in for a kiss, a mere brush of her lips against his. "You can trust me."

They parted and Kevan straightened, allowing her to pass through the doorway. She felt a hot ache in her throat, and the tears trembling on her lashes threatened to fall. The fantasy was fading away, and now she was like every other one-night-stand girl in the world—walking away from her lover, never to meet him again. *Oh, God.* She was such a sap.

"I had a great time, too, Janie. The next time I'm in Vegas, I'll give you a call."

"Don't make that promise, Kev." She pushed the button for the elevator, but didn't turn to face him. No way would she reveal her emotional state. He wasn't a bad guy. In fact, he was a damned decent man who would probably try to make her feel better. No, she could do without that sort of kindness. Mercifully, the elevator arrived and the doors opened. She stepped inside and turned, schooling her features into a cheerful smile.

"Good-bye, Kevan." She waved, hoping she presented a happier outside than she felt inside. He stood in the foyer, watching her, and waved back. Then the doors shut . . . and her dream date with Kevan Rune was officially over.

Angela's efforts to engage Ralph in conversation met with no success. She hung around the elevator, taking occasional walks around the lobby and front desk to see if anyone famous might arrive and do something worthy of news. No such luck. Where were Julia Roberts and George Clooney when a reporter on her last desperate assignment needed them?

At one A.M., Kevan and his mystery woman had not come down, so she went to the potty and to grab a quick bite from the twenty-four-hour café. When she returned, she met Ralph's replacement: Mark from California. He was a nice-looking African-American male who looked bigger, stronger, and meaner than ol' Ralph. His main responses to her pestering were fierce smiles, but he looked so handsome, she couldn't decide between feeling lustful or fearful. In the end she settled for both. Unfortunately, Mark's tolerance for her presence was far lower than Ralph's. After her fifth attempt to get him to talk, he had her escorted out of the lobby.

Now she loitered outside the Bellagio, hoping Kevan would appear. It was almost ten A.M. The Las Vegas sun was round and beautiful in the June sky, but the intense heat sucked the sweat from her skin and the air from her lungs. She was hungry again, and she needed a shower. A long, cold one. Maybe she'd bathe in ice cubes.

The doors opened and Angela looked up. If it wasn't Kevan Rune, she was going back to her hotel room and sacking out. The person emerging from the hotel was not Kevan. The silver dress sparkled in the daylight, the black lace wrap hanging limply from slumped shoulders. Angela grinned. The mystery woman revealed. *Ha!*

Her joy was cut short.

The doorman waved a waiting taxi forward and opened its door for the lady. *Shit!* Angela snapped off some rounds with the digital camera, but the woman scooted inside the cab too quickly for a good face shot. Hurrying to the doorman, she threw a fiver into his palm as he helped her into the next taxi.

She thrust twenty dollars at the driver. "Follow that taxi!"

The man had skin like dark chocolate and long, intricate braids of varying lengths and colors. He took the twenty-dollar bill and looked at her, brows raised. "That's ol' Harry, miss," he said in an unmistakable Jamaican accent. "How 'bout I just call 'im and ask where he be takin' the lady?"

"Uh . . . yeah," said Angela, collapsing to the seat. Her excitement fizzled. "That will work, too."

chapter five

After Janie left the Bellagio, she went home, got dressed in comfy jeans and a well-worn T-shirt, and drove to the chapel.

Seven years ago she'd loved walking through the door. Planning weddings had once brought her joy. Watching two people commit to their love by saying their vows in front of God and man . . . she used to adore the whole ritual, no matter how serious or how silly the ceremony. That joy had long since faded, even before her business had turned to shit.

No weddings were scheduled today or tomorrow—or hell, even next week. She'd owned the chapel longer than she'd been married, and now, after ceaseless work and plugging every nickel she had into it, her wedding business was failing as miserably as her relationship with Dale had.

"Why do you have to sign another confidentiality agreement with Kevan Rune?" asked Bev, waving a sheaf of papers at Janie as she entered the Wedding Veil's small office.

"Hello to you, too." *Argh!* She didn't want to deal with her sister's gentle haranguing. "It's no big deal."

She plucked the agreement from her sister's hand and took it to her desk. Kevan had lost no time at all getting her the paperwork. She'd left the Bellagio less than two hours ago. She didn't begrudge him the extra protection, but her stomach still felt like she'd swallowed lead filings. If only their night together had meant more to him . . . if only he had felt one-tenth of the way she had felt this morning. Her whole world had changed, and not just because she'd slept with a movie star. For a few hours last night she'd ceased thinking about Kevan as a Hollywood hunk.

"Stop with the suspense already. What happened with Mr. Gorgeous?"

Janie signed and initialed and dated the agreement, then stuck the pages into the fax, typed in the return phone number, and smacked the send button.

"We had a nice dinner. We talked. I drank too much champagne and walked to the Motel 6. Sherie put me up for the night."

Bev, who was shorter, thinner, and blonder than Janie, looked at her with narrowed eyes. "That's a great story for other people. But you can tell me what *really* went on last night."

Janie smiled and shrugged. She kept no secrets from her younger sister, but she'd promised Kevan her silence.

Bev stared at her, waiting; then her eyes widened. "Oh, my God! You had hot sex with Kevan Rune."

"I never said that."

"You did! You so totally did!" Bev clapped her hands and laughed, spinning in a little circle. "I can't believe it. What did he say? Do? How was he in bed?"

Janie pressed her lips together to keep from smiling and thereby confirming Bev's suspicions. Instead she bent her head and assessed the large stack of unpaid bills. At loose ends after ending a relationship and losing a job—in the *same* week—her sister had moved out here more than a year ago, right after Janie's divorce was final. Not even Bev's talent for squeezing every penny out of a tight budget had helped her pull out from the nosedive into financial hell.

"I'm going to lose the Wedding Veil." Even if she didn't exactly want the chapel anymore, deciding to sell it and losing it to creditors were two very different things. How had she gotten this far in debt? "You know Sean, right?"

"Duh. He's the Elvis impersonator who owns the Chapel of Love."

"He wants to open a second location, and he's been asking about buying the Wedding Veil. I don't know if selling the chapel will get me out of debt, though." Janie picked up the electric bill and shuddered. She didn't want to see the money owed for keeping the chapel air-conditioned during the summer months. She sighed so heavily the envelopes on the desk fluttered. "I almost wish winning the Cupid, Inc., contest had gotten me a huge cash prize instead of a date with Kevan Rune."

"Oh, honey," said Bev, dropping her playful interrogation. "We'll figure something out."

Angela's heart thudded in her chest. Sneaking into the chapel— way too much pink, *ew*—had been a big risk. The cabbie had gone to the mystery woman's home then followed her to the downtown chapel, but all that chasing had cost her a bundle. *Oh, so what!* As she crept away from the cracked-open door to the back office, she knew she'd gotten the biggest scoop ever in her career. Either the *StarNews* paid her what she was worth, or she'd take her information to another newspaper. She had a feeling, though, that ol' Harold, the editor in chief, would cough up serious cash.

She was, after all, the only one who knew that the woman who owned the Wedding Veil had won a date with Kevan Rune and, since Angela knew for a fact this Janie person had left the Bellagio this *morning*, the woman probably did the horizontal bop with Kevan. In addition to that juicy assumption, Janie's business was apparently going downhill in a hurry. *Hmmm. I can't prove any of it.*

She tiptoed out of the chapel, and the second she hit the concrete steps she ran across the tiny fake green lawn, under the white lattice arbor, and melted into the tourists headed toward Fremont Street.

More research was needed before she put together the story. She'd learned that with a *StarNews* article, she had to skirt a fine line between fiction and fact. Without a direct quote from Kevan or Janie confirming what they'd done in his Bellagio suite, she was left with the yellow journalist's key tool: innuendo. But first she'd find out about the Wedding Veil, then dig up the dirt on Cupid, Inc., and the contest that paired fan-shy Kevan Rune with plain Janie.

That same afternoon Janie sat at her desk, fluctuating between hope and despair as she went through the endless pile of bills. Her stomach growled, adding hunger to her emotionally chaotic state. Bev had left a couple minutes ago to pick up an early dinner. She sighed as she gazed at the papers fanned across her blotter. Maybe she should throw them all into a hat and pick three or four to pay.

The phone on her desk trilled and she picked it up on the first ring. "The Wedding Veil. This is Janie."

"Hi, Janie. It's Kevan."

Her breath hitched. Kevan Rune was calling her? Yes! Pleasure curled through her. "Hi."

"I'm getting ready to hit the road."

The warmth ribboning through her dissipated like smoke. "Oh. Well, good-bye again."

Janie looked at the clock on her desk. It was almost five P.M. What had he been doing for the last several hours? She figured he would've hopped a plane to L.A. by now. She had to admit she felt bummed about his leaving. She'd managed not to think about Kevan—well, not *too* much—while she got back to real life, but hearing his voice brought back with painful clarity the heavenly night they'd had together.

"I also wanted you to know that I have your underwear."

"You have my . . . wait a minute. That's impossible. I didn't have any underwear to leave."

"I didn't say I found them in the hotel room. I'll talk to you soon, Janie."

"Kevan—"

"*Soon.* Bye for now."

"Bye."

Ten minutes later a messenger arrived with a small box wrapped in plain brown paper. She tried to tip the guy, but he only grinned and said he'd already gotten paid plenty.

Janie returned to her desk and tore off the wrap. Her breath left in a whoosh. Two words were scribbled in elegant black across the pink box: *Agent Provocateur*. Hands trembling, she opened the box and peered at the two items inside. She plucked a black leather thong from the pink tissue paper. In the front, laced through the top, was a strip of pink leather, a tiny bow in the middle. The other item was also black leather with the same pink leather ribbon and bow, but it was smaller than the thong. Way too small to be a bra. *What the heck?* She held up the piece, stretching it out, and peered at it.

Oh, my God.

A matching mask!

Her skin tingled and her heart revved into overdrive as she thought about prancing around in just a thong and a mask, daring Kevan to catch her and ravish her.

At the bottom of the box she spied a small pink card. She picked it up and grinned. Scrawled across the card were the words: *Next time, don't wear the bra.—K*

Angela's digital wristwatch blinked 5:14 P.M. She glanced over her shoulder, checking out the Wedding Veil, which was directly across the street. The tiny white building shared a parking lot with a Chinese restaurant. Other than a man who'd left a few minutes ago, no one had come in or out for the last half hour.

Sighing, she returned to perusing the T-shirts displayed outside the cheesy souvenir shop. The small, merchandise-crowded store was squeezed between a seedy bar and a pawnshop. Blinking neon signs and old sun-bleached posters of half-naked women in sparkly costumes were crammed into the big, dirty picture window. Underneath it were two rickety card tables filled with shirts. In between the tables, passersby could peruse a bin of one-dollar items that weren't worth stealing, much less buying.

Angela had spent the last few hours hunting down information about Janie Brown, Cupid, Inc., and the Wedding Veil. She had enough to create one hell of an article, but her plane to L.A. didn't leave until tomorrow morning. She figured it wouldn't hurt to see who might be hanging around the chapel—or if Janie would keep another rendezvous with a certain tall, dark, and handsome movie star.

The salesclerk stood in the open doorway and watched Angela paw through the merchandise. He was young, with long, greasy hair, a pierced nose, and rampant acne. He wore loose jeans, a faded concert T-shirt, and army boots. She caught his listless gaze.

"Shirts are five bucks," he said, "but you can get three for ten dollars."

Oh, for Pete's sake! Angela had no intention of purchasing three T-shirts for ten dollars. Aside from the dismal fact that she had no family and no close friends who might enjoy a souvenir from Sin City, she was faking interest in EVERYBODY LOVES A LOSER tees because it was the only way to keep an eye on the chapel without looking obvious.

"You keep scoping out the Wedding Veil," said the guy. "You gonna get married?"

Aw, crap. Caught by a slacker whose bloodshot eyes suggested he hadn't slept in several days or he'd just smoked some weed. Angela smiled brightly. "I don't know what you're talking about."

"Dude! You keep looking over your shoulder and peering at the chapel. Then you keep looking at your watch."

"I do not." Angela dug through the shirts as if she might find one that had been gold-plated. What kind of lame reporter was she? Here she was, thinking she was so cool and so smooth . . . Damn it!

"Hey, I'm chill," he said, shrugging. "I've seen grooms stand up their brides a million, billion times."

She blinked at him. "What?"

"You. Got. Stood. Up." He nodded sagely, as if telling her in a loud, slow voice somehow deadened the potential pain of being left at the altar.

Speechless, Angela stared at him. Did she have LOSER tattooed on her forehead? Not only did she suck at covert surveillance; she apparently had a "dumped bride" vibe, too.

"You gonna buy those?" he asked.

She looked at the T-shirts clenched in her fist. Just then a motorcycle roared up the street. The biker pulled onto the sidewalk and drove into the parking lot, taking the slot nearest the chapel. He pulled off his helmet and shook out longish black hair.

Holy shit. She watched the guy in the tight jeans and a black T-shirt open the chapel's big pink door and saunter inside.

"Aw-right. Your groom showed up!" Slacker Boy grooved his head. "You know something weird? He looks really familiar."

"Like Kevan Rune, right?"

"No. He looks like that other guy . . . Keanu Reeves."

chapter six

"You still wearing that bra?" asked a deliciously mellow and very male voice.

Janie nearly jumped out of her chair. She probably looked like a scared cat to the sexy movie star leaning against the doorjamb and gazing at her with heat in his eyes. Her pulse beat an unsteady rhythm, and she felt the familiar do-me-now response of her body that seemed to arise anytime Kevan was within ten feet of her person. Smoothing her hair and wishing desperately for some lip gloss and a breath mint, she stood up. "You scared the bejeebers out of me."

"Bejeebers?" He walked into the room. "You have an interesting vocabulary. I wanted to ask about your accent. Are you from Texas?"

"Bite your tongue. I'm an Okie."

His brows rose.

"Born and raised in Oklahoma," she clarified. Nervous energy sparked in her stomach as he rounded the desk. His gaze landed on the Agent Provocateur box. He grinned. "I don't suppose you put on that thong, did you?"

"I couldn't wear the ensemble because that little bra you sent with it didn't fit."

For a moment he looked nonplussed . . . then he laughed softly. His thumb traced the curve of her jaw. "I can't get you out of my thoughts. And I don't want you out of my bed." He dipped his head for a light kiss. The soft press of his lips caused a delicate shudder to run through her.

"Ditto." She wrapped her arms around his neck and kissed him deeply, trying to put into her kiss what she could never put into words.

"Oh. My. God! You're locking lips with *Sean?*"

Bev's astonished voice broke the sensual spell. Talk about a mood killer. Janie sighed as she reluctantly removed her lips from Kevan's and turned to face her sibling. She stood inside the office doorway holding a big paper bag. The spicy scent of fried egg rolls wafted into the room. Janie watched with some delight as her sister's eyes widened and her mouth flapped open and shut. The Chinese takeout landed with a splat on the floor.

"I'm not seeing this. Nope. Not me." Bev picked up the bag and backed out of the room. "You're not Kevan Rune. She's alone in the office. And I'm on my way to get a drink. See? This is me leaving and I'm locking the door behind me, too." She grabbed the knob and yanked the door almost closed; then her head reappeared and she said, "Carry on, people."

Her sister shut the door and they heard the key turn in the lock. *Oh, hell.* Now Bev would never buy the story that Janie and Kevan had enjoyed a simple dinner last night, much less shut up about finding them liplocked.

"Who's Sean?" asked Kevan.

"He's the Elvis impersonator who owns Chapel of Love," answered Janie. She tilted her head and considered Kevan's profile. "I never thought about it before, but Sean sorta looks like you—when he's not dressed up like the King."

"You wouldn't believe how many times I've been asked to play Elvis Presley."

"You're kidding."

"That's what I said."

The fragrant scent of egg rolls lingered, reminding Janie that Bev had just taken off with the food. Janie lightly punched Kevan's shoulder. "This is the second time I've missed out on dinner because of you."

"I'll make it up to you at breakfast."

Her stomach fluttered. She couldn't believe Kevan was standing in her office saying things both naughty and sweet. Doing so was far beyond his duties as a contest prize. She could only hope that he had tracked her down and bought her lingerie because he was as emotionally affected by their night together as she was. Maybe it was possible that a relationship *could* blossom between them. Yeah. It was just about as possible as her winning a Megabucks jackpot.

Kevan stared at her, and she suspected he was gauging her reaction to his presence. She smiled, hoping her gaze conveyed the invitation to touch her—*now*. Kevan got her message—loud and clear—because his hand stole under her T-shirt, drifting up her rib cage. He cupped her breast and swiped his thumb across the nipple. The tip hardened immediately, and a zingy thrill went from breast to groin in 0.2 seconds.

"You are a breast addict," she accused, pressing closer to encourage optimum groping.

"Guilty." His other hand joined in the fun. Now both of her

breasts were being fondled with an efficiency and enthusiasm that left her breathless. Tiny shivers danced along her skin as he alternately stroked and twisted her nipples through the thin material of her bra.

She pushed her pelvis against his; the hard-on straining his jeans gouged her with yummy precision. "Do you know what it's like to walk around in wet panties?"

"Never worn panties," said Kevan, unsnapping the top of her jeans and lowering the zipper. He tugged on the waistband and allowed the jeans to drop to her knees. One hand continued to play with her breasts—*thank God*—but the other feathered its way across her stomach, one finger slipping inside her underwear to swipe her clit.

"Oh, Lord." She went boneless, shuddering with delight as his finger slid lower, lower, *lower*. When he dipped inside her she felt herself get wetter and hotter and needier. She squirmed against him, panting and moaning. He lowered his mouth to her neck and completed his pleasurable assault on her person by employing the breathy-kissy technique. Her vagina contracted, squeezing the finger thrusting inside her, and she felt slightly faint. Was it possible to pass out from being too sexually excited?

Janie fumbled with the buttons of his jeans, nearly ripping off the material in her haste. The jeans dropped . . . the boxers dropped . . . and his hard cock jutted out, ready to play.

Kevan removed his wicked hands long enough to help her onto the edge of the desk. Then he was lifting her shirt, unsnapping her bra, and freeing her breasts. His mouth ravished her aching nipples, but his hands stayed on her hips, tilting her back as he maneuvered between her legs. Both of them were still entangled in their own jeans, but who wanted to take the time to get undressed? *Not me.*

As Kevan took a condom from his jeans pocket, Janie wrapped her hand around the thick length of his cock and stroked vigorously, wishing that very soon, say, within the next five seconds, Kevan would be stroking her.

Wish granted. Kevan rolled on the condom and slid his cock inside her. He didn't attempt a slow seduction. She wanted it fast, and apparently he did, too, because he plunged into her quickly, shuddering and groaning.

Janie pressed her knees against his hips and wrapped her arms around his neck, unable to do more than hang on for the ride. His strokes were limited by the constriction of their clothing, but he was, nevertheless, effective in revving her engine into overdrive. The orgasm slammed through her—a sudden, exquisite rush of pleasure that overwhelmed her ability to think, to breathe.

"Oh, Janie!" Kevan penetrated deeply, stilling, trembling, his fingers digging into her hips as he came, his face buried in her shoulder as he strove for breath.

They held on to each other. After a while Janie's heartbeat returned to normal and she could use her lungs again. Kevan lifted his head and looked at her. His stunned gaze reflected her own amazement. Maybe he had hot, sweaty, incredible sex all the time, but until this moment she had never experienced the kind of soul-stealing pleasure she found with him.

"Whoa," he said.

"Yeah."

He moved back just enough for her to scoot off the desk; he bent down and pulled up her panties and jeans, zipping and buttoning. Then he reached around her back and rehooked her bra, pulling down her T-shirt with obvious reluctance.

She smiled, hoping he saw the promise shining in her eyes. "I didn't get to wear the lingerie."

His lips hitched into a grin. "My bike's outside. And I brought an extra helmet—just in case."

"We'll go to my house." Janie grabbed her purse, tucked the lingerie box inside it, then turned off the lamps and followed Kevan out. It only took a sec to lock up the office. Kevan waited for her in the aisle. He snagged her hand as she joined him and waved his free arm at the decor. "This is a lot of pink."

"Yeah." Janie tried to see the chapel through Kevan's eyes. The walls were painted a light shade of pink. Five rows of white pews lined up on each side of the aisle, draped with ribbon and silk roses. In the front, a ten-foot-by-ten-foot platform offered enough room for a podium, a preacher of choice, and the couple speaking their vows. The backdrop was a huge mural of a pink rose, dew on its petals, the lush green of its stem the only color contrast in the space.

"Don't tell anyone, but I like pink. There's a particular shade I have in mind, too." Kevan leaned down and captured her lips; she gladly indulged the eagerness of his mouth. Joy and lust wound through her, coiling inside her belly, arrowing down to her core.

No matter what happened next, this moment was perfect.

The front door creaked open and a female voice purred, "Mr. Rune, have you officially tied the knot with Janie Brown?"

chapter seven

The stupid-ass question shattered the perfect moment.

Kevan leaped away from Janie as if her skin had turned acidic. She didn't blame him for reacting that way, but it still made her feel rejected—like a secret mistress denied public affection.

They both turned and found an ecstatic Angela Marleaux standing less than a foot from the front door, a small digital camera in her hands. Obviously she had clicked off a few shots of them kissing. Chances were good the nitwit had a minirecorder somewhere on her person, too, and was waiting for one of them to utter a phrase or two that could be misconstrued.

"Did you sign a prenuptial agreement, *Mrs. Rune?*" asked Angela with sadistic delight. "Did Kevan promise to save your failing business in exchange for a quickie marriage?"

Janie rolled her eyes. The woman was crazy and her logic flawed. "This is private property. Please leave."

"Oh, c'mon! You win a date with Kevan Rune that lasts all night and suddenly you're kissing him in a wedding chapel." Angela's gaze turned sly. "Maybe this whole thing was a setup for Kevan. You know he has problems with his ex-girlfriend, and you figure you'd screw him, too, and make a quick buck, right? I know! You'll shut up about what happened at the Bellagio if he'll put up the cash."

That scenario was scarily logical. Janie glanced at Kevan. His jaw was clenched, but other than that, he'd fallen into a loose-limbed slouch and remained stoically silent. Did he really believe she was capable of such betrayal? After what they'd shared, would he think she'd trade her memories and feelings for money? Bonnie had done just that—and she'd been involved with Kevan for more than a year. Why should Kevan trust Janie—a woman he'd known less than forty-eight hours? *Damn, damn, damn.*

Janie thrust her hand into her purse and dug around for the cell phone.

She flipped open the phone and dialed 911. "Yes, I'd like to report an intruder at the Wedding Veil. There's a woman on my property refusing to leave, and I'd like to press charges for trespassing."

Angela raised the camera and snapped off some more shots. She hastily backed away. "See you in the papers!" she shouted. Then she whirled around and burst through the door, leaving it open as she booked down the street, melting into the shadows.

"She's gone, Officer. No, I don't want to make a report. Thank you for your help." Janie clicked off her phone and put it away. She inhaled a fortifying breath before facing Kevan. "I would never, *ever*—"

"I know." Kevan's expression was neutral, his gaze carefully shuttered. "I'm sorry, Janie. I made a mistake."

"I don't consider anything that happened between us a mistake." She felt sick to her stomach. Angela's surprise assault had forced reality into their little fantasy world. Now they both had to remember that Janie was a nobody—a not-thin, not-blond, not-rich nobody, and Kevan Rune was a movie star. She swallowed the hot ache lodged in her throat and blinked back tears. "What will happen when Angela's story breaks?"

"I don't know. But the best way to handle bad publicity is to stay silent and wait out the shit storm."

"Sage advice." She tried for a grin and failed. *Damnation!* She wasn't an actress and had never really been good at hiding her emotions. Waiting for Kevan to leave was pure torture. Why the hell was he dawdling? Her chest hurt and her eyes felt puffy, and if she didn't get chocolate in the next five minutes, she was gonna lose it completely. Gathering her courage, she stuck out her hand and Kevan grabbed it, shook firmly, and let go quickly.

"It's been a pleasure," she said, with just a touch of wickedness.

A smile ghosted his lips. "Ditto." Then he turned and walked away, never looking back.

At eleven A.M. on Monday, Kevan met his agent, Irwin Sark, for lunch. Lunch with Irwin was always in the man's spacious but chaotic office, ordered in from local eateries, and usually included the weird Hollywood fare Kevan abhorred. Sometimes living in Los Angeles was like living on a different planet.

Irwin owned the Creative Artists Collective Agency and had been Kevan's agent for fifteen years. He was big and loud and sported a bald head and a fat gray mustache. He wore expensive jogging suits and cheap sneakers, liked cigars and gold jewelry, and was one of the sharpest men alive on the planet.

Irwin had been responsible for getting him the role in a movie that was a modest success in his early career. Unfortunately, that film had also been responsible for Kevan being thought of as clueless, a perception he tried to fight with a combination of offbeat roles in small productions and big-budget action films. *Fast* had been his breakthrough into the A-list. Still, he hoped that one day soon he'd be able to take time off from his movie career and act onstage.

"Burgers," said Irwin, pointing at the Styrofoam boxes on his desk. "With French fries or American fries or whatever the hell we're callin' 'em these days."

Kevan grinned. Finally! Something he wouldn't gag on. He opened the box and salty, beefy steam wafted from the carton. Toasted sesame-seed bun, thick meat patty loaded with veggies, and served up with wedge-cut fries.

"What's up?" asked Kev as he hoisted the mondo burger. "You never order decent food. Where's the tofu-alfalfa-sprout-bean-curd salad with gluten-free wheat crackers?" He took a bite and chewed. *Nothing like a slab of beef to cheer up a guy who's having a tough time forgetting about a certain woman.*

"Didn't feel like salad," said Irwin. "I ordered Boca Burgers."

Kevan frowned. "What the hell is a Boca Burger?"

"A meatless patty made with soy protein." Irwin took a bite and sighed in pleasure. "Damned good."

"You suck." Kevan put down the sandwich and picked up a fry. "Are these made from real potatoes?"

"Organically grown, but yeah, they're real potatoes."

Kevan chewed on a fry. "So why the meeting, Irwin? I'm still slated for *Rogue*, aren't I?"

"Yeah, yeah." Irwin waved a chubby paw. A gold ring glittered on his pinkie, a huge square diamond in the middle of the thick band. "You know how you've wanted to do *Macbeth?* Well, Trillion Studio is putting up the cash for the film version. As long as you don't mind being directed by Mel, you'll get the lead."

"You're not shitting me, are you? Because I'll kill you if you're joking about this."

"Gibson will direct; you'll play Macbeth, but there are a few things Trillion wants—and you get one guess what the *numero uno* request is."

"Settle with Bonnie."

"She's taking away publicity from your last movie—which didn't do so great. Harrow House offered her half a mil for the rights to her tell-all book." Irwin's gaze locked onto Kevan's. "You're richer than God. Pay off the bitch and get her tied into a legal knot so tight that if she burps, it'll put her in breach of contract. Then you'll get your dream project made on Trillion's dime."

Maybe Irwin was right. Hell, Kevan couldn't work up annoyance toward his ex, much less the anger that had roared through him six months ago. Bonnie and her machinations seemed like a bad dream. She was a wound healed. But Janie, sweet, cinnamon Janie . . . He still felt raw about her. His thoughts were crowded with images—the dimple when she smiled, the way her breasts looked when they were topped with whipped cream, the glitter of tears in her eyes when he said good-bye.

What was wrong with him? He'd had one-night stands before. Hell, he'd had one-weekend stands before. What was so different about Janie?

Forget about it.

Forget about her.

"Earth to Kevan."

He shook his head as if doing so might realign his thoughts. "How much does Bonnie want?"

"A million."

Considering Bonnie knew his net worth, he was surprised she'd settle for a mil. Hollywood had been good to him the last few years. He was making $20 million a picture these days. While Bonnie's antics no longer infuriated him, he was still loath to give in to what amounted to blackmail.

"Kev, you've been in the biz long enough to understand the difference between truth and perception."

"Bonnie stoked the media fires, not me." Kevan's words lacked heat. He had the money for the settlement, he wanted to do the movie, and Bonnie no longer had the power to hurt him—on any level. "I'll pay her. And you know what? The only thing Bonnie wants more than to be rich is to be in a big-budget film. Get her a part in the movie."

Irwin's mouth dropped open and his mustache twitched. Then he grinned. "You're brilliant, kid. It'll show everyone you've made nice, and she'll want to promote the movie, drawing attention away from her sudden silence about you."

"That's the idea."

"Once you settle with Bonnie, maybe you can work out a deal with what's-her-face . . . Jodie, Jackie, Joanie. . . ."

"Janie. There's nothing to settle. She signed two confidentiality agreements."

Irwin wiped his fingers on a napkin and leaned back into his chair. "The sharks are scenting blood again, thanks to Angela Marleaux's crappy exposé."

"I saw the special edition they released this morning. The pictures weren't that good."

"They don't have to be. It's the story that delivers the worst sting. I can't believe you agreed to that Cupid, Inc., nonsense."

"I owed a favor and the debt's paid." Kevan abandoned all pretense of eating and waited for his agent to drop the next bomb. Dread whispered through him, a cold dagger gouging his spine. "What else, Irwin?"

"Your weekend bedmate is hosting a press conference today."

An immediate denial died on his lips. Why did he feel compelled to defend Janie? Screw the confidentiality agreements—he'd believed her, took her at her word. Lust had stupefied him, and yeah, he'd abandoned his common sense, but still, deep in his soul he'd really believed that Janie wouldn't sell him out. *Aw, hell.* He set himself up by agreeing to the contest—and by giving in to his sexual whims.

"What did you expect?" asked Irwin. "Angela was right about Ms. Brown's bad financial situation. She's in debt, out of options, and you're her meal ticket."

"She's not Bonnie."

Irwin shrugged. "Bonnie's never managed to get live coverage from E! Entertainment Television." He gestured to the flat-screen television that hung on the wall opposite the desk. "It starts at four o'clock."

Four and a half hours. Kev turned around in his chair and looked at the big screen. Turned off, it looked like an abstract metal painting. He faced Irwin, trying to stall the sense of trepidation crawling through him. He couldn't help but think of the famous line from the first scene in *Macbeth:* "Fair is foul and foul is fair."

Which would Janie be . . . fair or foul?

chapter eight

J anie stepped out from the chapel's office. The pews were filled with people—mostly reporters, but also a few gawkers. More than one camera crew had arrived, too. *Damnation*. Her heart pounded fiercely and she felt nauseous. Would she be able to go through with this?

"You're doing the right thing," said Bev, standing next to her, surveying the chaos.

"Then why does it feel wrong?"

"Because taking risks and changing your life sucks."

A chuckle burst from Janie, overriding the wail of despair lodged in her throat. She pressed her trembling lips together and straightened. She took a step forward, but Bev grabbed her arm.

"Before you go face that madhouse, take this." Her sister placed a chocolate truffle in Janie's hand. "I have an emergency box stowed away. We'll crack it open after this mess is over."

Janie popped the truffle into her mouth and chewed. Instant calm filled her as the sweet melted. "Oh, yeah. That's the stuff."

She swallowed, swiped her teeth for good measure, and grinned. "How's my smile?"

"Truffle-free. Go get 'em, girlie."

Sean waited for her on the platform, standing to the left of the white-wood podium. His smile encouraged her, as she leaned forward and spoke into the microphone.

"This morning a story appeared in the *StarNews* linking me with Kevan Rune. Ms. Marleaux, the illustrious"—she said the word in a tone that suggested she really meant *idiotic*—"reporter, penned an article that was entertaining, if you like fictional accounts."

"Ms. Brown," yelled a young man from the back row. "Are you saying Ms. Marleaux lied?"

"She strung together coincidence, mistaken impressions, and innuendo with consummate skill," replied Janie. "I did win the Cupid, Inc., contest. I did spend Friday evening with Kevan Rune. Truth be told, he's as handsome as the devil, but nowhere near as ornery."

Laughter rippled.

"Ms. Marleaux has pictures of you exiting the Bellagio in a rumpled evening gown. It is well-known that Kevan keeps a suite at that hotel. You can't deny the pictures of you and Kevan Rune kissing in this very chapel. If you're challenging the veracity of the *StarNews* story, how do you explain the photos?" The question came from a blond woman in the front row. Next to her was a cameraman, his video cam pointed straight at Janie. She exhaled a nervous breath and clenched the sides of the lectern.

"Bellagio has good craps, and I roll a mean pair of dice," said Janie. "Tourists aren't the only ones allowed to have fun in Las Vegas. We locals enjoy the tables, too."

"And kissing Kevan Rune in a wedding chapel?" persisted the blonde.

"As Ms. Brown said," Sean interjected, "Ms. Marleaux's article may have included mistaken impressions."

"Who are you, sir?"

"My name is Sean Donnelly, and I'm the new owner of this chapel. In the fall it will reopen as the Chapel of Love, Too." Sean smiled. He was dressed in jeans and a black T-shirt, his longish black hair worn down, mimicking Kevan's hairstyle.

The blonde's eyes narrowed. Janie could practically see the gears whirring in the woman's mind. *Go ahead, honey, make the leap. . . .*

"You bear a resemblance to Mr. Rune. Will you confirm that *you* were the man in the chapel on Saturday night?"

"I'll only confirm that Angela Marleaux isn't a very good photographer."

Chuckles erupted from the crowd.

"Ms. Brown, did Kevan give you any details about his relationship with Bonnie Braden?" asked an older gentleman standing in the aisle. He held a pencil and a small notebook at the ready, but his expression was one of jaded boredom.

"No," said Janie, tamping down the flare of anger. "But I'm sure you'll find all the information you need in the back issues of *StarNews*—if you trust Angela Marleaux as a reliable source."

"To clarify," said a voice somewhere in the middle of the pews on the left side, "you have not kissed, spent the night with, dated, or married Kevan Rune. Is that correct?"

"What woman on this earth wouldn't want to kiss, sleep with, date, or marry Kevan Rune?" asked Janie. "Unfortunately, none of those options were available in the confidentiality agreement I signed with Cupid, Inc."

"Ms. Brown!"

"Do you—"

"Are you going to—"

"Is Kevan—"

The machine-gun questions were fired from everywhere, melding one into another as the reporters strove to outshout one another. Pain throbbed between Janie's eyes. Was it any wonder Kevan hated to do interviews or talk to reporters?

If Janie didn't get out of there soon, meltdown was imminent. Sean, bless his soul, sensed her frazzled state. He put an arm around her shoulder and scooted her to the side, leaning down to speak into the microphone. "Ms. Brown has another engagement, but I can take questions about the Chapel of Love, Too, opening this August. We will have a full-time Elvis impersonator, a Unitarian minister, and I promise you, everything pink will be painted, burned, or destroyed."

Janie left the platform and hurried to the office, afraid one of the jackals might thwart her attempts to get away and use a psychic mind-meld to find out the truth about her and Kevan. *Good Lord.* She shuddered to think about what it would be like to face this kind of journalistic harassment all the time.

With a sigh of relief she slammed the door shut behind her. Bev sat at the desk, a guilty expression on her face as she shoved a white-chocolate truffle into her mouth. The large gold-foil box on the desk still had plenty of treats, but that was irrelevant.

"Thanks for waiting, you cow."

"I couldn't take the pressure of being in the same room with Ethel M.'s glorious tribute to candy," said Bev, pushing the box across the desk.

Janie plopped into the cushy chair on the opposite side,

vaguely wondering about the last time a client had sat in it, and plucked a little paper cup of goodness from the box. "I didn't lie. Skirted the truth here and there, but I didn't tell outright fibs."

"Can you help it if the press draws its own conclusions?"

"Nope."

They contemplated the mouthwatering variety of calorie-rich, fat-infused, carb-filled delights. Janie chose a coconut cup. Bev took a foil-wrapped liqueur-filled morsel shaped like a tiny barrel.

"I wish I'd been able to spend one more night with Kevan," said Janie. "How selfish is that? Hellfire! He shouldn't have bothered to show up on Saturday night."

"Makes you wonder why he did bother. Did you ever think about the possibility that he was into you? That maybe hot sex wasn't the only reason he wanted to be around you?"

Janie almost choked on the coconut nugget. "Get real."

"Who knows what would've happened if that asinine reporter hadn't interrupted the two of you? No matter what else happens, Janie, you keep hold of the fact that Kevan Rune came back for you."

"He also left me the minute he realized our little get-together would be publicized. And let's not forget he called me a 'mistake.' "

"If you're going to enjoy your memories of Mr. Rune, you'll have to edit out those parts. Just remember the way you felt when you were with him. Nothing else matters."

Janie slumped in the chair and studied the small, crowded office space. None of it was hers anymore. She'd signed the paperwork this morning, selling the Wedding Veil and everything in it to Sean. It wasn't as painful or as difficult as she'd thought it would be—after all, she was giving up the business she'd tried to put her heart and soul into for the last seven years.

Her marriage to Dale had failed long before they'd gotten a divorce. She'd held on to the chapel with all her might because it was the only thing she had left, but truth be told, her joy for running it had disappeared long ago. She'd been a successful wedding planner in Oklahoma. When the opportunity came to move to Vegas and buy the chapel, she took it. She'd spent years ushering couples into marital bliss. Well, at least guiding them through the arduous and confusing world of planning a wedding. But she knew from experience that one day of joy did not a lifetime of love make.

Maybe it was being married, or maybe just being married to the wrong person, that made her subconsciously realize she didn't want to plan weddings anymore. In that awful moment in the chapel, with her lips swollen from Kevan's kiss and her ears ringing from Angela's verbal assault, she had begun to reevaluate her life.

"Mom is thrilled we're moving back to Oklahoma," said Bev. "I can't wait to get a home-cooked meal. I'm even looking forward to her fussing over us and giving us advice we don't want."

Janie laughed. "Me, too. It won't take long to get the loose ends tied up. The realtor can handle the house sale without our actually living here. All we really have to do is get packed, pay the rest of the outstanding debts, and wish Sean the best."

"Sean is an all-right guy. I still can't believe he handed over a cashier's check. No banks, no loans, no problem." Bev licked chocolate from her fingers. "We'll have fun starting our new business. Do you think Oklahoma is ready for Romantic Nights?"

"Hell, yeah. Creating the perfect romantic encounter with

lingerie, toys, food, locations . . . whoo-wee, girl, we're gonna have a lot of fun." *Okay, so I'm not as jaded about the love business as I thought.* She and Bev had stayed up until three A.M. this morning brainstorming ideas for their new business. Instead of fanning the flames of new love by planning and executing weddings, they'd stoke the embers of lasting love by planning fabulous getaways for already committed couples. "You know what? We're brilliant."

Bev's concerned gaze assessed Janie. Then she looked away, apparently finding the wall behind Janie absolutely fascinating. *Jeez. I must look more miserable than I feel.* That was impossible. She felt like raw meat, stomped on, cut, and bloody, as raw and wounded as she'd ever been.

"Are you going to miss Las Vegas?" asked Bev.

"You know what the Las Vegas Convention and Visitors Authority says . . . 'What happens here, stays here.' " Janie reached into the box for another piece of candy.

"Tell me the truth, sis. What about Kevan? How do you feel about him?"

"It was just a fling." The sudden tears in her eyes surprised her, but worse still was the hurt that crushed her chest. Bev had asked for the truth. Why not admit to her sister what she could never convey to Kevan? "Who am I kidding? I fell for him. He's funny and sexy and handsome and wicked and . . ." She gulped a breath, tried to steady herself. The cherry cordial in her hand was clasped between trembling fingers. "It would've been nice to get to know him better, maybe find out what we could have together." She sighed. "That's what I really want."

"Me, too."

When she started at the sound of the male voice so near her

ear, the chocolate in Janie's hand went flying. It smacked the desk, rolled off, and landed on the floor, right side up.

Janie stood and turned around, her heart pounding. Blinking away the unshed tears, she stared at the Elvis impersonator standing just behind her chair. He had long black sideburns, big gold glasses with red lenses, and wore a white jumpsuit studded with gems. But the hideous glasses couldn't hide the soulful gaze she knew all too well.

Unable to formulate a coherent sentence, she looked over her shoulder at Bev. Her sister was rescuing the cordial projectile. "I will ignore the abuse of chocolate on this one occasion. I am also getting the heck out of here, because, quite frankly, I've always thought the seventies Elvis was five kinds of creepy." Bev hurried out, winking at the impersonator as she passed him. The knob rattled and Janie knew her sister had locked the door.

"I was under the impression you'd never play Elvis," she managed, even though her insides shook like Jell-O in an earthquake.

"For the right woman, a man will do just about anything."

Her thoughts crashed together. She couldn't wrap her mind around the idea that Kevan Rune was standing in front of her, dressed as Elvis, for cripe's sake, and admitting he wanted to be with her.

"The reporters . . . Kev, you can't—"

"No one looked twice at me. Only in Vegas would a getup like this be considered mundane."

"But why did you—"

He grasped her arms and pulled her into his embrace, kissing her with an eagerness that left her weak-kneed and mind-wiped. When he lifted his head, she clung to him because she was afraid her legs might give out.

"The press conference was inspired," he said, his fingers tracing the line of her jaw. "You rescued me again."

"And my thanks is a bad impersonation of the King?" She grinned wickedly. "Are you going to sing to me?"

"I would never torture you with the horrible sounds of my crooning. Besides, you remember the last thank-you gift? You used the roses as lethal weapons."

Janie laughed, and the tears fell, but they were joyous. She wrapped her arms around his neck. "You still owe me dinner."

"We'll eat whatever and wherever you want," he said. "As long as I get you for dessert."

Staff Meeting
Conference Room B
Ten A.M.

"It's nice of you to move the meetings to later in the morning," said Eros, watching his wife shimmy across the room and bend over the conference table to get the pitcher of ice water. He sat at the far end of the table, sifting through applications, but paused as he considered the sexy wiggle of his wife's ass. She wore a white miniskirt, and as the material stretched he saw the teeny line that suggested a thong.

"You're doing that on purpose," he accused, unable to keep the laughter from his voice. She wiggled some more as she poured a glass of water, then turned, her lips curved in a wicked smile. He felt a surge of heat in his groin. "Keep tormenting me, my love, and I'll show you a new definition of *board meeting*."

"For Zeus's sake! This is a boardroom, not a bedroom," Aphrodite snapped as she appeared in a shower of pink and gold sparks. All three Graces ringed her, their heads bowed in the ceaseless show of loving submission they always gave to their goddess.

"Grace. Grace. And Grace," said Eros. The lithe beauties smiled; their wide blue eyes both guileless and wise. "All three, Mom?"

"I've been summoned to your grandfather's house for lunch. Hera has taken her 'goddess of hearth and home' title way too far. *She's cooking*. Thousands of years without a single interest other than poking her nose into other people's marriages and following Zeus around like she's in an episode of *Columbo*, and now she decides to take up the kitchen arts." Aphrodite sat down, her white silk scarf billowing behind her like a renegade cloud.

His mother was dressed head-to-toe in white, from her Versace dress to her Manolo Blahnik beaded mules. He recognized the brands only because Psyche had trained him well in the art of shopping. He sighed as he considered the effects such knowledge had on his manhood. Somehow it wasn't right for a guy to know the difference between a beaded mule and a beaded slide. There was much a husband suffered for the love of his wife.

"I didn't have a lot of time to help with Kevan and Janie," said Aphrodite.

"Didn't have a lot of time to interfere," muttered Psyche as she bent to kiss Eros before taking her seat.

Aphrodite cast a suspicious look at her daughter-in-law, and Psyche smiled sweetly.

"Do we have an update?"

"They've been together six months and are deeply in love. The press fawns over the two of them, and Kevan handles his fans and the media a little better these days." Psyche grinned. "I've been thinking Angela might need a love life. She's not evil—not really—she just needs direction. I think she needs a boyfriend, and I think she should write romance novels. She's not a very good reporter."

Eros and Aphrodite stared at Psyche in astonishment. She returned their stares. "What? It's true."

"She's not our client."

"Not every love match has to be made through Cupid, Inc."

"Psyche—"

"Okay, okay. Sorry I brought up the possibility. But if she does come to us—"

"She's all yours."

"Yes," agreed Aphrodite. "*All* yours." A delicate shudder racked his mother's shoulders. "Shall we move on to . . . er . . ." She looked at the paper in front of her. "The Mile High Club? Zeus's lightning bolts! We're scheduling sex on planes, too?"

"After that episode with Pegasus, Athena forbade us to borrow him."

Aphrodite eyed her son suspiciously. "You made love on a flying horse?"

"We don't need to go there," interrupted Psyche.

Eros grinned. His beloved didn't want Mom to know what was physically possible for two naked people on hovering horseback. "Karee Lomen works as an associate editor for *Love* magazine, the romance periodical run by heiress Veronica Martori. We're partnering Karee with Bret Jernigan."

"And he is . . ." asked Aphrodite.

"A man who won the lottery," answered Eros with a laugh.

Psyche bopped him with her notepad. "Karee won't find it funny that he's joining the Mile High Club because he won a stupid office wager."

"He won't exactly find it hilarious that she plans to write a very detailed article about her experience."

"Excuse me? Bret is the managing editor for *Max-Out* magazine. He has every intention of writing his own article, and it won't be an essay about the romantic aspects of acting out a sexual fantasy."

Poof!

Hera appeared in a cloud of white smoke, which was not magical at all, but rolling puffs of flour. Eros breathed it in, tasting the powder as he waved it away from his face. He heard sounds of coughing and hacking from the Graces, as well as the belabored inhalations of his wife and his mother. The air took on the thick scent of uncooked dough.

"Aphrodite," said Hera in a soft but commanding tone. "You've been invited to lunch with me and your father."

Hera inclined her regal—and flour-sprinkled—head to Eros, then to Aphrodite. Despite the rumpled and stained state of her simple T-shirt and jeans, her red hair shone as bright as a shiny apple. Her perfect complexion glowed with health and beauty, marred only by some sort of brown, gooey substance clinging to one alabaster cheek. She turned again to Aphrodite. "I need help in the kitchen."

Psyche gasped, her shocked gaze following Eros's to Aphrodite. *Horrified* was too tame a term for his mother's expression. She looked as if Hera had said, "You must throw all your Manolo Blahniks into the bonfire."

"The Graces . . ." Aphrodite gestured weakly toward the three women gazing at Hera in perplexed awe.

"No. They are hassled enough by your selfish whims. *You* will help me." The tone was imperious, though Hera's face showed no trace of her famous temper. "You are finished with your meeting?" she asked Eros, which was not a polite question, but a firm command.

He knew better than to mess around with his stepgrandmother, and he nodded, sweeping his hand toward his mother as if to say, *Take her. She's yours.* A puff of flour shook from his outstretched arm and enveloped his mother. She coughed, her teary eyes promising retribution.

Aphrodite's paybacks weren't fun, but they were child's play compared to the torments Hera could devise. Hera protected marriage and family with a ferocity that sometimes bordered on manic. She was kind, particularly to suffering women, but her love for Zeus was her only true weakness. She took no sass from mortals or from inferior gods, and that pretty much covered everyone in the entire universe.

"Come along, Aphrodite."

His mother rose, resigned to her fate. Not even the goddess of love dared to defy Hera, wife to Zeus and queen of the gods. Hera looked around the room with considerable interest. "Zeus has told me about this venture. It interests me. We will talk soon, Eros."

In another cloud of white, this one all magic, Hera, Aphrodite, and the Graces disappeared.

Psyche dusted off her shirt and shook out her hair. "You don't think she's serious, do you? Hera helping us is too terrifying to consider."

"I wouldn't worry about it. Mother might stoop to cooking to avoid Hera's wrath, but she'll draw the line at *Grand-mère* treading on her territory."

"What about Karee and Bret?"

"They are a match. But like everyone we pair together, they must take risks and make sacrifices or lose true love."

Eros's gaze dipped to his wife's soiled blouse and, with a mere thought, made it disappear. Next he dissolved her pink bra and revealed her perfect breasts, as succulent and sweet as ambrosia. She looked at him, one eyebrow quirked. A wicked grin tilted her lips.

"In the meantime," said Eros. "Why don't you show me what you've got under that miniskirt?"

One Mile Up . . . A Little to the Left

chapter one

*S*he sat in the first-class section of the airplane with no idea why she was on a plane, much less where she was going. The weirdest thing, though, was the fact that she was bare-assed naked.

She rose and stepped into the tiny aisle, then walked through the curtain separating first class from economy. Searching for something . . . and it wasn't a robe. Nudity, schmudity. She liked being nekkid. No, she didn't want clothing. Her need to find whatever it was drew her toward the back of the aircraft.

Every seat was empty, yet she knew someone else was on this plane. She reached what should have been the galley, but saw only shadowy darkness. She took a single step forward. . . .

The next thing she knew, she was in the plane's lavatory, sitting on the edge of the tiny sink, her arms and legs wrapped around a strong male body. She couldn't see his face, but she could feel the hard length of his cock sliding into her.

Kerplunk!

Karee Lomen jolted awake and found herself sprawled on the floor, her hip throbbing and her arm bent at an odd angle. *Shit.*

Sitting up, she rubbed the sore spot near her thigh and looked re-proachfully at her crappy old couch. "One of these days," she muttered, "I'm going to *finish* that dream."

It was the second week of December, one of the few times of the year Las Vegas hotel casinos were desperate for visitors. Just be-fore Christmas was a primo time for tourists to visit Sin City, be-cause hotels offered outrageous deals, including discounted room rates, free food, gambling coupons, and other kinds of goodies. But right now Karee cared less about the hotels' misappropriation of the Christmas spirit and more about getting to the offices of *Love* magazine. Working her way through the crowd of people in the lobby of the Palms Resort & Casino, she managed to get to the elevators with only three calls of "Move it, people!" and one purposeful elbow jab.

When she got upstairs, she stopped by her office long enough to drop off her purse and to sneak a truffle from the Ethel M.'s box she kept stashed in her desk. Then she was hurrying to Veronica's office. Vee was boss, mentor, and friend—a lucky combination for Karee, who had little time for forming and maintaining friendships.

Ten minutes later Karee sat with a whoosh on one of the of-fice's expensive white leather chairs and sighed in delight. Her story about Kevan Rune's new L.A.-based dessert-and-coffee café, Apples, had gotten a thumbs-up from Veronica. Her boss was on the phone, chatting up yet another celebrity while scribbling notes in a huge black day planner.

Next on the to-do list was to figure out which dress—the black backless sheath or the red-beaded mini—to wear to the party hosted by the Bellagio Gallery of Fine Arts. Tonight the just acquired collection of Monet paintings would be unveiled to media and to Las Vegas's glitterati.

Karee stared out the floor-to-ceiling windows. The sumptuous yet über-hip headquarters of *Love* magazine were located on the twenty-eighth floor, best known as the former setting for MTV's *Real World: Las Vegas*. Less than a mile away was Las Vegas Boulevard, also referred to as the Strip. In the daylight it was just a bunch of gaudy buildings, tourist-cluttered streets, and snaking traffic. But at night, when Lady Luck put on her jewels, the Strip turned into shimmering temples filled with awestruck worshipers.

"Mel, darling, I haven't seen you since the birthday party for Night," cooed Veronica. "What do I have to do to get an exclusive about the film version of *Macbeth*? I hear Kevan Rune is playing the Scotsman."

Karee grinned. Vee was great at schmoozing. Veronica Elsworth Martori was an heiress who had more money than she could spend in three lifetimes. The woman was the world's most ardent fan of love, though she hadn't been much good at keeping a long-term relationship. The magazine she created was a mixture of book reviews, celebrity interviews, short romantic fiction, travel pieces, and carb-lush recipes. It had done fabulously well, much to the surprise of Veronica's parents and the publishing world.

Just five years ago, fresh from the University of Las Vegas with a degree in journalism, Karee had applied as an assistant for the upstart publication. She hadn't realized then that *Love* magazine was the ticket to her dreams, but it turned out to be the very thing she wanted. She loved everything about working for the magazine—the more difficult, the better. God, she relished the challenges of the publishing world. She hoped her hard work and her obvious passion for *Love* would gain her the managing editor position. Then she'd have more input on stories, layout, pictorials . . . it thrilled her to think about having more artistic control.

"When's the last time you went home?" asked Veronica as she hung up the phone.

Karee blinked away her musings and looked at her friend. "Last night."

"Wow. The first time in almost two weeks."

"The advantage of working in such a huge and fantastic suite is the availability of bedrooms."

"Don't you have a plant or a cat to take care of?"

"There is nothing alive at my apartment—unless you count the science experiments growing in my refrigerator."

Veronica blanched. "TMI, sweetie. You really need something to do outside of writing for *Love* magazine."

"My social life has increased exponentially because I write for your magazine. I go to clubs, museums, restaurants, pool parties, and—"

"And who do you bring with you? Who do you meet that you actually continue to have a relationship with after the articles are finished?"

"I can't believe *you're* lecturing *me* about permanent, fulfilling relationships."

"Retract your claws, my dear. Even if I keep meeting Mr. Wrong, at least I'm trying to find Mr. Right. I can't remember the last time you had a real date."

"Well, I had a really hot dream last night. Does that count?"

"Let me guess! Mystery man in the lavatory with a penis."

"Har. Har. Har."

"Did you get to the end of the dream?"

"Nope. I not only woke up, I fell off my couch."

Veronica laughed; then she stood up and rounded the massive desk, leaning against the edge and crossing her arms. Her pink blouse rose just a tad above her pink jeans, showing a strip of tanned tummy and the glitter of a diamond-pierced navel. Veronica was tall, very thin, and blond, with blue, blue eyes. She never wore any color other than pink, mostly to annoy her father, who thought his daughter should act and dress more corporate.

"We need to be prepared for the museum's soiree tonight. *Max-Out* will have reporters there, too, and chances are very good they're not showing up to do a serious article about Monet's masterpieces."

"You mean we should expect one of their famous practical jokes. After what happened when the Bellagio unveiled its newest water show, it's a wonder they got invited back for something as classy as an art shindig."

"Hmph. They hired six strippers to take off their clothes and jump into the water just as the dancing fountains started the routine to 'Love Me Tender.' Bellagio got more publicity than Britney Spears's drunken nuptials. Three months later, the publicists are still talking about it. They're probably hoping *Max-Out* will do something crazy and boost interest in the Gallery."

Max-Out magazine might be considered the male version of *Love* magazine, except that it reveled in its ability to make fun of everything about love and relationships. Despite its use of crass humor, skimpily dressed women, and encouragement of all things debauched, it still was well written, funny, and wildly popular— at least with most men.

"You think Mad Max will be there?"

Veronica shrugged. "Mad Max" was Maximillian Rutledge,

owner and publisher of the magazine. He had the same kind of background as Veronica: rich, famous, and a schmoozer of the first order. In fact, he and Veronica had dated for a while, but why they broke up was a mystery to Karee. The subject was verboten. Not long after the relationship ended, Veronica started *Love*, and not long after that, Max started *Max-Out*. Karee suspected that even after five years, her friend still carried a torch for her old beau.

"Gird yourself for battle," said Veronica. "We'll need shields and swords to survive Max's minions."

Karee grinned. "Don't worry about me. I have the perfect dress."

"These days fashion doesn't allow for sword sheaths."

"I guess my Jimmy Choo heels will have to do."

Vee gasped. "You bought them? Oh, my God. The red ones with the tiny straps that go around the leg?"

"Suede, open-toed, three-inch heels. Damn straight I bought them. Merry Christmas to me."

Chuckling, Veronica returned to her desk and opened a drawer. She withdrew three red-wrapped rectangles and a pink envelope. "Speaking of Christmas, I have prezzies for you."

Karee's eyes widened. *Oh, no.* She hadn't yet attempted to find a gift Veronica might like, want, or need. What did you buy a woman who owned everything in the world? Hell, who *owned* the world? "You know I don't celebrate holidays, Vee."

"You don't celebrate anything. That doesn't mean I can't buy you a present."

"You do this gift-giving thing every year." Karee groaned.

"And you argue about it every year." Veronica strode across the room and handed her the packages. "Now open your fucking presents and shut up."

"Oh, all right."

Karee had to admit that she experienced a small thrill from Vee's kindness. She hadn't celebrated Christmas since her parents lost their lives in a car accident her sophomore year of college. Orphaned at age twenty. She'd been the only child of a mother and father who were also only children. Both sets of grandparents had passed away before she'd been born.

When Mom and Dad died, she'd lost the last familial connection she had in the world. Writing became her obsession, her solace, her excuse to cut off emotions. Instead she wrote about them with the objective eye of a reporter. It wasn't that she had a cold heart. No. Not at all. She had, without conscious intent, protected herself from other people by simply never forming any lasting relationships.

The wrapping ripped easily, and she found herself the new owner of three DVDs. "Oh, you are so, so funny." Karee held up each one. "*Airplane, Hot Shots,* and *Airport.* I should have never told you about the dream."

"Oh, come on! That's a hot dream. But I've saved the best for last." Vee gave her the envelope, excitement in her gaze, her grin wide.

Karee stared at the pink invitation. " 'Welcome, future member of the Mile High Club. You have been given a fantasy to join the Mile High Club from Cupid, Inc.' " *What the hell?* She looked at Vee. "Please do not tell me you hooked me up with some kind of weirdo dating service."

"It's not a dating service. It's a sex service."

The pink paper fluttered from her hand. Veronica had lost her damned mind, and Karee wasn't going to travel down the same path of insanity. "I'm not that desperate."

"Yes, you are. You are scheduled to go to Cupid, Inc., this afternoon and do all the paperwork and exams. Your fantasy is scheduled for the twentieth." Vee waved her manicured hands around like a Cachucha dancer. "It's a fantasy, Karee. You'll get your groove on with a handsome man you'll never have to see again. Talk about flying the friendly skies!"

Her pulse did *not* stutter. Her mouth did *not* go dry. Her mind did *not* consider the possibilities of such a ridiculous gift. She wasn't turned on *at all* by the idea of fucking at thirty thousand feet. No, nope, *nada* . . . this Mile High Club fantasy did not appeal to her in the least. So what if she had an opportunity to literally make a dream come true? *Oh, hell.* Who was she kidding? She could be as wanton, as sexually open and free as she'd always desired, and not worry about emotional judgments from her partner.

"This is some Christmas present," said Karee, unable to articulate her acquiescence.

"If it'll make you go, then let's say I want an article for *Love.* In fact, I do want an article about the experience. Now, you'll have to do it"—Vee snickered—"in the name of journalism."

"Well . . . if it's for journalism . . . I suppose I have no choice." Excitement tingled through her. *Whoo-hoo!* This would be one assignment she'd gladly endure for *Love*.

chapter two

"I'm going to schmooze," said Veronica. "You guard the quiches."

"Yes, ma'am," said Karee, saluting. She stood post near the food-filled tables while she watched her friend saunter through the crowd and make nice with socialites.

The speeches from publicists, bigwigs, and art critics had ended just a few minutes ago, and with a snip of red ribbon people surged into the large room that housed the Monet collection. However, the focus wasn't the Impressionist paintings lining the walls, but the gourmet spread at the end of the room, featuring prawns, stuffed mushrooms, baby quiches, chocolate-dipped fruit, and a champagne fountain.

"I'm Bret," said a handsome man who approached her with two glasses of champagne, offering her one.

"Thank you." Karee blinked in surprise. She wasn't used to gaining male attention—at least not at fancy events.

"Are you here with anyone?" he asked. "I don't want to tread on a lucky man's territory."

Pleasure surged through her at the compliment, making her

feel tingly and warm. It had been too long since she'd allowed herself to flirt, much less date. And this guy was gorgeous. He had short blond hair, melted-chocolate eyes, and a muscled physique. He was only about three or four inches taller than she. Without the three-inch stilettos she was five-eight, and with the ankle abusers strapped on, she and Bret were about the same height. He wore khakis, a light brown oxford shirt, brown loafers, and a gorgeous brown leather jacket.

"To be honest, I'm bored out of my skull, my dress is itchy, and if I have to hear one more canned comment from a publicist, I'm going to scream." She leaned closer to him and said in a low voice, "I'm seriously thinking about stealing a tray of quiches and making a break for it."

Bret's eyes widened and he laughed. "Well, itchy or not, that's a hell of a dress."

The red beaded minidress hit her midthigh. It was strapless, low-cut, and the sewn-in bustier gave her some great cleavage. Her only jewelry was a pair of one-carat diamond stud earrings that she had purchased for herself as a birthday gift last year. No bra was necessary, so she wore only a pair of red thong underwear, stockings, and the Jimmy Choo heels that made her legs look sexy, but tortured her feet.

"So, Bret, what do you—"

"Excuse me, ladies and gentlemen," boomed a loud male voice. Every head turned to the center of the room, where a tall, broad-shouldered man dressed in a purple crushed velvet tuxedo stood next to a six-foot-tall block of Styrofoam.

"Mad Max!" exclaimed Karee. She looked around for Vee and found her on the opposite side of the room watching Max's show. Veronica, dripping in diamonds, was dressed in a pink Versace sheath. Her pale blond hair was swept up, glittering with carefully placed gems. Her friend shook her head as if to say, *Show your sword and ready your shield*. Her narrowed eyes moved from Karee to Maximillian, and if looks were laser beams, ol' Max would be a pile of ash.

"In honor of the Bellagio's unveiling of this fabulous Monet collection, the staff at *Max-Out* magazine would like to bestow this gift to the hotel." Two burly men dressed in gray jumpsuits pulled apart the Styrofoam. The material squeaked and crunched, but revealed its prize without too much fuss.

The voluptuous nude woman appeared to be an elaborate ice sculpture. Droplets of water slid down her crystalline skin, but Karee realized the moisture was stationary. Then Max patted the statue's round little butt, and the thumping of his signet ring revealed that the porn-star beauty was made of glass.

Her expression was the typical oh-baby-do-me look that graced the faces of *Max-Out*'s models. She had huge breasts, an impossibly thin waist, and a Brazilian bikini wax. Her arms were extended in front of her flat stomach, holding something rectangular that was covered by black plastic. Momentarily shocked, Karee felt herself becoming angrier and angrier.

"This is Moana," said Max, grinning broadly. "That's spelled M-o-a-n-a. And she's here to add some beauty to this otherwise ugly display of artwork."

His statement garnered a few chuckles, but most gazes were riveted to the rectangle of black poised between Moana's hands. Not even Bellagio's publicists had moved, though Karee had no doubt security would be called in at some point.

With great ceremony, Max ripped off the plastic. The sign read: I MELT FOR MONET.

"Clever," said Karee, not really meaning it. The idea must've fallen flat for most of the people in the room, too, because the silence reeked of disapproval. The wave of rancor rolled through the crowd so heavily that not even Max could ignore the sudden tension.

"Oh, come on, people! She melts for Monet." He pointed to a droplet. "See?"

"I see that your little joke has just about as much class as you do," said Veronica. "In fact"—she joined him in the center of the room and peered through the side of the statue—"I can see right through it."

People laughed and the tension broke. Conversations started again, and most everyone turned away from the spectacle. Max looked uncomfortable, his expression almost sheepish. He probably wasn't used to his brilliant schemes backfiring.

Karee turned to her new companion, smiling, and opened her mouth to render a scathing opinion of Mad Max. *Well, so much for successful flirting.* Her mouth snapped shut and her heart dropped to her toes.

Bret was gone.

On the morning of December 20, Karee found herself ensconced in a room so pink, it was like sitting in a pile of cotton candy. The bed took up half the space; it was covered with new (not washed—*new*, or so insisted the flight attendant) pink silk sheets. With shag carpeting, an awesome heart-shaped Jacuzzi, and a large pink cabinet that looked like a minibar, it might have been a Las Vegas hotel suite instead of a Boeing Business Jet.

Other than working on her articles for *Love*, searching eBay for a one-of-a-kind something for Veronica, and thinking about the disappearance of Bret, the man with no last name whom no one knew . . . she'd spent way too much time preparing for this day. Her credit cards had gotten a workout, but despite the fact that the whole purpose of paying for a fantasy was to simply get laid, she still wanted it to be the best experience ever for her—and for her mystery man.

Cupid, Inc., gave minimum information about partners. He was male, five-eleven, in excellent shape, disease-free, and he had to be loaded, too, because the Mile High Club Fantasy cost a fortune. She couldn't believe how much money Veronica had shelled out! And his name? She had no idea. Apparently the exchange of names was an option. She could be Sheila the Man-eating Slut, for all he knew . . . and he could be Rocko the Hard-dicked Caveman. She grinned at the silliness of her thoughts.

For an unfathomable reason, she'd been unable to stop thinking about that idiotic Bret. He'd been so cute, so flirtatious, and so enigmatic. Had something she'd said or done turned him off? It hardly mattered now. After all, she didn't really want to date anyone. Eventually she wanted a loving, long-term relationship, even though the very idea of commitment scared the shit out of her. To love someone, to risk for someone . . . only to lose him . . . no, she couldn't bear it.

Any armchair psychologist could point out that her parents' deaths had affected her so deeply she kept emotional distance from all other human beings. Work had become her friend, lover, and keeper. She would never admit to Veronica that she was lonely, that she might just be willing to make the leap for love. Truth was, she was probably ready to risk a little heartache, if she met a man worthy of the sacrifice.

Where the hell was her date? Antsy, she paced the area between the bed and the Jacuzzi. Nervousness ate away at her confidence. What if the guy thought she was ugly? Chubby? Slutty?

Get a grip, girl!

She couldn't control the attraction factor, and she might have commitment issues, but she didn't have low self-esteem. She also had every damned intention of being a slut for the next few hours. If Mystery Man wanted a plain old sexual encounter, he wouldn't have paid for a fantasy. She looked down at her outfit. See-through negligee, barely-there bra, teeny-tiny thong . . . shit, she looked *good!*

Just for something to do, she walked to the pink cabinet and opened it. It wasn't a minibar. It was a sex shop in a box. *Holy crap!* Vibrators, nipple clips, handcuffs, flavored gels—what the hell was *that?* She picked up the plastic-encased device and read the label. *Oh, no way.* She was not sticking that thing anywhere near her . . . Karee's gaze found a packaged pink vibrator and grabbed it. She also discovered a metal tin of Honey Dust with its own little feather duster.

Well, she had some time . . . why not use it?

"Brunette. Red dress. Killer legs. Hang on a sec, Max." Bret Jernigan plugged the headset into his cell phone, inserted the earbud, and made sure the tiny mike hovered near his chin. "Her first name was Karee. Ring any bells?"

"Nope."

Bret looked out the limousine's tinted window. When the sleek black machine showed up at *Max-Out*'s offices to pick him up, he breathed a sigh of relief that Cupid, Inc., hadn't given in to ultimate cheesiness by painting its vehicles red or dotting them with hearts and flowers.

"Speaking of beautiful women, we got some great photos of Bellagio security trying to haul Moana out of the room. One guy slipped and got a big handful of glass tit. I wouldn't be surprised if he got a bruised palm from her nipple."

"I can't wait to see the pictures." *Not.* Bret had joined *Max-Out* magazine three months ago. He'd been a freelance journalist for a number of years, but the lifestyle wore thin. Too much travel, too much living on fast food, and too much uncertainty about paychecks. Taking the magazine job meant a permanent home, a substantial salary, affordable health insurance, and the chance to settle down in other ways, too. He hadn't had a long-term commitment since college, and he had to admit, if only to himself, that it would be nice to have someone to share his life with.

Max-Out was an ideal workplace. If Bret could change anything, it would be to lessen the manic attention Max paid to his ex-girlfriend, Veronica Martori, who ran some sort of chick mag based in Las Vegas. He hadn't had time to check it out, but Max's opinion was that the periodical was an ode to all things estrogen and therefore must be avoided.

And yet, Max's need to get this Veronica's attention—or maybe it was his need to get her goat—was his main motivation for creating such elaborate jokes. Bret had missed Max's last practical joke at the Bellagio, coming aboard just days after it happened. He'd thought unveiling *Melting Moana* at a classy museum event was too tactless even for *Max-Out*, but he sure wished he'd been there to witness strippers swimming naked in the pristine blue lake in front of the hotel.

Max claimed the crazy stunts were publicity efforts for *Max-Out*. *Yeah, right*. Maximillian didn't need to do anything special for attention—he was one of the richest bachelors in the world and had made *People*'s Most Beautiful list no less than five times.

"Bret? You there?"

"Sorry. I got distracted. You were saying?"

"You missed all the fun with Moana last night. Where'd you disappear to?"

"Slight case of food poisoning," Bret lied. He'd felt a little strange flirting with Karee on the eve of his Mile High Club induction. Even though the fantasy would be a consensual one-night, er . . . one-day, stand, he still felt some loyalty to the woman who'd paid for a fantasy in which he'd have a starring role.

And, well, if he were really honest, Bret had seen Karee's unfavorable reaction to Moana and let cowardice rule the day. He hadn't felt like explaining that he not only knew the guy making an ass of himself in front of Las Vegas's rich and famous; he was the managing editor for the magazine said ass owned and operated.

He'd felt instantly attracted to the lady in red, not only because she had a body that would give Moana a run for her money, but also because of the wit and intelligence that had shone in her gray gaze. He'd felt she was someone he'd be able to laugh with, someone who was impetuous. She also had confidence in spades, as evidenced by the wowzer dress she wore, but he suspected she had a streak of practicality that tamed the adventuress.

Damn. He wished he'd at least gotten her last name, or maybe even a phone number. Who was she? Who did she work for? Maybe the *Las Vegas Review Journal* or *Nevada* magazine. He was still learning who was who in the Las Vegas media. He hadn't recognized many faces last night; most of the people attending were journalists and, of course, Las Vegas's upper crust.

"Hel-lo, Bret."

"Oh, sorry. What did you say?"

"Never mind, Romeo. Check in when you're finished with your Mile High Club fun."

"You got it, boss." Bret ended the call and tucked both phone and headset into his jacket pocket. As managing editor, he shouldn't have participated in the lottery for this assignment. He had more to worry about than . . . He chuckled. Than what? Enjoying sex with a beautiful, willing woman on a luxury airliner? Still, if he'd taken the assignment for himself without holding the lottery, it would've fostered resentment among the guys. He won the drawing fair and square.

He just hoped the prize was worth it.

chapter three

The limousine pulled into the parking lot of the Cupid, Inc., executive air terminal and drove to a gated entrance. Bret knew from his research that Cupid, Inc., was only one of two private businesses that owned property at McCarran Airport. Most of the small airlines couldn't fly into McCarran; they used the airport in North Las Vegas and bused tourists to and from that location.

After the security officer buzzed open the gate, the limo pulled onto the runway. In minutes, the limo arrived at the Boeing Business Jet, one of the most opulent jets made for corporate travel. Less than a hundred were in use in the world, and for good reason: The BBJ cost roughly $45 million—without upgrades or made-to-order cabins. This particular jet had been outfitted for Cupid, Inc., and took the idea of sumptuousness to a whole new level. Indeed, the brochure he'd read bragged about the king-size bed and the hot tub for two.

Bret Jernigan had to admit that his jaded reporter's soul was impressed so far. Cupid, Inc., was the exact opposite of sleazy. He had yet to find a flaw with the sex-fantasy business—everything was top-notch. He had believed it was simply another version of the service so-called private dancers advertised in the Las Vegas Yellow Pages.

Most people thought prostitution was permissible everywhere in Nevada, but the world's oldest profession was illegal in Clark County, and that included Las Vegas. He figured the owners of Cupid, Inc., ran a "dating service" that matched johns with working girls under the guise of putting together adults who shared the same sexual fantasies. If a human being just wanted to screw around, why not answer a personal ad or go to one of Vegas's swing clubs or make the hour-long drive to Pahrump for a legal brothel? And yet . . . all his research indicated that Cupid, Inc., was on the up-and-up, which was disappointing for the reporter, but opened up all kinds of possibilities for the man.

The limo driver opened his door and Bret exited, tipping the guy a twenty. No luggage needed for this flight. They would fly around a while, supposedly to allow him and his new lady friend enough time to indulge their sexual appetites several times; then the BBJ would return to McCarran.

Just as he reached the stairwell, his cell phone rang. He took the credit-card-size device out of his pocket and flipped it open. "Hello?"

"Good morning, Mr. Jernigan, this is Psyche with Cupid, Inc. I wanted to make absolutely sure you haven't changed your mind about the confidentiality agreements."

"Has my fantasy partner changed her mind?"

"No. As you requested, we found someone suitable who was willing to forgo the confidentiality agreements. You understand that neither you nor Cupid, Inc., will have recourse if your experience is revealed to others in any way, shape, or form?"

"You have my signature, witnessed by three other people, that states I understand the repercussions of not utilizing a confidentiality agreement. I believe my partner has done the same?"

"Yes, even though I advised her against such action." Psyche sighed. "Very well, Mr. Jernigan. Enjoy your flight."

Bret pressed end and pocketed the phone. He walked up the stairwell to the open hatchway and stepped inside.

"Welcome aboard, Mr. Jernigan. I'm your flight attendant, Meddie."

Dressed in a gold-striped black pantsuit, the young woman sported a heart-shaped tag on her lapel that declared she was, indeed, Meddie. She was probably no more than five feet in height, and her most interesting feature was the hair that fell in ringlets to her shoulders. It was the blue-black of a raven's wing, except for several random strands around her face—those were emerald green.

Her face was pale perfection: cherry lips, high cheekbones, and almond-shaped eyes nearly the same bright shade of green as the colored ringlets. She was almost too pretty. How odd to feel both revulsion and fascination at the same time. He fought an insane urge to look away from her—as if to stare at her for too long were like gazing into the sun. Eventually he would go blind from the indulgence. He noticed the thin scar around her neck and couldn't help but ask, "What happened?"

Her fingers touched the line that circled her throat. "Are you familiar with the Greek myth of Perseus and Medusa?"

Bret cast around the memories of his high school literature classes. "Medusa was some sort of evil creature with snakes for hair. Anyone who looked directly at her was turned to stone. Perseus was the hero who cut off her head."

She smiled. "Ah, yes. Well, it was something like that, only with a happier ending. May I take your jacket?"

He took off his black leather jacket and handed it to her. She folded it neatly over her arm, then gestured for him to continue moving to his right.

Bret strode through a large galley of such beauty and quality, a five-star chef would turn pea-soup green with envy. He glimpsed high-polished wood cabinets, marble countertops, and the silver sheen of matching metallic microwave, oven, and dishwasher. He slipped through the tiny hallway and halted.

Holy shit.

The spacious cabin looked like the inside of Austin Powers's private playroom. The carpet was thick purple shag, the tables were metal and curvy, and the plush chairs and two couches were a variety of funky colors: sherbet orange, Play-Doh yellow, pistachio green, and hot pink. He counted at least five lava lamps. A disco ball suspended from the ceiling slowly twirled, bathing the outrageous room in sparkles.

"It looks like the nineteen sixties threw up in here," he said, eliciting a laugh from Meddie. He looked at her over his shoulder. "Believe it or not, the room is missing one thing."

"Your date." She put away the jacket in a closet. "See that lovely wall?"

He looked where she pointed. It looked like the room had slammed against a silver plate. Splats of neon colored the tinny surface. He barely made out the outline of a door, but its big purple handle was easy to spot.

"Yeah."

"She's in there. If you think this space is psychedelic, wait till you see the suite."

Anticipation wiggled through him. What did his anonymous woman really want from this experience? The fantasy never matched up to the reality. What if two people partnered for a fantasy had no chemistry? Just because Cupid, Inc., put a couple of humans into a sensual situation didn't mean the potential lovers would fall ravenously upon each another. He couldn't help but think there was a Nervous Nelly waiting for him, probably coming up with excuses about why she changed her mind.

"Your partner has requested that you join her after takeoff. Please sit down and buckle your seat belt. Once the pilot gives us the all-clear, please feel free to . . . do whatever you want."

Meddie directed him toward a puffy orange chair. He sat and buckled the seat belt. Suddenly he felt like Nervous Nelly himself. What if the woman didn't like him? What if she didn't find him attractive? Or she thought his penis was too small? *Ha.* He smirked, arrogance rescuing his ego. He wasn't a slouch in the bedroom, and his Mr. Happy was just fine in the length and width department. If he and his date could both just relax, they'd have a good time, and best of all, he'd get a great story for *Max-Out.*

"There are call buttons at several stations in the aircraft. If you need anything, use the system to contact me. Otherwise you will not be disturbed for the duration of the flight."

"Gotcha."

"Do you have any questions?"

"No."

"Enjoy your flight, Mr. Jernigan."

"Thank you." Would a man ever enjoy an airplane ride more than he hoped to enjoy this one? If all went according to plan and fantasies really did come true . . . he would not only be a member of the Mile High Club, he'd be one cheerful son of a bitch.

Not long after Meddie retired to the crew rest area, located just beyond the galley, the pilot announced takeoff. Within ten minutes the plane taxied onto the runway and roared into the sky. In no time at all he was free of his chair and approaching the door to the suite.

Should he knock and try to act like a hammy Adam Sandler? Open the door slowly and do a sexy James Dean impersonation? Burst in and scream, "Stella! Steeeeelllllaaaa!" with a Marlon Brando scowl?

Bret grabbed the handle and . . . hesitated. He wasn't sure what he expected from the woman who signed up to have hot sex during a long flight. A straitlaced, fully clothed conservative sipping tea from delicate china . . . a Catwoman wannabe in tight black leather with a whip in her hand . . . a *Playboy* Playmate wearing only a see-through teddy and high, high heels.

Any of those scenarios would do just fine. Inhaling a fortifying breath, he yanked open the door and entered the suite.

Shocked from the onslaught of intense color, he took two strides and stopped. The door swung shut behind him, slamming into place.

Everything was pink—from the huge bed to the heart-shaped hot tub. The walls, chairs, sheets, pillows, carpets, curtains, even the champagne bottle and flutes . . . all items were varying shades of pink. *Good Lord!* How did they expect men to do the wild thing in such a pretty-princess room?

Feeling slightly dazed, he let his gaze zero in on the only thing *not* pink.

The brunette stood next to the bed, one foot planted on the floor, the other on the bed itself. One manicured hand wrapped around her hip as her shoulders thrust back to give him a spectacular view of her cleavage. It was a pose he'd seen many, many times in men's magazines. Was it any wonder that particular stance was so popular? Seeing a woman model her body like half Siren, half sex kitten was fucking erotic.

His heart stuttered to a stop before resuming its beat at a frantic pace. His temperature shot to three hundred degrees. It was her. *Karee*. The lady in red . . . now the lady in practically nothing. *Thank you, God. Thank you!*

She watched him with gray eyes, frowning as she looked at him. *Trying to place me. Sheesh.* He must not have left much of an impression on her last night.

The white lace negligee she wore hid nothing. His eyes feasted on what was underneath. That was the skimpiest bra he'd ever seen, and a mere wisp of lace served as panties. *Christ.* Her skin was tanned, and it seemed to shimmer in the low lighting of the room. It was almost as if she'd been dipped in gold.

He licked his suddenly dry lips. *Damn.* He couldn't stop looking at her legs. Her toenails were painted a pearlescent white. Her calves were sleekly muscled . . . pretty knees—the woman had *pretty* knees—and her thighs were toned, and her . . . he gulped. The underwear couldn't hide the neatly trimmed pussy. The curls pressed against the lace triangle, barely covering the pink flesh of her vulva. Sweat broke out on his brow. He wanted to taste her. *Now.*

"N-nice thong," he managed.

chapter four

"I know you," she said. "Bret, right?"

"Yes. And you're Karee," he responded, his voice hoarse. Well, damn, he might be able to speak more coherently if she weren't standing there looking almost naked and all-the-way scrumptious. "I haven't stopped thinking about you since we met yesterday."

"Is that why you took off?"

"I . . . uh, no."

"Black loafers, black jeans, black shirt," she mused, checking out his form. "At the party you looked like a café mocha, and today you look like a licorice whip."

"Do you like licorice?"

She smiled, a quirking of the lips that suggested she not only liked candy, she did wicked things with it . . . things she might do with him if he played his cards right.

Then he caught sight of the object she gripped in her other hand.

It was six inches long.

Two inches wide.

And pink.

"Is that what I think it is?" he asked.

"It's a vibrator. You should see all the stuff in the toy chest! Sex aids I've never seen before—I mean, a Rubik's Cube would be easier to figure out than some of those devices. Anyway, it works like the minibar in a hotel room." She grinned as she crawled onto the bed. "If you break the seal on the fridge, you know that the maid is going to count how many beers are left."

Her words were rapid-fire, like the report of an Uzi. Her skin looked flushed and she seemed agitated. No, not nervous agitation . . . squirmy and breathless. She pointed the pink dick at him and waved it around.

"I like to think I'm adventurous, but we might as well set the ground rules. I'm not into anything too kinky—no BDSM. No anal play, but oral sex is high on my to-do list. I've never tried sixty-nine, so that might be fun. Oh, hell! Are you going to stare at me like I'm crazy or come over here and kiss me?"

Bret jolted. The sixty-nine position? Didn't mind getting tied up? Liked using sex toys? *Dear God.* His mind malfunctioned, going offline due to sensory overload . . . then it rebooted, slowly, since all the blood had rushed to his penis, leaving hardly any in his brain for little things—like thinking.

His dream woman now sat in the middle of a huge bed holding a plastic cock and demanding a kiss, and he was standing there like a drooling moron. He shed his clothes in record time and leaped onto the bed, taking Karee down like a wrestler trying to win the world championship. The vibrator flew from her grasp and landed with a soft thud somewhere on the bed.

"By the way," she said as he peeled off her negligee, "I'm not a slut."

"Sluts don't pay for fantasies," said Bret. "You're an adventurous woman living out a sexual dream, and I'm thrilled to be part of it."

"You should probably know that I get really horny on airplanes."

"Why?"

"Do you want to know now or would you rather fuck me and hear the story later?"

"The second thing you said."

"What about my kiss?"

"Okay." He tossed away the negligee and settled between her legs. He planted a soft kiss on the thong's white lace triangle and was rewarded by Karee's low moan.

"That's not exactly what I meant," she said in a choked voice, "but I appreciate your interpretation of the request."

He kissed her inner thigh and paused at the sweet tang on his lips. Experimentally he licked her from hip to pubic bone, and tasted the faint sweetness again. "Your skin has flavor."

"Honey Dust," she whispered.

That explained the gold shimmer of her skin he'd noticed earlier. The Honey Dust smelled as good as it tasted, and he found himself feasting on her legs, thighs, hips, stomach. His hard-on gouged his stomach, protesting its imprisonment, and his balls tightened, joining the complaint. Uncomfortable genitals, though, were not reason enough to stop exploring the lovely body of Karee.

Bret had the desire, but not the ability, to rip off the thong.

With trembling fingers, he pulled the scrap of material off her hips and down her legs, and flung the panties onto the floor.

He licked her labia with slow strokes, drawing her juicy clit between his lips. Warm and sweet. As ripe as a peach plucked on a summer day. Desire rippled through him; he swallowed a groan. *God, yes!*

"I-I have a confession," Karee said.

"Hmmm?" He delved into her vagina and thrust his tongue rapidly inside. He couldn't wait until his cock had the joy of slipping inside her tight warmth and stroking them both to heaven.

He felt the dive of her hands into his hair, the lift of her hips, a silent encouragement for his continued efforts. He returned his attention to the plump flesh of her outer labia, allowing his tongue to flirt with the inner lips as he worked his way to the jewel in the crown. The clitoris hid under its tiny hood like a shy bird. His tongue swirled around her clitoris, flicking and sucking and teasing. He lifted his head just enough to remind her, "Confession?"

"I . . . uh . . . oh, Lord." She sucked in a breath, her fingers digging into his scalp. "I was messing around with the vibrator before you arrived on scene. So I'm incredibly close to—"

She screamed, pressing his face against her vulva as she came. Writhing, bucking, panting . . . she was wild in her ecstasy. He pushed his tongue inside her to feel the vibrations of her pleasure; his mouth flooded with her nectar. Finally she sank to the mattress, obviously replete. With slow care, he soothed her clitoris, and all the while his cock begged for playtime.

The effects of the orgasm still ricocheted through Karee as Bret did a sensual crawl up her body. Within seconds he'd disposed of her bra. His mouth was warm and wet, his tongue raspy as he sucked her nipples into hardness.

Renewed desire tore through her, ripping away the soft complacency left by her incredible orgasm. Bret's devotion to her breasts made her squirmy and hot, but her excitement revved into overdrive at the prospect of Bret's hard cock thrusting inside her.

With eager hands she worked her way across his chest, down the six-pack stomach, all the way to the luscious hard-on. God, he had muscles on his muscles. His warm flesh felt as smooth and hard as burnished wood.

Speaking of wood . . . Her fingers swirled around the plumed head of his cock before sliding along the shaft. She could tell by feel that his penis was circumcised. It was also thick and long. *Jesus.* He shifted to give her more room to play; bless his multi-tasking heart, he didn't stop his lustful assault on her breasts. She wrapped one hand around his penis while the other cupped and massaged his balls. She and Bret wiggled against each other, skin sliding, hips bumping, moans escaping.

"You smell so good. Taste so good," he muttered. "Honey Dust rules!" He deftly turned her sensitized nipples into aching points of contact—amative zings from nipples to clit sizzled through her. It felt like her nervous system had been electrified.

"Kiss me," she whispered. "Fuck me."

He wrapped his arms around her and kissed her breathless. His tongue danced with hers, mimicking the movement of his cock as he parted her legs and slid his hard length into the soft wetness of her pussy. She wound her legs around his waist and matched his thrusts, her hands clutching his hair, her mouth attacking his with fervor.

"Oh, Bret!"

He slid his arms under her back, holding tightly as he rolled over. Karee found herself on top, his delicious cock embedded inside her. She was so greedy for him. *Again.* With eager anticipation, she planted her hands on his chest and rode his cock.

Bret filled his hands with her breasts, kneading the flesh, tweaking the nipples. She pushed her clit against him, rubbing harder and faster, slamming herself onto the beautiful, hard dick of her lover.

"Yes, Karee. Oh, yes." He grabbed her hips and shoved deeply inside her.

She responded by clutching him with her pelvic muscles.

"Wait. Shit. Damn." He stilled completely and sucked in slow breaths. He stared at her with a mixture of pleasure and pain in his eyes. "If you do that again, I'll cum."

"So the Kegel exercises are worth the effort?"

He nodded. Then he said, "Condom."

"It's a little late, don't you think? Besides, if we weren't healthy, disease-free, and at least one of us on birth control, we wouldn't be in this fantastic bed in this fantastic plane having fantastic sex." Karee inhaled a shaky breath. This was her fantasy. *He* was her fantasy. "I've always wanted to try a particular position."

"You're trying to kill me, aren't you?"

"There are worse ways to die." She slid off him and flipped around so that she faced his legs.

"You have a really nice ass," he commented.

"Thanks." She did what amounted to a half backbend over him. Her feet went on either side of his thighs, her hands settling on each side of his chest. "Just so you don't worry about my flexibility, I practice Ananda yoga every morning."

He made a gurgling sound then. "I've never seen this particular gymnastic move in the Olympics." His hands slid along her buttocks and squeezed the rounded flesh. "Let's go for the gold."

Feeling like a scuttling crab, she scooted forward and squirmed onto his penis. With slow precision she moved her hips, sliding up and down his length. *Oh, God.* As she got more comfortable with the position, she increased her pace. That sweet cock hit her G-spot with erotic accuracy. Pleasure spiked in her belly.

She felt the curl of Bret's fingers around her waist; he slipped his other hand over her hip. "Look what I found," he said. A soft whir alerted her that he'd located the toy she'd lost in the bedcovers.

The minute the vibrator touched her clit, her core filled with the first tendrils of tingling pleasure. "Bret, you're going to make me cum."

"I hope so, because—"

As the orgasm bloomed into sparks of heat and joy, she took all of him, all the way to his balls, rejoicing when she heard his prayerful gasp, felt the clench of muscles, the stillness of his hot, hard cock right before . . .

They came together, a torrent of *soundfeelingemotionmovement.* She was robbed of sight, of breath, of thought. For this one unending moment, all she knew was the beating of her own heart and the purity of her own bliss.

chapter five

"I think that's why I've always wanted to fuck on an airplane," said Karee as they lay on the bed and talked. Neither one of them had moved since they collapsed next to each other, but they'd spent a pleasurable half hour talking about a variety of subjects. They had the relationship thing ass-backward, didn't they? Hell, maybe it would be better if human beings tested the physical attraction first. Nothing was worse than liking a guy because he was smart, funny, and kind . . . only to find the sizzle was missing in the bedroom.

"Ol' Bobby Dalton kissed you senseless in the airplane bathroom?" Bret rolled onto his side and traced shapes on her stomach. "That's not a bad way to end an exciting high school band trip to Hawaii. What instrument did he play?"

"If you expect me to say the flute, forget it." She laughed. "He played the drums. I played the flute. Er, but not *his* flute. Unfortunately, that kiss was the only thing I ever got from Bobby. It was a great kiss, too. Maybe that was the beginning of what my friend calls 'uppis hottis hornyitus.' It would explain why I get . . . um,

squirmy on flights and why I keep having that recurring dream."
She sighed, feeling oh, so relaxed. "Anyhoo, after we got home,
Bobby forgot my name."

"High school boys are assholes." He encircled her navel. "I
know. I used to be one."

"You've improved with age," she said, capturing his roving
fingers.

"Not really." He sighed. "I need to tell you something."

Cold dread punched her in the stomach. She'd been with Bret
for almost two hours and she was already getting the "we need to
talk" speech.

"Shit. You're gay."

His brows rose. "Uh, no."

"Married."

"Nope."

"You live with your mother."

"I like girls, I've never walked down the aisle, and my mother
lives on the East Coast."

"Well, how bad could it be?"

"I signed up for the fantasy in order to write an article for *Max-
Out* magazine. I saw how you reacted last night to Max's little
show, and I bailed so I wouldn't have to admit to knowing anything about it. I swear to God I didn't know you were my date for
this little adventure."

"You write for *Max-Out*?"

"I'm the managing editor."

Karee grappled with the idea that she'd just had incredible sex
with the right-hand man of her boss's sworn archenemy. *Crap.* At
this moment she could care less that Bret worked for *Max-Out*.
Veronica, though, would care greatly and would probably de-

mand some sort of scathing commentary about Bret's sexual prowess. *No can do, Vee. This guy curled my toes—and a few other parts.*

"I'm sorry, Karee. I probably should have said something before I jumped your bones."

"Hold on, cowboy. You're not the only one who has a confession."

"If you're gay, I'm all for your girlfriend joining us."

Karee rolled onto her side and faced him. "I work for *Love* magazine. This little trip is part Christmas present, part assignment."

Bret blinked. His mouth opened. Closed. "You work for Veronica Martori."

"Yeah. And you work for Maximillian Rutledge."

Silence ensued as they considered the magnitude of the revelations. Finally Bret asked, "Is Veronica as wild about Max as he is about her?"

"If by 'wild,' you mean antagonistic, vengeful, and incapable of speaking about Max without screaming and breaking something valuable, then yeah, she's wild about him."

"Thought so."

Karee considered Bret's impressive nudity. He gave her the same kind of once-over as they marshaled their thoughts. So they were both writing stories about the Cupid, Inc., fantasy experience. No doubt his contribution would be sardonic and humorous in ways only men would appreciate. He'd probably give it a silly title like "One Mile Up . . . A Little to the Left," and include a sidebar that covered some stupid aspect like "Twelve Things to Lick at Thirty Thousand Feet."

"Since we're both writing stories for opposing magazines, and we both didn't sign confidentiality agreements for apparently the same reason, can we at least agree not to use real names?" she asked.

"Agreed. Do you have a preference?"

"I've always liked Loralee. And make it so that I'm from Georgia. I've always wanted one of those sultry Southern accents."

Bret grinned. "Anything else, Loralee?"

"What about you? What name do you want?"

"Tiger."

"You want me to call you Tiger? Who am I, Mary Jane talking to Peter Parker? Ha. No way."

"Aw, c'mon."

"Bret!"

"All right, already. Call me Bubba. And I'm from Florida."

"Terrific. These two should get along great—a redneck and a debutante."

He laughed. "It can't be any weirder for them than it is for us. Are you going to tell Veronica the truth?"

"Hell, no. Are you telling Max you slept with the enemy?"

"No." He looked at her. "So . . . what should we do next?"

Karee knew what Bret was really asking: *Do we continue to enjoy this fantasy or do we call the captain and tell him to turn this bird around?*

Oh, well. No matter what Bret wrote in his article, she was still having the best time she'd had with a guy in months . . . er, years. If it only lasted for the next couple of hours, she'd still count herself a lucky girl—at least in the sex department. Plus, she would have a hell of a story to report, too.

She leaned forward and brushed a kiss across his lips. "Why don't we investigate the Jacuzzi?"

In seconds they had slipped into the bubbling pink waters of the hot tub. There was enough room, barely, for two people to sit in it—one in each curve at the heart's top—and their feet met at the point of the heart's bottom.

"I can't believe they managed to put a hot tub onto an airplane. Amazing."

"And the water is pink," said Bret. "Is there nothing immune from that color?"

Karee laughed. "Hey! We forgot the champagne. We should have some bubbly and a good toast before . . ."

Bret's brows rose. "Before what?"

"Before you get a blow job."

If there had been an Olympic event for men leaping out of Jacuzzis, grabbing a champagne bottle and glasses, and returning, Bret would've gotten the gold medal. He handed her a glass, popped the cork, and poured the champagne. He put the bottle in the space between the heart's indentation; the pink tabletop was small but would accommodate the champagne container and the flutes.

"To great stories, insane bosses, and second meetings," said Bret, tapping his glass to hers.

"And to Cupid, Inc.," added Karee.

They drank. The champagne was sweet and fizzy; she drained half the glass and giggled. *Oh, Lord.* She was giggling. She hated giggling. But she figured that with a sexy man, good alcohol, and a killer spa . . . a girl was entitled to a few giggles.

She sank down into the water, enjoying the rest of her champagne and the feel of the hot, bubbling water on her skin. Bret did the same, though she knew without looking that he was staring at her. *Oh, poor baby.* She'd bet money he couldn't wait for her to put her mouth on his cock. She swallowed another giggle. She'd torture him for another minute or two.

"This water is divine," she said. "Isn't it, Bret?"

"Yeah. Terrific." He sounded put out. He placed his empty glass next to the champagne bottle. "It smells like strawberries."

Karee sniffed. He was right. The water was pink and scented. The whole room was a ten on the cheese scale, but . . . she liked it. She liked the room, the pink, the high cheese factor. But she especially liked Bret.

After she finished her champagne, she put down her glass and slipped between his legs, crawling forward to kiss his chest. "You're not pouting, are you?"

"A little."

"So you want me to suck your cock?"

He inhaled a sharp breath, his eyes going wide and dark. "Hell, yes."

"I don't have gills," she said. "It might help if that particular part of you was above water."

Water splashed as he lifted himself onto the edge of the hot tub. The grooved seat, cushioned no less, where he'd been sitting made a nice placement for her knees. His legs pillared on either side of her, and she was able to settle quite comfortably in position.

She peppered kisses on his inner thighs, licking away the droplets of water. "Would you believe this water is flavored, too? It's like lapping up strawberry juice."

"I care deeply about the flavored water," said Bret. "Really."

"Oh, well, I could go on describing its many qualities . . . or I could do *this*."

Karee licked the top of his cock, swirling her tongue around the plumed head. He was already halfway to full mast. He gasped, his hands diving into her hair. She kissed his shaft very slowly to his contracted balls and spent a few moments lavishing attention on his scrotum. He squirmed a little and moaned a lot, but she knew he was waiting for—no, *wanting*—her to take him fully.

Another slow traverse up his now fully hard shaft until she reached the head . . . then she rounded her mouth over the top and sucked. The grip he had on her skull tightened. Inch by inch she took him into her mouth, all the way to the base.

"Oh. My. God," he panted.

Her hands reached for his balls, squeezing gently as she licked and sucked his cock. His moans were louder now, his legs tense, his hands drifting to her shoulders. Making him hot was making her hot. Bringing him this kind of pleasure overwhelmed her senses; her nipples were tight and tingling; her skin flushed from the heated water; and her very core throbbed.

She released his cock and looked up at him, unable to articulate how she felt or what she wanted.

"Bend over," he said.

Karee scrambled to her feet and Bret stood, too. The water reached midthigh and lapped at their skin. They spent a few quality minutes stroking each other, kissing each other, ratcheting up the heat factor until it was in the red zone. Then Bret whispered again, "Bend over."

Karee turned around and accommodated his request, holding on to the edge of the hot tub as her rear end flounced in the air. Within seconds she felt the slow, hot slide of his cock, and she shuddered in delight at the deep penetration. Bret placed one hand on her hip and the other slipped underneath, his finger pushing along her slick folds to tickle her clit.

Then he was fucking her, his flesh smacking on hers, his finger working its mojo on her clitoris, and she loved it, loved the pseudo violence of it, loved that she'd turned him on that much, that she'd turned herself on that much. . . . *Oh, dear God.*

Already she felt the sparks before the explosion. Her body felt electrified, her clit so sensitive she could hardly stand the movement of Bret's finger; then pleasure crashed through her, over and over and over until she screamed from the intensity of it.

Moments later she felt Bret stiffen, her name on his lips as he held on to her buttocks and came.

Reality slowly returned and they parted, sinking into the water. Karee found herself sitting on Bret's lap, her arms around his neck as she continued to recover from the spectacular sex. He held her tightly, stroking her back, and she sighed contentedly.

"Karee," he said.

She lifted her head to look at him. God, he was cute. And funny. And so sweet. "Yeah?"

"This is the best fantasy I've ever had."

chapter six

"This is the best fantasy I've ever had?" repeated Veronica. "He *said* that?"

"Yep."

They sat in Veronica's plush office, Karee stretched out on the white leather couch, Vee curled into the chair. She felt incredibly relaxed. Life was good. Life was beautiful. Life was sexalicious.

"Then what?"

"Vee, it was incredible! It still makes me hot to think about what happened in that heart-shaped monstrosity." She fanned herself. "Say what you will about Cupid, Inc.'s methods—the whole thing was the most romantic experience a girl could hope for."

"Are you seeing him again?"

"We're having lunch today." Karee felt a little thrill at the prospect of seeing Bret again. Maybe what they'd experienced as newly inducted members into the Mile High Club was all flash and no substance. It wouldn't be the first time the opposite sex had let her down. Dating for her was akin to Inquisition-style torture. Just get out the thumbscrews and the rack—both were eas-ier to endure than trying to find a guy worth hanging on to.

All she ever wanted to do was write, and since she got the job with *Love*, that dream had expanded to include the other areas of magazine publication. But now, with Bret, for the first time *ever*, she was interested in something—make that *someone*—other than her job. It was both frightening and exciting. Damned if she didn't hope that the spark she and Bret had discovered together would not only burn brighter, but stay lit for a long, long time.

"Are you sure his name is really Bubba?" asked Veronica. She had sensed something off about Karee's story from the beginning, but Karee wasn't ready to reveal that she'd done the horizontal bop with Bret. Given Vee's hatred of *Max-Out* and its owner, chances were good she might never tell her boss the truth.

"Who the hell names their kid *Bubba?*"

Karee shrugged.

"Whatever. We're working on the February issue, so I need your article ASAP. We're putting it to bed this week. Make the Cupid, Inc., article good, sweetie. I want those issues to fly off the stands!"

"I will," said Karee, though she was strangely reluctant to write the story. Somehow, writing for the world what she and Bret had experienced seemed wrong. She wanted to keep that plane ride to herself, like her own little secret, a mental diary made up of memories that only she and Bret shared.

"It's too bad you won't be around to see the issue. I could mail you a copy."

Karee's musings about Bret turned into puzzled shock. Wouldn't be around to see the issue? *Huh?* "You're . . . you're fir-ing me?"

"I'm giving you a promotion, Karee. In London."

"London?" Karee Lomen stared at her boss, knowing her stunned expression probably amused her mentor.

"Yes, darling. *London.* You will be the editor in chief for the new U.K. edition of *Love* magazine. Just think of all that awaits you—shopping, shopping, and more shopping." Veronica put a hand against her brow and struck a pose of near fainting, which made Karee laugh.

"I've groomed you for this day, m'dear. You know the romance world inside and out. *Love* has made a mint in the U.S., and you must make sure our little venture does the same in the United Kingdom."

Karee smiled, tears in her eyes, and said, "What the fuck are you talking about?"

"Your dream job." Veronica grinned. "How many times have you told me about your desire to run the magazine? I'm giving you better than managing editor, dearest. You'll be editor in chief. You'll be setting up and running the U.K. edition—starting Christmas Day."

"Christmas Day?" Karee felt panic warble through her. "As in, I'm getting on a plane four days from now? Are you crazy?"

"Since you don't celebrate Christmas, I thought you might like to get away from all the, as you've put it in the past, 'sentimental bullshit.' You'll have a chance to familiarize yourself with London, get your flat in order, and look at the offices. I've been setting this up for you for the last six months, Karee. It's my gift to you as my best friend and as my best employee."

Why didn't she feel more thrilled? *Duh. Bret.* She'd known him all of two days, for Pete's sake! She'd been working toward this career goal for five years and had expected to work several more to get her very own magazine. She couldn't chuck it all out the window for a guy.

How many times had she seen coworkers give up their dreams for a man, only to get screwed over? *Well, shit.* Not many. Peggy the accountant seemed thrilled with life as a married woman, and Tamara just got engaged and seemed to have enough enthusiasm and energy for her career and planning a wedding, and there was Jennifer, her own editorial assistant, married for two years, who just found out she was preggers . . . .

Wait a fucking minute.

What was she doing? Thinking? Feeling? No, no, no. She was taking this job, she was flying to London, and she was saying *adios* to Bret. They didn't owe each other jack squat. Fantasy ended. Over. Kaput.

A howl of despair wailed inside her, an echo of pain and remorse for what might have been. But how could she keep a relationship going when Bret was in Las Vegas and she was in London? An impossibility. *Damn it.*

"Vee, I-I don't know what to say."

"Say yes, you idiot."

"Yes, you idiot."

Veronica laughed. "That'll do. Now go to lunch with Bubba and tell him the good news."

"Shit! I'm late!"

Bret put down his cup and goggled as the luscious and charming Karee, code name Loralee, grabbed her purse and dug through it. She tossed a twenty onto the table and scooted away, nearly tipping over the chair in her haste to rise.

"Karee!" He looked at the money, which would more than

cover their modest lunch, and scooped up the bill. He was a modern guy, but still old-fashioned enough to abhor the idea of "going Dutch." It gave him pleasure to pay, too. But Karee wasn't the type of girl who would allow him to take care of her—they'd gone to the mall before lunch, and all his attempts to buy her clothes, jewelry, meals, or flowers were met with lectures and refusals. Yeah. Karee was fiercely independent.

"Veronica's gonna kill me. I was supposed to be back at the office fifteen minutes ago."

"She won't kill you. She adores you."

"Only on Tuesdays."

Karee hugged the purse to her ribs, unintentionally pushing her breasts up and increasing the already pleasing cleavage of her sexy black dress. He ripped away his gaze from her breasts and met her stare, rewarded by the sensual regret he saw in her gray eyes.

"Have I mentioned that you're funny and sweet and . . . God, you look really good in those jeans . . . but I'm moving to London in four days?"

Bret felt as though he'd been punched in the gut. "What?"

"I just found out today. This morning. Three hours ago. Vee made me editor in chief of the new U.K. edition of *Love* magazine. She's done a lot of the prep work, but there's still a ton to do before we roll our first issue in June. It's the bridal issue, of course, which will be weird, because I'm not all that fond of weddings, unless it was my own, but even then, hell, I don't know. I think I'd hire a planner or just get hitched in Vegas. Easier that way, you know."

She was speaking fast again, and now he knew that the rat-tat-

tat of her words indicated her level of nervousness. He couldn't believe that he wouldn't have a chance to get to know Karee better. *London? No!* His heart clenched at the appalling idea that she'd be living in another country.

Bret rose and grasped her elbow, pulling her into his embrace. Damn the bulky purse blocking those gorgeous breasts from him! Her gaze traced his lips and he felt a response in his groin. His woman was so beautiful, so sexy . . . so elusive. Of course, the two of them would have to be careful until they figured out a way to break it to their bosses that they had not only joined the Mile High Club together; they had decided to date. No, wait. They couldn't date. England was one hell of a commute from Vegas.

For now, though, they had *this.* . . . He claimed her lips. She melted under his kiss, tasting like caramel cappuccino and the chocolate cake they'd indulged in with their coffees. Her tongue met his with eagerness, melding in a way that made him shudder to think what it would be like to have her underneath him again, meeting him thrust for thrust. She wanted him the way he wanted her. Always. They were really good together. No, they were fantastic together.

"You are the best kisser ever! But I gotta go. I had fun yesterday. The most fun I've ever had. I mean, ever. I'm sorry, *really* sorry, that we can't—you know. Oh, shit. I can't do this. Bye, Bret." She pulled away, tears in her eyes, her trembling hand against her kiss-swollen mouth . . . then she turned and stumbled away without a word or a glance.

Bret paid the check and hurried outside. He pushed through the doors in time to see Karee pull her silver Volvo to the parking lot's exit. Through the window he saw her, a big grin on her cute face and her hand flapping a sloppy good-bye.

His heart thumped erratically and his stomach felt filled with metal shards. With regret an ache in his soul, he watched the Volvo turn onto the street and speed away.

chapter seven

On January 21, Karee sat on her new red sofa and surveyed her apartment—or, as the English called it, her flat—through tear-filled eyes. Freshly painted lemon-yellow walls, toe-dipping white shag carpet, beautiful cherry-wood furniture . . . hell, she owned a bed Oliver Twist would kill to sleep on. Her apartment in Las Vegas had been an ode to sparse, barren, and dusty. Here she had the urge to create a more suitable living space. She wanted a home, not just a place to sack out at night.

Her puffy-eyed gaze sought the two magazines, next to her. The tears fell, and she indulged in yet another sobbing episode. She collapsed on the couch, a wad of tissues in her hand as she released the pent-up emotion. *What's wrong with you? You silly twit. Stop blubbering.*

The glossy mags were February issues. One cover featured a rain of white rose petals on a bed with red silk sheets. The other sported a scantily clad young woman with a sexy-naughty gaze, holding a bow and arrow in her hands. In bold red block letters each cover proclaimed: *Cupid, Inc.*

Instead of thinking about how she felt, Karee closed her eyes and let other memories wash over her. . . .

On Christmas morning Bret had appeared on her apartment doorstep with mistletoe, fruitcake, and a gold necklace with a heart pendant. He also gave her another gift: a reason to celebrate the holiday season.

She should have known that very moment that she was head over heels for him. What kind of idiotic, goofy, darling man brought *fruitcake* on Christmas Day to a woman he'd laid without consequences or expectations? Here was probably the only guy on the planet who didn't use the get-out-of-jail-free card. She was leaving for London, and he'd stopped by because he wanted to kiss her good-bye. And that was all he did, despite her invitation to come inside and do more, *much* more.

When Karee arrived in London, she threw herself into her new job. The last four weeks were a blur of putting together the office, hiring editors, and decorating her new apartment. Anytime thoughts of Bret interfered, which was far too often, she battered away the terrible yearning that clawed through her with more work, marathon shopping, or Valium-induced sleep. Until today, she believed she would get over him and that— tough luck, ol' girl—they weren't meant to be together. Then Vee, that cruel, cruel woman, FedExed her the issues of *Max-Out* and *Love*.

Her eyes flicked open and she slowly eased up to a sitting position. Once again, she found herself staring at the stupid magazines. *Oh, Bret! You . . . you idiot!*

The phone rang and she leaned over the sofa's overstuffed arm to snatch up the receiver. " 'Lo."

"Did you get the magazines?"

"Yes, Vee."

"You hate me?"

"A little."

"You'll get over it. When's your flight?"

Karee sniffed and blinked away more tears. "I never said I was coming back to Vegas. I have work to do."

"*When* is your flight?"

Karee sighed, giving up. Of course she was flying to Vegas. No way could she let what Bret had done stand—and she needed to face him. "Tomorrow morning." She gave her boss the flight information, said good-bye, and hung up.

Karee Lomen sat in the first-class section of the airplane with her thighs pressed together. Her laptop case covered, appropriately, her lap, hiding from the too-solicitous flight attendant the rigid clench of her legs, easily visible given the tight fit of her jeans.

The plane hit a pocket of turbulence and shook violently for a few seconds before smoothing out again. She bit her lip to keep from moaning. Her fingernails dug into the leather armrests, and she sucked in a shaky breath.

"Everything okay?" asked Maureen, the svelte blonde who had asked the same question about forty times since takeoff. "You look flushed. How about another glass of champagne?"

Karee stretched her lips into a smile and shook her head. "N-no, thanks."

"Everything will be fine. We're almost there." The woman's voice held a note of sympathy.

Almost there was damned right. If the plane hit another rough spot, Karee would be *there* without benefit of landing gear. She pressed her thighs together even though the muscles were already straining with effort. Little zings slithered between her legs, and she clenched her teeth.

Her skin reddened. Sweat gathered between her breasts. Delicate shudders racked her. Groans stalled in her throat. Karee had endured this insanity almost the entire way. She'd flown seven hours from London to New York City and another five hours on a nonstop from NYC to Las Vegas.

Tiny quakes issued from her agitated clitoris. Her nipples were distended, scraping against the lace of her bra. Her whole body felt sensitized; even her toes curled inside her boots. Her socks were gonna have holes, for Pete's sake! What the hell was wrong with that pilot? Was one freakin' unruly air pocket too much to ask? If the orgasm rolled over, instead of spiking her with tiny whoo-hoos, she'd be able to finish the rest of the flight in relative calm.

She stared out the window, thanking the flight gods that no one sat next to her. In fact, most of first class was empty, leaving her to deal with her sexual excitement in relative privacy. She bit her lip hard to rein in the deep moan trying to escape her throat. It was Bret's fault she felt like *this*. Before joining the Mile High Club, she'd been able to handle a long flight without an overt sexual reaction. She'd managed the flight to London a month ago only because, thanks to Sominex, she'd spent most of the time asleep.

Screw it. I'm going to the bathroom and take care of this. Static issued from the speakers, then Maureen's cultured voice spoke. "Good evening, ladies and gentlemen. We are fifteen minutes from McCarran Airport. Please fasten your seat belts and put your trays and seat backs in the upright position. Thank you for flying with us, and we hope you enjoy your stay in Las Vegas."

So much for the bathroom. It was an excruciating, frustrating fifteen minutes, but the pilot, damn his soul, made a landing so smooth, no orgasm-producing jolt occurred. If only Bret were here to expedite matters . . . *Yeah, right.* It was probably a good thing she didn't orgasm; only the seat belt cinched around her waist would've prevented her from jumping up and screaming, "Oh, yeah, baby!"

The minute the flight attendant released the passengers to disembark, Karee lugged her laptop case, her small purse tucked inside it, and her carry-on suitcase into the aisle. Her panties were freakin' soaked, her body trembled, and she felt feverish.

Maureen met her at the door, her gaze so weighted with empathy, Karee felt the heat of embarrassment creep into her cheeks. "There, now, honey, that wasn't so bad, was it? I think you were very brave. It's difficult for people who are afraid to fly to get on a plane." The nice woman patted her on the arm. "You have a good time in Vegas."

"Thanks." Then Karee was out the door, down the causeway, and hurrying toward the escalators that took passengers to baggage claim. With her laptop case hanging from her shoulder, she picked up her carry-on suitcase and stepped between the lazy-assed people waiting on the moving steps.

She spotted Bret at the bottom of the escalator waiting for her. Her heart skipped several beats, then started pounding furiously. He looked as he did the first time she'd seen him, in khakis and a brown shirt and that brown leather jacket. And yeah, he still looked as delicious as a café mocha. *Damn it.* She hadn't had a chance to marshal her thoughts or figure out what she wanted to say to him.

When she joined him, he asked, "You read the article, huh?"

"It was the most . . . the most . . ." She felt tears crowd her eyes. *Aw, crap.* She'd done enough crying already! "The *most* wonderful thing I've ever read. You could've called or e-mailed, you know? It's been torture these last few weeks trying not to think about you. And then you go and make something that should've been purely about sex and bodies and sweat into something beautiful . . . and romantic." The words flying out of her mouth slowed to silence; she inhaled a breath. God, she felt so nervous.

Bret pulled the suitcase out of her hand, whipped off her laptop case and purse, and laid a kiss on her so fervent she forgot everything except the feel of his mouth on hers. He held her close, like a thief embracing the crown jewels. After a minute she managed to free herself. She stared up at him, unable to formulate a single sentence.

"What we shared was beautiful and romantic. And sexy and sweaty." Bret grinned and kissed her again. "How was I supposed to know how you felt? I couldn't risk that you'd ignore a phone call or an e-mail. I didn't want to hear the 'we can be friends' speech. So I used the article. It was hell waiting for your reaction."

"How did you talk Vee into it?"

"After she decided not to kill me, she agreed my piece would make a nice *Love* article. Max grumbled about its mushiness, but I think under all that testosterone, he's got a heart."

"What about me in London and you in Las Vegas? That's a really long-distance relationship."

"Oh. Didn't I tell you? I quit as managing editor for *Max-Out.* I'm going back to freelancing, and I'm relocating to London."

Joy sputtered through Karee, joy and confusion. "You're moving to London?"

"Have computer, will travel."

"But there's . . . We haven't exactly known . . . Are you sure?"

"If you're worried about whether or not I'm crazy for quitting my job and moving to England just so we can explore the possibilities of our relationship, you're right." He leaned close, looking directly into her eyes. "I'm crazy about you."

Her emotions collided with the agitated state of her body. She felt on fire, her panties were *still* soaked, and she throbbed for release. "Where's your car parked?" she asked, breathless and frantic.

Bret looked her over, a smile playing on his lips. "You look like you're about ready to launch into outer space. Must've been a great flight."

Karee flashed him a grin. "Not really. I'm very . . . needy right now. So where the hell is your car? I'm going to jump your bones."

She picked up her laptop case and purse; Bret grabbed the handle of her carry-on. He guided her around the baggage carousels, threading her through the crowd and bypassing the security turnstiles.

He pulled her past the car rental agency booths and made a sudden right, pushing open a door and leading her into a stairwell. He dropped the suitcase and she put down her laptop case and purse; then he was backing her against the wall, his mouth hot on hers as he unsnapped her jeans and thrust his finger inside her panties.

"I know you're almost there," he whispered as he traced the

shell of her ear with his tongue. "You like flying on planes, don't you, honey?"

"God, yes."

He shoved up her T-shirt and sucked her nipples through the lace of her bra. Pleasure electrified her as he twirled his tongue around the hard peaks, using the soft material to agitate her aching breasts. "Bret! What about you?"

"We have plenty of time to be together, love," he whispered. "Just enjoy this."

Plunging two fingers inside her, groaning, panting, swearing, he lapped at her breasts—one, then the other, suckling her nipples until she went crazy with lust. Again and again he thrust his fingers inside her, his palm rubbing her clitoris, his mouth on her nipples. "Oh, God. Oh, God!" she cried, her hands clenching the butter-soft material of his leather jacket.

"Come for me," he demanded.

The orgasm burst, and wave after wave of bliss rolled through her. She went blind and mindless for a moment, completely lost in the sensations shuddering through her. Her knees felt like pudding, and her brain felt wrapped in cotton. Bret was holding on to her, his head buried against her neck, his palm flat against her vulva as he waited for her to recover.

"You know something?" she asked in a whisper.

Bret raised his head and looked at her, his expression a mixture of amusement, desire, and pride. "What?"

"That's the kind of flying I like the best."

Staff Meeting
Conference Room A
Ten A.M.

"And that's why you should never cook with Hera," concluded Aphrodite. Her rapt audience included Grace and Daphne. She put down the laser pointer and, with a snap of her fingers, turned on the lights and made the transparencies disappear. "Any questions?"

"Yeah. Aren't we supposed to be talking about matching clients with fantasies? I mean, no offense, Di Di, but that kitchen fiasco with Hera happened in December. This is February." Daphne waved a careless hand. Her shiny purple nail polish glittered in the overhead lights.

"The lasting lesson, my dear Daphne, is to always hire caterers."

"I'll write that down in my *Book of Great Advice.*"

Aphrodite rolled her eyes. She liked Daphne. She really did. But the child had a razor-sharp tongue. She had never understood Apollo's attraction to the girl. "All this talk of food has made me famished. Let's go eat."

With a snap of her fingers, the three women were transported from Cupid, Inc.'s boardroom to the sidewalk in front of the Manzana Café. The restaurant located in downtown Las Vegas was squeezed between its small parking lot and an empty building. A couple blocks away was the noise and frenzy of the Fremont Street Experience.

"Di Di, have you ever considered traveling by car like a normal person?"

Aphrodite noted that Daph looked slightly nauseous, and grinned. "I am neither normal nor a *person.* Thank Zeus. Besides, cars are ineffective transport."

They entered the café, the bell on its glass door tinkling merrily. A lovely young woman with sparkling brown eyes, caramel skin, and a genuine smile led them to a booth by a large picture window. The view of the street wasn't exactly a look into Demeter's garden, so Aphrodite eschewed it for the menu.

"My name is Helen," said the woman, flipping open an order pad and taking out the pen tucked into her white apron. "What would you like to drink? We have fresh-squeezed orange juice, coffee, chocolate milk, or, if you're really adventurous, cold water with a lemon wedge."

Aphrodite ordered coffee, Grace asked for orange juice, and the too-thin Daphne chose water. Aphrodite had been to this little café a few times, and, though she wouldn't admit it to Dionysus, the coffee rivaled his creations. The food was simple fare, but excellent. She had kept an eye on the waitress, whom she knew was also the daughter of the proprietor. Helen was sweet-natured and polite even when patrons were not. But there was a look in her eyes Aphrodite recognized—a longing for an adventure. How often had Helen wondered, *Is this all there is?*

"Aphrodite," said Daphne, "let's get down to business."

"Of course. You have the paperwork."

Daphne displayed the many applications, placing them on the Formica table.

Aphrodite looked at the thick paperwork and sighed. "As you all know, Eros and Psyche are celebrating an anniversary—"

"I thought their wedding anniversary was in March."

"Not that anniversary, Daph. First kiss, first dance, first abduction—one of those. While they celebrate the nauseating minutiae of their love, they've left me in charge of matches. Although I must say, it is I who should do the bossing around. After all, I was the first goddess of love—"

"That's not what Isis says."

"Isis! She's not a love goddess. Putting together her dismembered husband is impressive, but it doesn't make her queen of the human heart."

"I heard she couldn't find his penis and she made one out of clay."

"I heard it was made from gold," said Grace.

"The world's first dildo."

"Daphne," said Aphrodite, "do you have any updates that don't include fake penises?"

"Only one. Bret and Karee are living together in London and seem very much in love. I suspect we'll get a wedding invitation by the end of the year." Daphne tapped the papers. "You ready for the first case of the day, Di Di?"

"Don't call me that." Her gaze landed on Helen. She was behind the counter preparing their beverages, humming and dancing a little as she went about her tasks.

"We have a Spy Fantasy to set up. Do you know anything about James Bond?"

"What would you like to know?" asked Helen, arriving just in time to hear the question. She passed out the drinks, then placed the big metal tray against her hip. "I'm a huge fan of Ian Fleming. I've read all his James Bond books and seen every movie at least twice."

Aphrodite smiled. "If you had a chance to indulge in a Spy Fantasy—action, adventure, hot sex . . . would you?"

"In a heartbeat."

After Helen left, Daphne hissed, "What are you doing?"

"Helen is bored out of her mind, and she is a huge fan of James Bond. She's perfect for the Spy Fantasy. And I know the perfect man for her. In fact, his mother is an old friend of mine, and she's been trying to find his match for years."

"We don't have paperwork or payment or permission."

"Oh, please. I've been the love goddess for thousands of years. This idea of filling out forms and taking money is appalling."

"What do Psyche and Eros do with the money?" ventured Grace in her soft, sweet voice.

"They give it to various charities. Gods might not have any use for money, but the humans sure need it," said Daphne.

"Dionysus does the same with the profits from his cafés," added Aphrodite. She caught Daph's frustrated glare and rolled her eyes. "Oh, all right you . . . you papermonger." She waved her hand, and a filled-out application appeared on top of the stack. Stapled to it were the requisite forms—medical report, signed confidentiality agreement, and partner questionnaire.

"Psyche and Eros are going to kill you."

"Pish-tosh. All the information is correct and true. I'm simply expediting matters."

Daphne picked up the top sheet and studied it. "Helen Manzana and Paul Aris. Hey, Di Di, got a pen?"

Another hand wave and a pen appeared between Daph's fingers. She peered at the form and then scribbled on it. "That's what I thought. How cool is this?"

"How cool is *what*?"

"Paul Aris. If you write P and period then his last name, voilà!" Daphne held up her notepad: *P. ARIS*. "Paris! Helen and Paris. C'mon, Aphrodite, you of all people should appreciate these names." She frowned. "Of course, the last time you messed around with two people named Paris and Helen it didn't exactly turn out great."

"True. All I got for my efforts was a golden apple and a ten-year war. And that ungrateful cow Helen returned to her husband after Troy was blasted into dust." Aphrodite sipped her coffee, chancing a look out the window. Trash blew down the sidewalk. She watched a crumpled newspaper bounce along the curb, then a plastic beer cup scoot into the street. "That wasn't one of my better love matches."

Daphne grinned. "Here's a second chance to make sure things go right."

Helen picked up the gray plastic tub and headed toward the table just abandoned by the three beautiful women. She'd seen the blond lady in here before, and she always tipped generously. The glasses and empty plates clattered and clanked as she put them inside the tub. Once again when faced with pleasantly mundane task, she found her thoughts wandering among various fantasies . . . James Bond bursting in the door and begging for her help, Jason Bourne taking her on a wild trip through Europe as he attempted to escape the CIA, or joining Travis McGee on one of his Floridian escapades.

After she was finished clearing off the dishes, she picked up the receipt. *Whoa.* They'd left her a twenty-dollar tip. *Sweet!* Underneath the cash was a small pink envelope. *What the heck?*

She opened it and found a gift certificate to a place called Cupid, Inc. It read, *Good for one Spy Fantasy for Helen Manzana.* There was a phone number. She grinned. She'd heard of Cupid, Inc. A friend of hers who used to own the Wedding Veil down the block had won their contest for a date with Kevan Rune. Janie was now happily ensconced at a small ranch in Oklahoma running a new business and occasionally going on movie shoots with her soon-to-be husband, the movie star.

Helen stared at the showy gold lettering on the certificate and felt excitement rush through her.

If Janie Brown could get that kind of happy ending from Cupid, why not me?

The Spy Who Rubbed Me

chapter one

"I want you to steal Aphrodite's golden apple."

Paul Aris, reformed thief and newly appointed director of LifeStar Charities, stared at his mother in shock. "You want me to do *what?*"

"You heard me, darling boy."

At fifty-five, Elizabeth Sinclair Aris looked as gorgeous as ever. Blessed with high cheekbones, sparkling blue eyes, and alabaster skin, his mother remained a classic beauty. Her only concession to age was the monthly coloring appointments she kept in order to oust the gray from her honey-blond hair. He knew the one thing that vexed his mother about her appearance was her lack of height. As the heiress to the Sinclair Motors fortune, she had learned to be imposing at a young age, but since she was shy of five feet tall she often commented that she felt like a Lilliputian railing at giants. Tonight she wore a cream-colored pantsuit—Versace, if he wasn't mistaken—and four-inch open-toed stilettos. The staggeringly high heels were a sure sign she felt less than confident. Added to that, her usually jovial gaze held both determination and trepidation.

"What do you say, Paul?"

"I'm on the straight and narrow." When his mother handed him the reins of LifeStar, she'd given him more than a new start in life. She'd given him purpose. He had no plans to screw it all up, not when he was finally figuring out what he wanted from the world.

Paul grasped the brandy glass in both hands and sank onto the supple leather chair. He stared at the flames that popped and snapped in the copper-plated fireplace. The living room was cozy even with its vaulted ceiling, black marble floors, and oversize furniture. His mother had a way of creating warmth and comfort where none existed. Despite her vast wealth and her position as a respected society matron, she always had time and energy to make those who had nothing feel as if they had everything.

Her life's work was LifeStar Charities, an organization that catered to many different needs. She'd started it after his father passed away, pouring her grief into action. He'd been nine years old when Michael Aris died from a brain aneurism. Throughout the years, images of his father faded into vague recollections—the sound of his deep laugh, the smell of pipe tobacco, the calloused hand that showed him how to throw a baseball. But for his mother, each memory was shiny and new, and she mourned Dad every day. Maybe this latest scheme was yet another distraction from the loneliness she felt.

"Missing Dad again?"

"Paul, any fool who believes the pain of losing the love of your life fades with the passage of time . . . Oh, that damned fool has never really loved." She looked at him. "I want the same for you. Even though I had only a dozen wonderful years with your father,

I wouldn't trade that time for anything in world. I want true love for you."

An old conversation. His mother believed so deeply in affairs of the heart that she'd wasted too much time trying to pair him with women she hoped were soul-mate possibilities. What would he know about true love? The only mistress he'd ever enjoyed was thievery, and she was a clever, seductive one, at that. He could not deny that his mother and father had experienced a rare love, but that did not mean he would be so lucky.

"What does stealing Aphrodite's apple have to do with my finding true love?"

A secretive smile curved her lips. "Perhaps if Helen and Paris had met at a different time and a different place, their relationship might not have been doomed."

"Mother." Exasperation sharpened his tone. "Are you in danger? Is someone blackmailing you for the apple?"

She swirled the brandy in her glass, then sipped it. "I'm not in danger. This is more like . . . a mission."

Chills of fear crept down his spine. His mother did not keep secrets. She'd always told him that telling the truth stymied the most vicious gossip. If you hid nothing and admitted all, the world lost interest. Scandal was scandal only if the people involved lied, covered up, and cowered behind their publicists.

"Mum, it's been a while. I'm rusty."

"You were the best jewel thief in London."

He shook his head. "All fun and games. A spoiled rich boy who wanted the adrenaline high. You were right about that."

"It's important, Paul. Why else would I ask my only child to risk his parole and perhaps his life by committing a crime?" She placed her own brandy glass on the table by his chair, then knelt beside him. Her hand grasped his knee; he noted the fine trembling in her long, pale fingers. The only jewelry that glittered was the simple gold wedding band. "You know what Aphrodite's apple is?"

"A solid gold apple with 'To the most beautiful,' carved on it. It's a replica of the apple Eris, the goddess of discord, supposedly tossed to Athena, Hera, and Aphrodite to stir up trouble among the goddesses. It's made of solid gold and worth roughly thirty-five million dollars."

"I see you still know your treasure."

He shrugged, uncomfortable with her gentle teasing. He pulled his lips into a smile, though he felt more like growling. "I may have thought about taking the apple when it made the museum rounds in London."

"Ah." She patted his knee and rose, gliding to the fireplace to stare at the blaze. "Paris, the poor boy, was appointed judge of their beauty contest. The goddesses each attempted to bribe him, but he chose Aphrodite's gift: the most gorgeous woman in the world. You want to hear something funny? The apple is on display at the Troy Casino in Las Vegas."

He said nothing. Of course he knew the apple was at Troy Casino. He may have given up the ol' game of snatching beauties out from under the noses of their owners, but that didn't mean the urge had been excised. He would never admit to his mother that he played a little game of creating ways to steal exceptional pieces like Aphrodite's apple.

Paul sipped on his brandy as he thought about what his mother had told him and what she wanted from him. There was no question that he would go to Las Vegas and steal the apple. His mother could ask him for the moon and he'd do everything in his power to snatch it from the sky. He owed her too much not to help her. She had never given up on him. Not once.

"Eve tempted Adam with an apple from the tree of knowledge." His mother sounded bemused. "And now a mother tempts her only child with the same forbidden fruit."

"It seems apples have a tainted history, Mum."

The faint scent of mesquite infiltrated the air, mixing with the fragrant aromas from the abundant vases of flowers placed throughout the room. His mother loved flora—from the elegant rose to the lowly carnation. No room in the house was without fresh-cut blooms of some sort.

"When's the last time you went out with a young lady?"

The abrupt change of subject was damned odd, too, but somewhat of a relief. Discussing his love life with his mother was only slightly better than discussing his reentrance into burgling.

"I haven't dated in a while. I've been too busy with LifeStar."

"You should never be too busy for love." She crossed the room, her heels clacking on the high-polished floor. Against the wall opposite the fireplace, an original Monet hanging above it, was an antique rolltop desk. He knew that desk had been his father's, and he always thought she'd kept it around for sentimental reasons. But now he was surprised to find that it was fully stocked with pens, notepads, check registers, and files. Extracting a sheaf of papers, she closed the desk and returned, thrusting a pamphlet at him.

" 'Cupid, Inc. Your fantasy is our business,' " he read from the glossy front panel. The logo was a red heart pierced by a glittering gold arrow. He opened it and his jaw dropped open. " 'Sexual fantasies for discerning adults.' Mum, have you lost your mind? Asking for me to do a burglary . . . Bloody hell. Now you want me to . . . have sex?"

"I have a friend who coordinates the liaisons. Cupid, Inc., arranges for the spy couple to steal the apple. Of course, at the time of the 'theft,' casino personnel switch the real apple for a fake. The bogus fruit is a keepsake for the couple. Isn't that cute?"

Paul rolled his eyes. "It's as wonderful as chocolate Kisses and champagne bubbles."

"Oh, do shut up." His mother sat in the chair opposite his and pinned him with a narrowed gaze. "You're thirty years old, Paul. You avoid commitment like it's the plague. Switching your obsession with thievery to an obsession for running LifeStar doesn't make you any less a workaholic. Life is so much better with someone to share it."

Wait a bloody minute. "Mum! You don't intend for me to steal the apple at all. You've . . . Oh, my God! You've hooked me up with a blind date!"

Her eyes twinkled merrily. "You're not usually this slow on the uptake. For the record, I have not 'hooked you up.' You'll spend an exciting day dodging bullets and planning heists, and, if you're lucky, you'll get to make love with a beautiful, willing woman."

"I don't have time for this ridiculous endeavor. You nearly gave me a heart attack with all this talk of stealing treasure." He grinned. "Really, Mum. Are you so desperate for grandchildren?"

"Absolutely."

Maybe a day off wasn't such a bad idea. Dating and sex were both fond memories. His only lover lately had been LifeStar—and she was a greedy woman with many needs. He couldn't believe he was considering this insane plan. Mum had tried numerous ways of putting him together with girls for the soulmate test. Signing him up for a sexual fantasy was her wackiest scheme yet.

Once his mother made up her mind, that was that. If he re-fused now, she would find one way or another to gain his consent. *Oh, hell.* What was one day of leisure? LifeStar wouldn't fall apart without his guidance. It was very satisfying, often exhausting work, but it did not fill the emptiness of his home, and it could never offer the same warmth and companionship he would find with a woman.

"All right, Mum. I'll go on your little adventure."

"Wonderful! I've made all the arrangements. You leave tomor-row morning."

"Of course I do." Paul laughed. "You always win, Mum."

"In matters of the heart, darling, I will always fight for the happy ending. So should you."

chapter two

The man burst into the Manzana Café. The bell above jangled crankily as the all-glass door shuddered with the violence of his urgent entrance. It was just after the morning breakfast rush, and only two customers were left, the beautiful blond lady lingering over coffee and a young man so startled by the abrupt intrusion, he dropped his egg-filled fork onto the floor.

Clad in a rumpled tuxedo, an ominous red stain marring the perfect white of his shirt, the man's handsome face was crumpled in agitation and his chest heaved as if he'd been running. He gulped breaths of air, glancing over his shoulder as if expecting to see someone behind him. Then he looked straight Helen, who was behind the counter, her mouth hanging open in shock, a pot of coffee dangling from her left hand.

"Helen Manzana!" cried the crazy guy in a delicious English accent. "I need your help!"

Helen managed to put the carafe onto the counter just seconds before the James Bond wannabe launched himself over the Formica and dragged her down to the floor. He put a finger to his lips and scrunched close to her, his blue eyes sparkling with humor. She grinned, knowing she probably wore the same expression. It was happening! Finally! After days of suspense and wondering when—

The bell jingled the announcement of another arrival.

"Hey, you. Blondie. You see a guy in a tuxedo run in here?" The deep baritone carried an accent that was all Bronx and had a scary undertone that made Helen's heart pound faster.

"He ran out again," said the blonde in a low, cultured voice. "Down the street."

"Oh, yeah? Sure he did." The clomp of booted feet passed close to the counter. Obviously the creep was headed toward the pretty woman. "Maybe you're lying."

"Maybe you should invest in a breath mint," said the woman. "Or—and here's a suggestion you may not get often enough— brush your teeth once in a while."

"What are ya? A dentist?"

"Do I look like a dentist?"

"Maybe if all dentists looked like you, I'd go see one." He guffawed at this clever comment. "You look sugary enough to eat. And I got a sweet tooth."

"I'm flattered," the woman said in a tone that suggested the opposite. "Is there a reason you're after a man in a tuxedo? Didn't he kiss you good-bye after your *nuit d'amour deux?*"

"I don't know what them fancy words mean, but I don't think I like what you're saying. Maybe I ought to show you I'm a real man."

"You're such a flirt."

The swinging door that led to the kitchen slapped open. Helen's annoyed mother, five feet tall with graying black hair, olive skin that revealed her Hispanic heritage, and a soft body shaped like a pear, stepped out. She wore a hairnet, sported a white apron over her plain black dress, and held a large spatula. For all the sweet appearance of her mama, Helen knew the woman had a core of steel. She looked down at Helen and the man; then her gaze traveled to the right, probably landing on the bad guy and the cool blonde.

"Hey, *estúpido!* You bothering my customers?"

"Mama!" Helen whispered fiercely. Sure, this was all a show, but still, her mother didn't need to point the spatula like it was a six-shooter instead of a kitchen implement.

"What is it with broads and fancy language today? I'm just asking some questions. You seen a guy with a tuxedo?"

"In here? Go check the cafés at the Bellagio. Rich folks don't buy their huevos rancheros from me."

"Maybe I feel like getting a cup of coffee."

"Maybe you feel like getting my foot up your ass." Mama crossed her arms. "Get out or I'll call the police."

The booted feet returned in a leisurely walk that indicated a don't-care attitude, and stopped just about where Helen and the mystery guy huddled. They tried to scrunch under the two-inch edge overhang, hoping Mr. Grouchy wouldn't lean over far enough to notice them. Janie watched her mother march forward until her belly pressed against the counter; then *smack!* The spatula landed against flesh.

"Ow!"

Smack!

"Shit, lady."

Smack!

Mama spurted a stream of angry Spanish. Helen caught *es-*

túpido (stupid) and *cerdo sucio* (dirty swine), but the rest was incomprehensible.

"I'm going! I'm going!" The boots retreated and the bell rang as the door squealed open. "But I'll be back."

"Don't worry. I have more spatulas!"

After a moment Mama looked down at them. Her head jerked toward the handsome man on the floor. "This is the guy?"

"Yes."

"And this is what you gonna do today? Run around like geese and let *estúpido* chase you?"

"Probably."

"Ai, yi, yi. The young are so silly."

"Dearest madam, we will also save the world in the process." The man in the tuxedo grinned. He rose, giving Helen a hand up. Then he turned to Mama and executed a little bow. "Aris. Paul Aris."

"Rosa Maria Conchita Manzana," said Helen's mother. She smiled. "It was fun to smack the big one. If he come back after this little game, I make him big breakfast. *You* treat my girl well or . . ." She raised the spatula and flapped it.

"I will give her every courtesy."

Mama rolled her eyes, then made shooing motions. "Go on then. Your cousin Rico will help me while you play spy." She grabbed Helen and hugged her. "You find your happiness, *mi hija.*"

"I will, Mama."

After watching Paul and Helen exit into the kitchen, probably with the idea of sneaking out the back door, Aphrodite scooted from the booth, leaving twenty dollars to pay for her coffee. She left through the front door and walked toward Fremont Street.

This part of downtown was crowded with buildings and long alleys filled with trash and sometimes a homeless person trying to sleep. She had just passed the storefront of an adult bookstore when two strong male hands snaked out and pulled her into the alleyway.

"What's shaking, doll face?" said a man in a thick Bronx accent.

She shook loose from the man's grip and he let her go, a nasty smile twisting his lips. She assessed him casually. He was short and stocky, obviously muscled, with a broad, flat face and a squashed nose. His small eyes looked like black pebbles, and his dirty brown hair was cut military style. His maroon suit, complete with black tie, screamed, "I watch *The Sopranos*." Gold rings glittered from his cigarlike fingers.

"Honestly, could you be any more clichéd?"

The man laughed. His shape stretched and popped, morphing into his real self. One moment he was a mobster's hit man, the next, a tall and gorgeous god with a dangerous gleam in his eyes. As was typical Ares, he wore head-to-toe black, from the tight-fitting T-shirt and black jeans, to the tips of his snakeskin boots. Even his curly locks were as black and as shiny as a cobra's gaze. In his god form he was more than six feet tall, with broad shoulders, lean legs, and muscular perfection. Her heart stuttered, as it always did when she was in his presence. Ares was the only god to inspire in her the gut-bunching lust that felled so many others.

"C'mon. I put on a good show."

Aphrodite graced him with a smile. "Yes, you did."

"This situation seems vaguely familiar. Paul and Helen . . . Helen and Paris." He reached out and cupped her chin, stroking the underside of her jaw. "Ah, yes. To win a golden apple, you offered a young prince the most beautiful woman in the world and gave him Helen, the very married queen of Sparta. And, if I recall, you started a war that lasted ten years and cost hundreds of lives."

She stepped back and his hand dropped away from her cheek. "You are the god of war, Ares. How many mortals have suffered because of your whims?"

"We are who we are, my dear Aphrodite."

"And that is both blessing and curse."

"Don't wax philosophical, *Di Di*."

He grinned at the narrowed look she sent him. Then, with the puff of black smoke he always used so dramatically, he disappeared and left Aphrodite to face the stained brick wall and her own doubts.

"What are we doing here?" asked Helen as Paul guided her into the lobby of the MGM Grand. In front of them was the check-in counter, to the right, elevator banks, and to the left, the casino.

"We're here for the clue." He kissed her knuckles, an oddly formal gesture that jangled her nerves.

"Are we really going to chase down clues like a bad version of *The Da Vinci Code*? I expected something . . ." She waved her hand in lieu of suitable words.

"You mean like a building blowing up or us getting shot at or someone shoving us into a car trunk?"

"Yeah."

"That's a bad version of *CSI*."

She laughed. He brushed another kiss across her knuckles before heading toward the check-in counter. She watched him weave through the clusters of people holding children and suitcases, and noted that the tux showcased his ass in a very nice way.

While Paul followed the directions he'd received from Cupid, Inc., Helen ambled to the edge of the casino and gazed at the rows and rows of buzzing and blinking slot machines. She gazed over her shoulder and saw Paul talking to a man behind the counter. Paul Aris, her very own spy, was silly, but cute. *Really* cute.

Light flowery scents perfumed the air, but not strongly enough to filter out ashy whiffs of lit cigarettes. The potpourri aromas were pumped throughout the casinos to mask the unpleasant smells of smoke, unwashed bodies, and cheap cologne. In a casino as large as the MGM, the smell-control attempts usually succeeded.

The one-armed bandits whirred musically, competing for the attention of passersby with neon glam and flashy lights. Some sported familiar icons of old TV shows, and every so often Helen heard snippets of *The Munsters* and *Green Acres* theme songs. Among the show tunes, she heard the occasional *clink-clink-clink* of dropping coins. That sound was as prevelant as it used to be.

Many of the casinos, especially the big ones, had installed gambling machines that issued tickets. Instead of the tinny drop of nickels or quarters or the satisfying thunk of dollar coins, a long white paper would emerge. It didn't feel or look like money—just a receipt to be redeemed at any cashier's cage or, better yet, slipped into the next machine.

A male hand dropped onto her shoulder. Startled, Helen turned around and faced Paul. He still looked deliciously rumpled, though he managed to cover the red stain (ketchup, he'd admitted with a boyish grin) with a pinned-on carnation. He had sandy brown hair that feathered across his brow, sky-blue eyes, and a face just shy of handsome. Paul reminded her of the character Alec Baldwin played in *Beetlejuice*: studious, forthright, and kind . . . with a wee bit of Satan's charm.

"Got it!"

"The clue?"

"No. The key to the clue." He held up a plastic key card. "We take this to room five-oh-two and pick up the clue."

Helen's heart stuttered. "Y-you don't think it's . . . uh, a hint to . . ."

He stared at her, his wicked grin unrelenting, but in a mischievous way that diminished the devilish curve of his lips.

"Wasn't this your fantasy, Helen? To make off with a dashing spy and have your way with him?"

"Yes, of course, but not—"

"Don't worry so much, love." He brushed his finger across her cheek, and that slight agitation of skin on skin caused chills of anticipation. "Shall we?"

She took his hand, and together they hurried to the elevators and to the clue.

chapter three

As they entered the grand tower room, Paul leading the way, he heard Helen ask, "Are you British?"

"Born in Oklahoma, actually. I spent most of my childhood and much of my school years in London. I'm afraid I picked up the accent and it stuck."

"So you're an Okie who sounds like James Bond?"

"I never thought of it that way. But I probably sound more along the lines of Austin Powers."

They entered the main part of the room. The layout was similar to that of thousands of other hotel rooms on the Strip: The door opened into a small hallway, with the bathroom entrance on one side and the closet on the other. The room itself housed a comfy bed with nightstands on either side of it, each topped with small lamps; an armoire housed a TV and drawers; a simple desk with its own chair crowded against the same wall as the bed; and finally, arranged under the huge picture window were a big chair, a sofa, and a coffee table.

The decor was an ode to brown and beige, warm and vaguely

appealing. Even the artwork was a bland attempt at pleasant. The room might have been the hotel's attempt to offer a place of respite for the overwrought gambler or, more likely, a psychological counterpoint of the more exciting, garish, brash, fun world that existed in the casino.

The square neon-pink envelope propped on the king-size bed stood out like a red rose in a white-rose bouquet. Paul plucked it from the coverlet and opened it, sliding out the paper.

"What does it say?"

Paul looked at Helen, hesitating to reveal the envelope's contents. She seemed reluctant to share physical space with him . . . at least so far. Downstairs she'd looked nervous, almost fearful, about the sexual side of their spy fantasy. He hadn't expected his date to hop into the sack during the first second of their meeting, but still, was it possible she wasn't attracted to him? *Get a grip, ol' boy.*

She waited a couple of feet away in the hotel room, ignoring all the available places to sit. Her brown eyes glittered with excitement as she watched him and waited for his answer.

She was lovely, so very lovely.

Helen wore her auburn hair chin-length and straight, styled in a way that gently curved around her heart-shaped face. Her lips looked like a Christmas bow, red and shiny and waiting to be opened. *Oh, that juicy mouth.* The slow heat of arousal crept through him, and he inhaled a shaky breath.

Her caramel complexion required little adornment. She played up the curve of her cheekbones with the merest hint of blush, and gold shadow glimmered on her eyelids. Her thick lashes and careful application of black liner gave her a dreamy, doe-eyed gaze.

"Paul?"

Tiny gold hoops, three on each lobe and each smaller than the next, were revealed only when she turned her head just so. No other jewelry dangled from her neck or encircled her fingers. She looked like a girl with simple tastes. That appealed to him. He didn't want complicated or expensive or shallow. He'd had enough of beautiful, money-grubbing women to last a lifetime.

"*Paul!*"

He blinked. "What?"

"The message?"

"Oh. Uh, right. I'm sorry . . . you know, well, it's just that you're . . ." He cleared his throat, tried to slow the sudden stuttering of his heartbeat. "You're very pretty." *Good Lord.* He sounded just like an untried schoolboy. He imagined Helen would scarcely believe that he had once been called "scathingly witty" by GQ magazine. *Ha.*

"The note says 'Helen Manzana is very pretty'?" Laughter weaved through the words, though she managed to keep a straight face.

"Note?"

"The one in your hand. I'm guessing there's a message written on the card . . . unless it's hieroglyphics?"

"No. But just so you know, I'm a whiz at Mad Libs." He grinned and handed it to her.

"It says, 'The first clue is yours, but you'd better not delay; the next one you'll find at Mandalay Bay.' "

"Which explains this hotel key," he said, plucking the plastic card from the envelope. He tucked it into his pants pocket.

"Shush. I'm reading. 'This challenge is more than a dream come true; it's also about who is spy one and spy two. Before the danger you must flee, share answers to these questions three.' "

"Dr. Seuss strikes again." He frowned. "Wait a minute. What does it mean 'Before the danger you must flee'? Is it talking about the big, ugly guy who chased me into the diner, or is it warning us that we're supposed to expect company?"

She shrugged. "Does it matter? We're spies, and spies have enemies. Besides, it's all a game. No one will really get hurt."

True, but a shiver of foreboding crept up his spine anyway. He'd been on his way to the Manzana Café when the jerk jumped out of a car, yelling obscenities, and charged after him. At first he'd believed some thug was trying to take his wallet, but then he realized Mr. Bronx was only an actor. Cupid, Inc., obviously wanted its fantasies to be as real as possible.

"What's that?"

Helen flipped over the paper. "It's a big T."

"So . . . we have a word puzzle. I assume the next clues will have letters printed on the notes' backsides, too."

He hadn't expected to find Helen so charming or pretty. It had been a very long time since he'd dated anyone seriously. Thanks to his mother and her endless society soirees, he knew more than his fair share of willing women who tried to snag Elizabeth Sinclair Aris's son. Yet those encounters left him feeling empty and vaguely unsettled.

Since he left college, his every waking hour had been consumed by work. At first the work had been stealing the riches of the rich. Then, after getting caught, he managed to get his jail time reduced to months instead of years by helping out Interpol with a touchy situation. Now work meant a legitimate job helping people. Being the director of his mother's vast network of charitable organizations was fulfilling on professional and personal levels. Despite Mother's almost manic fulfillment of her role as a society matron, she cared deeply about many issues and was fearless when it came to speaking out for those who needed help.

"Earth to Paul. You're cleared for reentry."

He looked at Helen, feeling sheepish. "Sorry. I didn't mean to zone out."

"It's cool. Are you ready for the questions?"

"Shoot."

"What is your favorite food and why?"

"Strawberries." Should he say something sexy and cool, like, *I've loved strawberries since I watched that scene in 9½ Weeks?* Or stick to the truth? He'd spent a lifetime mucking about in perceptions, exaggerations, and one-upmanship. So . . . the truth, then. "When I was eight years old, I spent a hot week in June at my grandmother's farm in Oklahoma. She had this little place outside Henrietta.

"We went into the garden with metal pails and plucked big, red strawberries from the tangled growth that snaked all over the ground. Our hands got dirty, and the sun beat down on us, but it smelled like summer—all earthy and wet. She let me eat those berries straight from the vine. They were warm and sweet—the sweetest things I've ever tasted."

That had been the last summer he'd felt like a kid, and the last time he'd seen his Granny Jo. Mother had loved his blue-collar father with all her debutante heart, but after he died she severed all ties with that world, including contact with Granny Jo. Paul supposed it was Mother's way of dealing with her grief, but denying all aspects of her previous life also meant denying her son the only human link left to his father. Granny Jo died a couple of years later.

Paul blinked away the memories and ventured a look at Helen. "Sorry to blather on like that."

Her gaze was sympathetic. "It's a very nice memory to have."

"Yes, it is. So . . . your favorite food is?"

"Chocolate. And the reason why is because it tastes like heaven and makes me feel like life is worth living."

"Fair enough." He tried to shake off the cobwebs of sadness that still clung to him. He hadn't thought about Granny Jo in a long time. He owned the little farm—it had been his from the day he turned eighteen. But he'd been busy and hassled, as usual, and had hired a company to look after the place.

"Second question," said Helen. "Well, sorta. Name one word you believe describes your partner."

"Adventurous."

She looked surprised and pleased. Her expression made him feel like a little boy who'd answered the teacher's question correctly. He'd been right to believe she was a woman who'd appreciate compliments on inner qualities rather than outer beauty, though her outer self was damned fine, too.

"And for you, Paul . . . I'll go with sexy."

"You are a perceptive woman." Grinning, he waved at the paper, eager to finish this part of the game. "What's the third question?"

She glanced at the paper. "It's not really a question, more like a suggestion."

Before Paul had surrendered the note, he'd glanced at it, and the last line had caught his attention. Would Helen be adventurous? Or would she chicken out? "And?" he prompted.

"It says, 'Kiss your spy.'"

The seconds piled onto one another. It seemed like a whole year had passed when she finally stopped staring at the pink card stock. Her eyes locked with his. "I'll kiss my spy," she said, "if you'll kiss yours."

"I'm willing to make the sacrifice." He grinned. "Shall we agree on a place for the kiss?"

For a moment her gaze went liquid, and he saw the blaze of desire. With one blink and a sweep of those amazing lashes, the lust melted away into polite interest.

"Where—above the belt line—would you like a kiss?" she asked, her voice as quiet and pensive as the rustle of silk.

His pulse skipped a couple of beats, rallied, then plummeted into a fast mambo. "What say we give lip-to-lip a whirl? Sound all right?"

"Sounds fine to me."

He waited for her to make the first move. If he were James Bond, he'd throw her onto the bed and kiss her until she melted into his embrace, giving in to his lasciviousness. Of course, if Helen were a Bond girl, she'd be wearing either a skimpy bikini or a barely-there lace teddy. *Hmmm.* What did she have on under those jeans and the V-cut black top? His gaze traveled to her feet and he noted that her sneakers were black, too, and probably worn for comfort as she tackled long days at the café where she worked. Then his mind returned to the question of her lingerie. Before he could imagine what kind of panties she might be wearing, she stepped into the circle of his arms and kissed him.

chapter four

Helen's heart pounded a furious rhythm as she boldly claimed the mouth of her very own spy. The pink note drifted to the floor, joining the envelope dropped by Paul. Excitement swept through her, a twisting heat that coiled in the pit of her stomach.

The kiss started as a series of brief, shy meetings. The brush of lips, the soft intake of breath, the slow return to taste . . . to touch . . . to tempt. Paul's hands rested on her waist, his fingers feathered on her hips, and she enchained his neck with her arms, pressing against him as his mouth worshiped hers.

"Helen," he whispered. It was half plea, half sigh.

Emboldened by his response, she dipped her tongue to each corner of his mouth, slowly tracing its seam. She licked the plump flesh, nibbling just a little on his bottom lip until he moaned. His lips parted, and she swiped her tongue against his. He tasted like mint chocolate. *Oh, God.* The man tasted like *chocolate!*

Pure lust zapped her.

She deepened the kiss, appreciating the way Paul allowed her to make the moves. He reciprocated the pleasures of meshing mouth and tongue only after she initiated each sensual action. The faint whiff of his cologne reminded her of winter in the mountains: the cold tang of snow, the sharp scent of pine trees, and cedar-tinged smoke curling from stone chimneys.

Twining her fingers into his hair, she drew him closer still and ravished his mouth, giving in to every sensual whim. She suckled his bottom lip again, tucking it between her teeth for a gentle bite. Then she thrust her tongue inside his mouth to savor the sweetness of him. She delighted in his tightened grip, in the low sound of his need.

Desire seared her as she planted small kisses on his chin and his jaw . . . until she was drawn back to the heat of his mouth. This kiss was a long, hot duel of tongues. She felt the slide of his hands to her rear end, the press of his hard-on in the vee of her thighs. . . . *Oh, God.*

They broke apart, panting and dazed, and stared at each other.

"Wow," she said.

"I second that."

"You taste like chocolate."

He reached into the front pocket of his tuxedo coat and showed her a few green foil-wrapped rectangles. "I'm somewhat of a chocolate addict, too," he admitted.

"Do you think—"

The phone rang. Surprised, they looked at each other, then at the phone. It sat on the nightstand closest to them . . . and trilled again.

Paul grabbed the receiver. "Yes?"

Helen watched his lips, still reddened from their kiss, pull into a frown. He hung up, then bent to retrieve the note and envelope. After tucking them into the same pocket that held the hotel key card, he grabbed her hand. "We need to go, darling. Apparently the 'danger we must flee' is on his way to our room."

"It's that guy? The one who chased you into the café?"

"Probably . . . unless Cupid, Inc., has employed multiple bad guys to harass us on this little adventure."

Paul's firm grasp sent tingles up her arm. She liked holding his hand. She liked the warm, sure feel of his fingers wrapped around hers. And even though it was less of a walk-on-the-beach occasion and more of a hang-on-we're-gonna-run situation . . . well, it was still nice.

He opened the door and peeked out. Apparently Big, Gruff, and Dangerous wasn't prowling around yet. They hurried down the hallway and punched the down button.

Almost immediately the doors dinged and slid open. Unfortunately the only occupant in the car was about as wide as a building and as mean-looking as any villain who'd gotten his butt kicked by Superman. Before she could mutter, "Oh, crap!" Paul yanked her out of the Bronx Hulk's range and ran to the end of the hallway.

They slammed through the metal door to the stairwell. Paul let go of her hand as they hit the concrete steps. Their tennis shoes scuffed and slapped as they hurried to the fourth . . . then the third floor. Above, the door screeched open and the bad guy pounded after them.

"I'm gonna rip off your heads!" he roared.

Helen's heart, already pumping furiously thanks to the impromptu workout, stuttered in fear. *Holy* frijoles! He was scary, that one. And even though they were playing a game, she was still shaken by the idea that *cerdo sucio* might catch them.

Minutes later, after escaping the stairwell with their heads intact, Helen and Paul ran through the MGM's casino and exited the big glass doors that opened onto the Strip. The only way to cross the street was to get to the sky bridge—the huge concrete connection above the Strip's car-crowded street. They took the escalator, weaving between the tourists who stood still while the moving stairs did the work, and jogged across the bridge until they reached the other side, which faced the New York–New York Hotel and Casino.

Helen pointed to the sky bridge that led to the Excalibur, which was a Medieval-themed hotel casino—all the way from its castle turrets to its water-filled moat. "We can take the monorail from the Excalibur to Mandalay Bay."

"I don't like the idea of getting trapped in a small, slow-moving vehicle, especially if our bad guy catches up to us and shares the ride."

"It's not that small, and it's not slow."

"Do we have an option B?"

"The hotels connect. You can walk from the Excalibur to Luxor and from Luxor to Mandalay Bay."

"Excellent. We can get lost in the crowds and, failing that, we'll have places to hide."

"The monorail is faster."

Paul looked at her, smiling. His fingers skimmed her jaw. "Darling Helen . . . don't you know faster isn't always better?"

Ai, yi, yi, yi. The man oozed sex appeal. Her mind wandered to the kiss they had shared in the MGM hotel room. The sizzle and pop of that experience made her hungry for more, *much* more. After all, this was a Cupid, Inc., adventure . . . and that meant she could have it all—hook, spy, and sinker.

*   *   *

They made it to the hotel room without incident. Helen wasn't sure if she felt disappointed or relieved.

Paul slid in the key card and opened the door. The first look down the short hallway revealed another typical Las Vegas hotel room—big and beige. Since it was Mandalay Bay, the decor included rattan furniture and floral patterns on the bedspread and curtains. Helen noted the bathroom on the right, the closet on the left, the view of the Strip from the floor-to-ceiling windows . . . and the king-size bed.

While Paul stood at the window and admired the afternoon view of Las Vegas Boulevard, Helen scoped out the bed and nightstands for another pink envelope. *Nothing.* "Where's the clue?"

"I'll help. Maybe it's hidden somewhere in here."

After a few minutes of searching places obvious (drawers, trash cans) and less than obvious (under the bathroom sink, behind the framed pictures), they found *nada*. They stood near the armoire that held television, minibar, and drawers and scanned the other possible hiding places.

"Do you think the bad guy got here before us and snagged the envelope?" asked Helen.

"I doubt it. So far his only job has been to pump up our adrenaline." Paul glanced at the bed. "Though maybe we're not supposed to be looking for clues so much as taking a hint."

Her pulse leaped at his interpretation. Was she ready to behave like a Bond girl? She trembled at the thought of the pleasure she'd find with Paul. Here she was, faced with a handsome man, a huge bed, and a once-in-a-lifetime fantasy, and she hesitated. Why?

Paul, on the other hand, suffered no hesitation. He leaned forward and kissed her, very lightly, and waited to see what she would do. The mere brush of his lips sent her senses skittering and heart galloping. If that small touch could make her whole body feel like a shooting star, what would it be like to be naked, skin-to-skin and lip-to-lip, with Paul buried inside her?

She wrapped her arms around Paul's neck and opened her mouth to his, inviting his kiss.

"My, my, my. Isn't this delicious?" asked a cultured female voice.

Helen found herself whirled around, Paul's warm hands on her shoulders. For a split second her backside met his muscled chest; then he shoved her behind him. She looked over his shoulder at the tall, thin woman who stood not two feet away, assessing them the same way a researcher might evaluate lab rats.

Her long black hair was worn straight, pulled into a sexy ponytail on the top of her head. Her obsidian gaze was as dark and cold as river rocks, her pale skin as pearlescent as a full moon. The only other color visible was the slash of red lipstick on her mouth and the polish on her fingernails. Dressed head to toe in black leather, she wore a vest and a miniskirt that hugged her body like a new boyfriend. The thigh-high boots had at least three-inch heels.

The most impressive item of her ensemble, though, was the 9mm in her right hand. It was aimed at them in a manner that suggested she not only knew how to use the weapon, but she relished the idea of pulling the trigger. Her red fingernails looked like droplets of blood on the gun's gleaming black handle.

"Where's the clue?" she asked politely.

chapter five

Even though Helen knew the spy fantasy was merely a very exciting game, something about this woman unnerved her. The air in the room seemed to crackle with electricity. Helen swore she smelled sulfur, the brimstone perfume of the underworld.

"My name is Eris, and I'll be your villain today." Her laughter was a sultry, dangerous sound that must have led many an unsuspecting male to a bad end. She gestured with her free hand. "C'mon. Hand it over."

Paul drew out the envelope, which held the pink note, and handed it to Eris. With one step she retrieve the pink paper. Not once did the gun waver in its deadly aim. "You know the thing that bothers me the most about spy movies? The way the bad guy always fesses up in the end. The downfall of every movie villain is the inconceivable need to explain his past actions, or worse, his big plan for destroying the world, before leaving the hero to his disastrous end."

"Eris," said Paul. "The goddess of chaos and discord."

"You better believe it." Her smile was not reassuring. Helen shuddered at the coldness in her gaze. If this lady was acting, she deserved an Oscar.

"Good name for a villainess," said Paul. "Eris threw the golden apple onto the table at the wedding feast and caused the big fight."

"Inscribed with 'for the fairest' or 'to the most beautiful.' Depends on which version of the story you like best."

"That one action led to the Trojan War."

"Who knew that much chaos would ensue from such a small trick? It turned out better than . . ." Her mouth dropped open. "Oh, you clever boy! Keep the villain talking and buy yourself some time. Tsk, tsk. I've become a cliché."

She aimed the gun at his head. *Oh, shit. Shit!* Helen flattened her palms on Paul's back and shoved as hard as she could. The unexpected action made him stumble forward into Eris and they both went down. Paul landed on top, defending himself against Eris's flailing arms. She landed blows on his face and neck, but he still managed to wrest the gun from her grip. He had no opportunity to aim it at her. She fought with too much ferocity. Eris landed a punch on his jaw that nearly wrenched Paul off her. He stayed, but the gun flew out of his hand, sliding across the beige carpet underneath the bed.

"You arrogant, stupid mortal!" she screeched. "How dare you!"

Helen dove for the gun, but couldn't reach it. With less than half a foot of space between the frame and the floor, there was no way for her to scoot under the bed. Her hand strained toward the 9mm, but it remained out of her reach.

The sounds of Paul's brawl with Eris—the squeak of leather, the grunt of struggle, the smack of palm against cheek—propelled Helen to every side of the bed. The gun had landed in the middle space, and the only way to retrieve it would be if her fingers suddenly grew two extra inches.

Damn it. She looked around the room for anything else that might help and grabbed the lamp on the bedside table. The cord stalled her efforts, and no matter how hard she yanked, the stupid lamp wouldn't release from the wall socket. She dropped the light; it clattered sideways onto the table.

"Get *off* me!" Eris yelled.

"If you would calm the fuck down," Paul yelled back, "I'd be happy to."

Helen watched as Eris responded to this suggestion by grabbing a hunk of Paul's hair and pulling it like a taffy machine gone wild.

Adrenaline pumped through her; this felt real. This whole thing felt real. Cupid, Inc., really went for the gusto. She hadn't expected to feel so terrified in a fake situation. And yet the fear icing in her veins mixed with the incredible heat of excitement singeing her nerves.

What could she do to help Paul? Her gaze landed on the bed and she grinned. She ripped off the bedspread, stepped onto the mattress, and walked to its edge.

"Heads up, Paul!" She tossed the cover into the air. It puffed open like a parachute and floated onto Paul and Eris.

She jumped onto the floor, avoiding the rolling, squealing blanket of death, and rounded it. Lifting its edge, she peeked under and found herself face-to-face with Eris. The woman managed to free one arm from Paul's grip; she latched on and flung Helen forward, right into Paul. They fell off Eris, taking most of the bedspread with them. Helen landed on Paul's chest, her arms by her sides, her face pressed into his neck. His cologne was the winter-woodsy scent she'd noticed before. *Great.* They were wrapped together like two mummies sharing a sarcophagus, thanks to her brilliant idea of flinging fabric at the wrestling enemies.

Eris freed the rest of her body by kicking the crap out of them. She wriggled out from underneath Paul's legs, screaming obscenities, and landed a few more nasty blows with her high heels before escaping. The bitch cursed and muttered. Then Helen heard the *snick* of the door opening and closing.

Long moments passed as they gathered their wits and their breath.

Helen felt fantastic. Utterly, completely *fucking* fantastic. Sweaty, hot, scared-out-of-her-mind, heart-beating-a-million-miles-an-hour fantastic. In celebration of her exhilaration, she licked a drop of sweat from Paul's neck, tasting salt and the slight bitterness of his cologne.

What was she doing?

Oh, who cared! She felt gloriously horny, this was a sexual fantasy, and Paul was here for the same purpose as she. What was wrong with giving in to her sudden desire? This wasn't an episode of *24*; she had more than an hour to find the next clue and save the day.

She licked his neck again, following another droplet's trail. Then she kissed all available flesh from shoulder to jaw.

"It's not that I don't enjoy what you're doing," Paul managed. "But what are you doing?"

"Nibbling." She paused in her exploration of his earlobe. "Think the bitch is gone?"

"Probably."

"Did she get the clue?"

"Probably."

"Want to have sex?"

"Prob—*What?*"

"I'm feeling frisky," she said. "It's all this spy stuff. It's so stimulating. I feel wanton and sexy."

"You're an adrenaline junkie," he accused, though she noticed that his hands had found their way to her buttocks.

"I guess I am," she agreed. "I never realized it before. I've dreamed about an adventure for so long. I'm greedy for everything . . . including you." Her mouth nuzzled on his neck, and she cursed the white shirt denying her the view of his chest.

"Should we get out of the blanket?" Paul asked.

Helen's answer was to sit up, which forced the bedspread to go with her. She tossed the fabric behind her; then, to the obvious surprise and delight of Paul, she pulled off her shirt and bra. Before he could do much more than gurgle his appreciation of her 36C breasts, she set to work taking off Paul's trousers. She tugged them down his thighs, taking along his black silk boxers. She had never felt this frenzied before.

Of course, she'd had all of two boyfriends. Paul was neither a clumsy teenager nor a foreplay-challenged male, like those lamebrains. Most of her sexual encounters resided on the tame side of the sizzle zone; she knew without a doubt that *this* encounter would be well past ten on that scale.

Paul watched her with a lazy heat, his gaze stroking her bared breasts with enough lust to make her nipples harden and tingle. She noted the rapid rise and fall of his chest, and knew he was not unaffected by her actions. Paul was merely a lion stalking its prey, awaiting the right moment to attack. The shock of that impression sent her blood raging. She couldn't wait for him to leap, to grab hold, to plunder.

Her gaze feasted on his cock. Already at half-mast, the blue-veined flesh was thickly rounded, and she wondered just how long it would be at full hardness. Could she take all of him?

Damn right.

The head looked as juicy and plump as a ripe plum, and she bent to taste it. Paul's groan was an unexpected reward. His hands dove into her hair, and the slight arch of his hips encouraged her sensual exploration. Her tongue twirled under the edge of the head. She kissed his cock from tip to base, tasting every ridge, every vein. She took a long moment to worship his balls, suckling, licking, tasting the male essence of him in every juicy mouthful.

His moan vibrated to her very core. She was wet, her panties clinging to the swelling flesh of her vagina. She wanted nothing more than to rip off her own jeans and slide onto Paul's cock, but first . . .

She returned to his fully engorged penis. No denying he was blessed in the family-jewels department. He was *big*—and she liked it. To show her appreciation, she made love to that hard, hot cock with mouth and hands, stroking and sucking until Paul writhed and moaned.

"Helen, you'd, uh . . . better, you know. Because, I might . . . oh, God."

chapter six

No, not yet, big boy. Helen released Paul long enough to toe off her shoes and socks. She shucked off the jeans. She didn't care that she was naked and he was almost fully clothed. It was sexier somehow, taking Paul like this, trapped by his own clothing the same way she was trapped by her own lust.

She retrieved a condom from her jean pocket and rolled it onto his cock. Then she lowered herself onto his dick inch by inch, shuddering as he filled her, stretching her with pleasurable perfection. For a few seconds she closed her eyes and inhaled steadying breaths. How was it remotely possible she felt on the thin side of orgasm? She was more turned on than she'd ever been in her entire life.

Paul's hands cupped her breasts, his fingers strumming the nipples into taut, aching peaks. Her eyes flicked open and she met his gaze. His blue eyes challenged her to finish what she'd begun; the sardonic curl of his lips suggested she wouldn't complete the race.

The enormity of what she'd started with a man she'd met only this morning hit her with the same velocity as a meteor tearing into Earth. Yet the shock waves brought not shame, but *pleasure*. Excitement. Naughty, naughty thrills.

It's a fantasy—my fantasy.

Helen planted her hands on Paul's chest and, forgoing anything like slow and easy, pumped up and down on his cock, squeezing and sliding and plunging. She wasn't exactly an example of precision and grace, but with the steadying hand of Paul on one hip and the strokes of his thumb on her clit, her eagerness more than made up for any lack.

"I'm already close," whispered Paul as he strained against her, stroke for stroke.

"Me, too."

He fondled her clit faster. She increased her pace, wanting him to cum inside her . . . wanting her own release. . . .

Sweat dripped between her breasts. . . .

Her buttocks slapped against the tops of his thighs. . . .

Moans and pants melded into one sound. . . .

The orgasm burst, a tsunami of bliss that stalled the breath in her lungs, the motion of her legs. *Oh. My. God.*

"Don't stop," begged Paul.

His cock threatened to slip out of her, but she lowered herself again and resumed her pace, all the while her orgasm crashed through her, the mind-fogging pleasure rolling and cresting like waves lapping at the shore.

His thumb stayed on her sensitive clit, still stroking, and she gritted her teeth against the almost painful agitation. To her surprise, the sure, small strokes threatened another onslaught of rapture, less intense than the first, but . . . *Day-amn.* She'd never had a double orgasm before. Just as another mind-blowing sensation rolled over her, Paul grabbed both of her hips. He surged upward, so hard and deep she swore she felt the tip of his penis at the entrance to her womb.

"Yes," Paul cried out. "Yes!"

He came, a violent jerking that suggested a really strong orgasm, and clenched his teeth, his eyes squeezed shut. After a long, shuddering moment, he went limp, his eyes opened, and their gazes met.

"That was . . . amazing," he said.

"Yeah."

"Helen, I mean it. I've never experienced anything that intense before."

"Me, either." She drifted down to his chest and smiled when his arms wrapped around her. "Just for the record, I never put out on the first date. Hell, I never kiss on the first date. You know something . . . I haven't had a first date in a long time."

"I haven't, either," said Paul. "Is that why you signed up with Cupid, Inc.?"

"Someone gave me a gift certificate," said Helen. "I love movies about secret agents, and I thought pretending to be one would be fun." She lifted her head and smiled at him. "I was right."

While Helen turned on the shower, Paul shed his tuxedo and thought about what the hell had just happened. True, he'd been attracted to Helen since the first second he'd laid eyes on her, but the incredible sex had been . . . surprising. After the strange and frightening experience with that bitch Eris, any other woman might've abandoned him and run straight home.

But Helen wasn't any other woman. She was ravenous *and*

cute. Not many females could pull off that kind of paradoxical behavior and still make him want to hang around. She empowered
him, in some weird way. He wanted to protect her; he wanted her
trust, her faith. . . . *Shit.* What was wrong with him?

Love pays no attention to time.

His mother's favorite phrase. *Oh, no, Mum. No, you don't!* He
didn't believe in true love. Maybe a relationship could sustain itself on mutual friendship and common interests, but the heart-
pounding, breath-stopping, rose-colored glasses world of true love
didn't really exist anywhere except romance novels.

You'll know when it happens, she'd told him time and time
again. *It's like a veil is lifted from your eyes and the world is suddenly
bright and beautiful.*

He felt that way now. Pure and dazzling and joyful.

Shit.

No way.

He thought about the way he felt, inside and out, with honesty
and clarity.

Shit!

To distract himself from the very idea that he might've fallen
for Helen Manzana, Paul decided to track down some different
clothes. He was ready to ditch the uncomfortable and unwieldy
tux and the black dress shoes. Mandalay Bay didn't have much in
the way of clothing stores, but the Luxor had a shop called Exclusive. He called them, ordered some clothes and a pair of sneakers to be delivered to the hotel room, and gave them his
credit-card number.

"Paul?"

He got off the bed and walked to the bathroom. Helen leaned
against the shower door as steam from the hot water billowed out.

Paul took another inventory of Helen's commendable figure, from the full, rounded breasts with their cocoa nipples to the flat stomach and gentle flare of her hips. She had long legs and beautiful feet, the toenails painted the same pearlescent pink as her fingernails.

"I need someone to wash my back," she purred, grasping his hand and drawing him forward. They stepped into the not-quite-scalding spray.

"Maybe I should start with the front." Paul cupped her breasts, enjoying the sweet weight of the firm flesh. His thumbs flicked across her nipples.

He leaned down and captured one peak, already puckered by the heat and the water. A soft moan and a slight shudder emerged from beautiful Helen. He smiled against her breast, pressing a kiss to the top, then the sides. Water pounded against his neck as he performed this ritual; he felt the scrape of Helen's nails on his arms. Desire slammed him, as heavy and thick as before, when Helen had offered herself without reserve, without extracting a single promise of devotion.

His tongue traced the edge of the areola, encircling the nipple until the only thing left was to draw the tender bud into his mouth. He sucked hard, suddenly greedy for the taste of her skin, the heat of her body. Moving to the other breast, he attempted to give it the same affectionate treatment, but the blood pounded in his skull, an ancient rhythm of lust and need that he gave in to willingly, gladly.

He dropped to his knees, the very image of a slave showing his loyalty to the goddess, and paid tribute to every inch of her skin, from rib to navel, from navel to hip, from hip to the edge of her pubic hair.

"Paul . . . oh, *Paul!*"

He took her cries for consent and delved into her soft core, licking the peachy flesh, opening the labia with his fingers to taste all that was hidden. He feasted on every centimeter, getting more desperate with his own passion.

Grabbing her buttocks and pulling her forward, he traced the vaginal opening slick with her juices. *Sweet God.* He thrust his tongue inside, his movements mimicking all that he wanted to do with his cock.

He felt the trembling of her thighs, the hard dive of her fingers into hair, the long moan echoing in the tiny bathroom. Water battered them endlessly; liquid pearls slid down Helen's skin, dropping into his eyes, into his mouth.

It didn't matter.

Only Helen mattered.

Only *this* mattered.

In seconds he imprisoned her clit in his mouth and played with the hard nub, torturing his prize with licks and sucks.

"Please," she begged. "Please, Paul. Make me come."

He doubled his efforts, flicking her clitoris quickly, over and over, until his mouth threatened to cramp and his tongue went numb. His cock was harder than a steel rod, and he wanted nothing more than to slip inside Helen, take his pleasure while she found hers.

Then Helen tensed, a stillness that lasted an eternity, and screamed.

chapter seven

Paul savored the nectar flowing into his mouth. He drank from Helen with voracious need until he felt the tug of her hands on his hair, drawing him upward.

When he stood, she kissed him. Long, hot, hard. Her tongue warred with his as her hands slipped down his chest to his buttocks. He felt the squeeze of her hands on his ass, the press of her pussy against his cock. *Oh, God.*

Then she was pulling away from him, stepping back, her eyes still glazed with passion.

"What are you—"

Her wait-and-see smile stalled the question in his throat. She turned around, bent over, and flattened her palms against the tile wall. Seconds ticked by as he looked at her gorgeous ass. Water pebbled on the brown skin, rolling down the lush curves. J. Lo had *nothing* on Helen Manzana.

"Paul? How much of an invitation do you need?"

Without wasting another nanosecond, he stepped forward, bent his knees, and held on to her hips as he pushed his cock between her thighs. Sensations ricocheted through him, registering high on the wow-o-meter. His thoughts were vague and floaty . . . all he could do was feel the soft slide of skin, the water turning tepid, the unsteady pounding of his heart.

Helen's fingers closed around his cock and she guided him into her tight, slick heat. He sheathed himself all the way to his balls and sucked in a breath. He waited, allowing her to adjust around him, then oh, so slowly withdrew. When he pressed inside her with the same unhurried precision, her inner muscles milked him. He bit his lower lip, shuddering with every sweet clench.

He might have survived this surprising internal seduction, but then she cried, "Fuck me, *mi amor*. Fuck me hard!"

That kind of demand, wrapped in the Spanish accent she had not displayed until now, made any thought of leisurely fucking disappear like mist in the sunlight. He grabbed her hips and plunged inside her, ramming his cock into her sweet flesh until the heat and the lust and the passion entwined, winding into a tight coil . . . and released.

"Helen!" The orgasm shook him to his core, roaring through his entire body with the fierceness of a summer storm.

A few minutes later they soaped and cleansed each other. They didn't speak, but it wasn't an awkward silence. When they were scrubbed clean, Paul turned off the water and stepped out.

He grabbed a towel and spent a pleasurable five minutes patting dry every centimeter of Helen. Her skin reminded him of a café latte; he already knew how sweet and creamy she tasted.

His cock stirred as lust built anew.

How many times could he make love to this woman?

He finished drying off Helen, dropping the towel. Smiling, she took a clean towel from the counter and performed the same service for him. When the cotton fabric rubbed on his half-hard penis, he closed his eyes and shuddered.

"My goodness," said Helen as she replaced the towel with the warm touch of her hand. "You certainly are . . . enthusiastic."

"I like you," he said, feeling somewhat embarrassed. He had never felt this attracted to a woman he'd known only a few hours. Though he could not deny he'd had intimate encounters with women that had been, well, very short-term, his feelings for Helen could not be relegated to mere physical excitement. "Perhaps I should be manly and brag that I'm a male version of the Energizer bunny."

"Are you?"

Her eyes glimmered with desire. She wrapped her fingers around his cock and stroked. He moaned as she caressed him into a full hard-on.

"I must admit that I've rarely performed so well without some rest between . . . adventures."

"Looks like you're ready again."

Paul grinned; he scooped a surprised Helen into his arms and took her to the bed. He tossed her onto it, which made her laugh, and joined her.

"We're lousy spies," she said. "We're supposed to be following the clues and saving the day."

"It's our fantasy," he murmured as he rolled on top of her and nuzzled her neck. "Right now, I'm still trying to follow the first clue's suggestion number three."

"Kiss your spy?"

"Yes," said Paul. "I missed a few spots."

"Hmmm. You should certainly be thorough."

"Well, darling, if you insist . . ."

*   *   *

The second clue was delivered via bellboy not long after Paul's clothing arrived. While Paul tied his tennis shoe strings, Helen opened the clue and read it.

" 'The second clue is yours to hold, use it to find Emperor's Gold.' " She flipped over the pink paper. "An R and an O."

While she puzzled over what T-R-O might spell, something round and heavy fell out of the envelope.

"What's that?" asked Paul. He walked from the bed to the hallway where Helen stood. She bent down and picked up the shiny object lodged near the closet door. She turned it over in her palm. It was an ancient coin. She'd seen these before—in an elegant little place tucked away at the Forum Shops.

"Oh my God. I got it! This is from Emperor's Gold."

Paul took it and examined the edges. "It's not gold."

"Emperor's Gold is a store that sells ancient coins and unique jewelry. It's located at Caesars Palace, in the Forum. That must be where the next clue is!"

After their yowzer interlude on the bed, they'd gotten dressed—she in her regular clothes and Paul in the clothes he'd ordered from Exclusivo. The fact that he could afford to shop there and pay outrageous delivery charges gave her some pause. Maybe, just maybe, she had entertained a thought or two about seeing Paul after their adventure was concluded. She'd been having such a good time she'd only just realized that while her fun came from the generosity of a gift certificate, Paul had surely paid full price for his adventure. She'd seen the package prices, and they were waaaayyy out of her range.

And so, it appeared, was Paul.

He had made love to her so beautifully in the bed. The frenzy of their first joining and the crazed lust of their shower play paled in comparison to the intense and gentle loving he'd shown her on the bed. Time had no meaning. There had been only quiet, powerful pleasure. He asked what she liked, what she wanted, and when he made her cum, *again,* he held her gaze. He hid nothing from her. She saw how her orgasm turned him on, made him happy . . . and mere seconds after she found her bliss, he found his.

And yet . . .

He ordered clothing the way others ordered Chinese food. He'd gone to school in London. He could afford Cupid, Inc. It was not a great leap to think he might be wealthy.

What if Paul was on a rich man's lark?

That would mean Helen was his partner in sexual satisfaction and silly fun—and nothing else. Her father, God rest his soul, and mother had been married almost thirty years before Papa had a heart attack and passed away. Their love had been filled with ups and downs, but she had never once doubted their bond. She would never settle for less than that kind of devotion.

Paul leaned down and brushed a kiss across her lips. "Ready to go?"

She felt, as her mama would say, goggle-eyed and gushy. Smiling, she took his hand and they left the room.

chapter eight

"Get in here!" The thug who had chased Paul into the café waved the Colt .45 toward the bathroom door. *Well, shit.* They'd taken the Las Vegas monorail to the Flamingo, then crossed one of the sky bridges to get to Caesars Palace. Mr. Bronx had caught them at the entrance to the Forum Shops and had pressed the gun into Helen's backside, ordering them here, to a bathroom that was under repair.

"Look, isn't getting hassled by one of you enough? Don't you think it's overkill for Eris to attack us in our hotel room, then you waylay us here?" asked Paul.

"Eris? What are you talkin' about?"

"Tall, thin, bitchy," said Helen. "She looked like the evil twin of Barbarella."

He smirked at her description, then straightened. "Ain't no one but me tailing your asses. Now, *get inside.*"

"Oh, fuck you," said Helen. She whacked the gun out of his hand. It popped out of his grip and slid along the floor, smacking the door to the men's restroom. Mr. Bronx's mouth dropped open in shock, and Paul knew that guy's expression mirrored his own. His Helen had some major balls.

"I can't believe I just did that!" she said, looking at him with wide eyes.

"C'mon!" He grabbed her hand, and they ran into the chaos that was the mall. He let Helen lead them through the crowds, around ornate fountains with talking statues, and into the recesses of the world that was the Forum Shops. Above them, the sky-painted ceiling melded from morning to afternoon to dusk, all within a few minutes.

Emperor's Gold was tucked between a Louis Vuitton luggage shop and an Ann Taylor boutique. The jewelry store was a small rectangle. The floors were marble, the walls eggshell white, the glass cases filled with gold, silver, and the occasional flash of gems. An elderly gentleman waited for them. Dressed in a well-fitting suit that Paul recognized as Armani, the old man grinned. "Ah. You look like a couple so much in love. You come to Alfredo's poor shop to find a special gift, eh?"

Alfredo was as Italian as Mr. Bronx was New York City. Paul smiled and presented the coin.

"Oh-ho! Lovers from Cupid, Inc. This coin, it brings you luck. And you give it to me, so I give you this." He handed them a big pink envelope. "When you get engaged, you come back and let Alfredo help you find something nice."

Helen glanced at him, her cheeks rosy with embarrassment. "We just met," she murmured.

"Love don't pay no attention to time," said Alfredo.

Paul blinked in shock, his heart turning over in his chest. How odd that this man would repeat one of his mother's favorite phrases. He could admit that he liked Helen, that they had explosive sex, but he couldn't begin to think about the L-word. They'd known each other six hours. Surely love needed a little more time.

"Go now," said Alfredo, waving his hands at them. "Shoo. Shoo. I see you soon, eh? Yes. You come back for the engagement ring."

Paul guided Helen out of the shop and to one of the elaborate fountains that sat a few feet away. She took the envelope and opened it. " 'You're almost there; the game's nearly done; by now you should know two is better than one. Go to where the first story began, except your lover's tale will have a happier end.' " She turned it over. "Look, a Y. That spells . . . Troy."

"Gee, thanks," said Eris as she plucked the envelope and card stock from Helen's fingers. "What you hope to get, I will possess long before you even know where it is."

"Where the hell did you come from?" Paul asked, making a grab for the clue.

"You've answered your own question, moron." Eris jerked out of his reach and grinned evilly. "I've been trying to get this goddamned piece-of-shit ap—thing for the last two millennia. I can't believe it's come down to stealing clues from humans to get to it. Honestly!"

She stalked off, melting away into the crowd before Paul and Helen could take a single step to follow her.

"Poop!" said Helen. "If she takes the clues to . . . I'm guessing . . . the Troy Casino, will she get our prize?"

Paul's anger faded. He knew where the clues were taking them. His mother had told him the endgame. *I want you to steal*

Aphrodite's golden apple. . . . at the time of the 'theft,' casino personnel switch the real apple for a fake . . . fight for the happy ending.

He looked at Helen. He wanted her to feel the kind of scary, strange, nearly unbelievable emotions he did. . . . He wanted her to keep . . . well, wanting him.

"Don't worry, love," he said, grasping her hand again. "The game's not over yet."

chapter nine

"Eris!" Aphrodite stared at the dark goddess in surprise. The poor dear really should reconsider the black-leather look. The color and material did nothing good for her pale complexion. "I haven't seen you since . . . well, I can't really remember."

"I've been hanging out with Hades—thanks to Zeus and his very poor sense of humor. I didn't know hiding his lightning bolts would make him freak out." She waved around two pink envelopes. "I can't believe I had to chase around two humans to get this information. Now, give me the apple, and let me get out of this realm. Humans smell bad, and they spit when they talk."

"The apple?"

"The one in the box behind you. It's the only fucking thing in this lobby I care to see." She shook the papers violently. "I followed the stupid clues. I mean, I only had the T and the Y . . . but shit, if I'd known there was a casino in Las Vegas called Troy, I would've figured it out sooner."

People milled around the lobby, some waiting to check in, some meandering around to look at the decor. Thick red velvet curtains draped most of the walls, the floor was black tile, and the low lights that dotted the ceiling changed colors. In a way, the lobby resembled a low-key disco.

The Troy Casino was small by Las Vegas standards, but it met the requirements for uniqueness. Shaped like the wooden horse that had won the Spartans the war and destroyed nearly all of the Trojans and their city, it was squeezed between the Mirage and Treasure Island. It had only a thousand rooms, and it was always booked. The hotel had been one of Aphrodite's better ideas.

"Why do you want it?"

"I don't. Zeus said if I brought him the apple, he would end my punishment in the Underworld. I've been broiling there for two hundred years."

Oh, he did, did he? Aphrodite would have a conversation with her father about sending minions to steal her possessions.

Eris, impatient as always, zapped the box. Sparks flew, but the metal casing around the glass held. When she aimed her finger to zap it again, Aphrodite waved her hand and made the power of it fizzle into smoke.

"Hephaestus made this box!" accused Eris. "Damn it!"

"You!"

Aphrodite and Eris spun to face Helen and Paul.

"Gods may not be able to break open the box, but a human can. You, the one called Paul, open this box immediately."

"With what? My willpower?"

Aphrodite watched in amazement as Helen fisted her hand, hauled back, and punched Eris in the jaw. The woman fell to the floor, as useless as Jell-O in a microwave.

Paul retrieved the two pieces of pink paper dropped by Eris, the prideful look he sent Helen not lost on Aphrodite. "We've brought the clues, and, I would like to point out, we managed to get here without them." He handed Aphrodite all three envelopes.

"Ah. Indeed." She presented them with a golden apple. "Technically, you were supposed to save the world by stealing this and returning it to Cupid, Inc."

Helen took the object and looked at it. " 'To the most beautiful.' It may be fake, but it's still amazing."

"It's yours. And so is this." She handed them a hotel key for the Aphrodite Suite. "This is an exclusive suite in the Troy Casino, and yours until tomorrow. Checkout is at noon."

Paul and Helen looked at each other and grinned. "Thank you."

Helen took the key and, with a smoky look at Paul promising all kinds of wicked pleasures, walked toward the bank of elevators. Aphrodite touched his shoulder as he passed, and he stopped. "Yes?"

"You do realize you've had the apple with you the whole time."

"Look, I get it. Love pays no attention to time. Fight for your happy ending. I can take a hint from the universe, okay? But Helen and I will make our own timetable."

"That's wonderful news, Paul," said Aphrodite. "However, I was referring to Helen's last name. Manzana."

"So?"

"It's Spanish for apple."

Epilogue

One year later . . .

"**W**hy is there a tree with purple leaves in the lobby?" asked Eros as he strode into the boardroom. "I've never seen that kind of— Oh."

Psyche grimaced. "Yeah. It's Daphne. Apollo came in a little while ago and made the mistake of asking her to lunch."

"She freaked out about eating a meal with him?"

"She might've been okay, if he hadn't explained it was a prewedding lunch that Emeril was cooking especially for them. He also said the real Elvis would make an appearance at their nuptials. He thinks Daphne likes 'Love Me Tender.'"

"Does she?"

"Nope. She likes heavy metal and punk rock."

"Maybe Apollo should give up."

Psyche's face formed a mock look of horror. "The love god giving up on a happily-ever-after? I'm shocked!"

Eros grinned and dragged her into his arms. "We've done okay in the happily-ever-after department." He kissed her, and the ever-present thrill of desire zinged through him.

"Oh, for the love of Zeus. Should I leave the room?" Aphrodite interrupted, but without her usual rancor.

Eros and Psyche parted and looked at the goddess, their grins unapologetic.

"Sit down, you two; we have a lot to discuss. Where's Daphne?"

"She's, um . . . rooting out a problem," answered Psyche as she took her chair.

"Sure is," said Eros sitting next to her. "She's getting into the thicket of it and going out on a limb."

He looked at his wife, and they both burst into gales of laughter.

"I can hear you!" yelled Daphne. "Just because I'm a tree doesn't mean I'm deaf!"

"Apollo came by, I take it?" asked Aphrodite. She shuffled through the paperwork in front of her. "We'll have to deal with that issue later. Now, to business. We've done very well in the two years since we've been open. Oh! That reminds me. We received a wedding invitation from Paul Aris and Helen Manzana."

"That's good news," said Eros. "Wasn't it touch-and-go for them?"

"Once Helen got over the shock that the man she loved was heir to the Sinclair Motors fortune and a reformed thief, she and her mother sold the café and moved to New York City. Helen helps Paul run LifeStar Charities, and they often go to Oklahoma. They're fixing up his Granny Jo's farm and making it viable again."

"What's next?" asked Psyche. "We've had more successes than

failures, but there's still a lot of work to be done. Lust is far easier to create than the bonds of true love."

"Indeed." Aphrodite waved her hand. More than fifty stacks of files, all at least three feet high, filled the huge table.

"Mother! Where did you . . . how did you . . . oh, Zeus's lightning bolts!" Eros stared at all the files representing the hearts and souls of human couples who wanted nothing more than to be loved and cherished. And if they got hot sex as part of the deal, all the better.

"It's a good thing we're immortal," said Psyche, eyeing the tower of manila folders in front of her. "This is going to take a while."